CU01455346

Echoes of Us

Aaron McLean

This book is a work of fiction. Names, characters, places, and incidents are product of the author's imagination or are used fictitiously. Any resemblance to actual events, locales, or persons, living or dead, is coincidental.

Copyright © 2025 by Aaron McLean. All rights reserved, including the right to reproduce, distribute, or transmit in any forms or by any means. For information regarding subsidiary rights, please contact the author.

No portion of this book may be reproduced in any form without written permission from the publisher or author, except as permitted by U.S. copyright law.

Aaron McLean | apmclean.com

Cover design by Kandice Coppala | www.kandicecoppala.com

Echoes of Us

Aaron McLean

I hope that you get lost in this story. Also, at the same time— I hope that in some way, you find yourself.
-Aaron

Aaron McLean | apmclean.com

Cover design by Kandice Coppala | www.kandicecoppala.com

Foreword

Why Romance?

I've been asked that question more times than I can count, and the answer is simple.

Because love isn't just soft kisses and whisperings of "I love you." It's teeth sinking into lips, fingers tangled in hair, a breathless "don't stop." It's obsession and surrender, the slow burn that leaves you aching and the wildfire that consumes you whole. It's the way a single look can make your skin tingle, the way someone's voice can wreck you in all the right ways. Love is messy, wild, and unapologetically raw—and I fucking live for it.

And yeah, I even love the pain that comes with it. The kind that shatters you, leaves you gasping, aching, asking yourself—"Why?". The kind that makes you stare at the ceiling at 2 a.m., replaying every touch, every moan, every promise that slipped through your fingers. The kind that reminds you that love is never safe, never predictable—but always worth it. Because when you come back from it, when you find it again, you don't hold back. You go all in. No games. No bullshit. Just the kind of love that makes you lose yourself—and find yourself at the same damn time.

And that's what I want for you. I want you to believe in the kind of love that stops time. The kind that crashes into you when you least expect it, leaving you breathless, shaken, and undeniably his or hers. That's fate, sweetheart. And when it finds you? Let it consume you. Let it ruin you. Let it *own* you.

So here's *Echoes of Us*. I wrote this to make you feel—to crave, to ache, to shatter, to come undone. Let it drag you under. Let it make you scream in frustration, clench your thighs, bite your lip, and maybe—just maybe—believe in love a little more. And if you end up breathless, wrecked, or needing a cold shower?

Good. That means I did my job.

Now, fall—hard, deep, and without restraint.

—*Aaron*

Echoes of Us

Aaron McLean

Prologue

LET ME TELL YOU a story.

Not the kind with a perfect ending. Not the kind that fits into some neat little box with all the right moments happening at all the right times. No, this story is messy. It's raw. It's full of every beautiful, painful, gut-wrenching thing that love is made of.

Because love—the real kind—doesn't follow the rules. It doesn't fit inside a timeline. It doesn't care about logic or reason or whether you're ready for it. Love happens *to* you. And once it's there? It never really leaves.

I learned that the hard way.

I used to think love was a choice. That if you were strong enough, disciplined enough, you could decide when to let someone in and when to walk away. That you could control it. Shape it. Keep it from wrecking you.

Then Savannah Monroe happened.

And nothing has made sense since.

She was never supposed to be mine, not really. Not in the way that counted. But that didn't stop me from wanting her. From loving her in a way that changed me. From losing her in a way that nearly destroyed me.

I used to sit on this dock and stare at the water, trying to convince myself that time would wash her away. That if I stayed still long enough, the ache in my chest would dull, that one day I'd wake up and not feel her absence like a ghost wrapped around my ribs. But no matter how many nights passed, no matter how hard I tried to move on, she was still there.

In the way the wind brushes against my skin.
In the way the tide rolls in, unrelenting, impossible to ignore.
In the whispers of the past that never quite let go.

I've spent a long time trying to rewrite the ending. Trying to be the man who lets go, who moves forward, who builds something new. But the truth is, some stories aren't meant to be rewritten.

Some stories are meant to pull you back in.

So, if you're looking for something simple, something easy—this isn't it.

But if you want the truth, if you want to know what it's like to love someone so deeply that they become a part of you, even when they're gone—then keep reading.

Because this?

This is the ***Echoes of Us.***

-Chase Montgomery

Echoes of Us

Aaron McLean

Beyond The Reputation

CHASE MONTGOMERY WAS THE kind of man everyone in Wrightsville Beach knew—some by name, others by reputation. He was the golden boy with a devil-may-care attitude, the kind of man who could walk into a room and turn heads without trying, who could make a woman feel like she was the only person in the world with a single glance.

He had it all—looks that made people stare, southern charm that made them weak, and a reputation that made them talk. The stories about him traveled faster than the tide, whispered over drinks at The Low Tide Tavern, passed between friends with knowing smirks. Some swore he had a new woman every weekend, others said he never called the same girl twice. And yet, for all the tales of his conquests, no one ever had a bad word to say about him. He was the type to leave a woman breathless, never broken.

At The Low Tide Tavern, the bartender barely needed to ask what he was drinking. He always ordered bourbon, neat, with the kind of slow, confident nod that made the act feel like a ritual rather than a habit. The waitstaff knew better than to bet against him in a game of pool. The tourists found him irresistible, drawn in by the casual swagger, the effortless way he made them feel like they were stepping into a story they'd never forget. And the locals? They simply accepted that Chase Montgomery was as much a part of Wrightsville Beach as the ocean itself—constant, unchanging, always there.

Women chased after him, but he never let anyone catch him. He played the game well, knew exactly what to say, when to touch, when to pull away just enough to leave them wanting more. He could be reckless, intoxicating, impossible to resist—but never cruel. He had a way of making women feel like they were special, even if just for one night. And that was the most dangerous thing about him. It wasn't the fleeting romances or the stolen kisses under the pier at midnight. It was the way he made them believe, even if just for a moment, that they were the exception.

But there was another side to Chase, one few got to see. The one who would stop in the middle of the road to help an elderly couple load their groceries. The one who knew the names of every fisherman at the marina, who made sure the old man who sat on the pier every morning had a hot cup of coffee when the air turned crisp. He was the guy who coached Little League when a buddy needed help, who took his mama to dinner every Friday night, who never missed Sunday lunch at his grandparents' house. He'd flirt with your sister, steal your girl for a dance, and then turn around and help your grandmother carry her bags to the car. A contradiction wrapped in a smirk and a well-worn pair of jeans.

The duality was what made Chase so impossible to define. To most, he was a smooth-talking, fast-living ladies' man, content to spend his nights tangled in someone else's sheets and his days running the consulting firm he built from the ground up. But the truth was, behind the smirk and the reputation, he was searching for something more. He wanted love—the kind of love that seeped into his soul, settled into his bones, and felt like home. The kind that wasn't rushed, wasn't reckless, but slow-burning and certain. The kind of love that wrapped around you like a warm breeze on a summer night, steady and unshakable. Not just passion in the dark, not just stolen moments that faded with the sunrise, but something real—something that made forever feel too short.

He had seen glimpses of it in the quiet corners of life. In the way his grandparents still held hands on their porch swing, their fingers effortlessly laced together, as if even time itself couldn't wear down the connection between them. He saw it in the way his grandpa still kissed his grandma's forehead every night before bed, whispering the same words he had for decades, "Sweet dreams, my love." It was in the way his mother still smiled when she spoke about the first time she met his father, as if that love had never aged, never lost its magic.

He heard it in the stories the old fisherman at the dock told, sipping whiskey as he spoke about the girl he let get away. The way his voice softened when he said her name, the way his eyes still carried the weight of a love unfinished. A love that had never quite loosened its grip on his heart. There was a lesson in that, one he tried to ignore, but it whispered to him in the quiet moments, in the spaces between all the faces he had memorized but never kept.

And then there were the nights when Chase lay in bed, staring at the ceiling, listening to the waves crash against the shore. Nights when the emptiness felt heavier, when he realized that, for all the faces he had memorized, not one had ever truly stayed. He wondered if there was someone out there who would see beyond the stories, beyond the smirk and the reputation, beyond the carefully crafted version of himself the world had come to expect. Someone who would love him not for the chase, not for the thrill, but for the man he was in the moments no one else saw.

Because Chase Montgomery didn't just want love. He wanted her—the one who would make every restless night worth it, the one who would turn a house into a home, the one whose love would feel like the softest place to land. The one who would kiss him slow, who would trace the lines of his face with fingertips that made him believe in something bigger than himself. The one whose laughter would echo through his days, whose presence would feel like the missing piece he'd spent a lifetime searching for.

And if he ever found her, he knew—he would never let her go. And when he finally had her beneath him, writhing, breathless, whispering his name like a prayer, he'd make damn sure she knew exactly what it meant to be his. Every kiss, every touch, every tangled sheet between them would be a promise—one he'd never break.

Coastal Echoes

Savannah Monroe had spent years mastering the art of control—control over her career, her emotions, and, most importantly, her heart. She had worked tirelessly to build a name for herself as one of Asheville's top real estate attorneys, carving out a reputation as a woman who never backed down, never folded under pressure, and never allowed herself to be defined by anything other than success. Love? That was something she no longer had room for. It had burned her before, left scars that time had yet to fully erase. So, she shut that part of herself away, buried it beneath contracts, closing deals, and the steady rhythm of work that kept her too busy to dwell on what she had lost.

But then, there was Wrightsville Beach.

The moment she stepped out of the car, she felt it—that pull, that quiet hum of nostalgia carried by the salty breeze. She closed her eyes for a second, breathing it in, letting it wrap around her like a memory she hadn't asked for but couldn't shake. This place had always been her escape, the one corner of the world where she had allowed herself to dream without limits. Summers here had meant freedom. It had meant waking up to the scent of the ocean drifting through open windows, running barefoot along the wooden planks of the dock, chasing sunsets on the water, and falling asleep to the lull of waves crashing against the shore.

She had spent entire seasons in this very house, a place built on love, on laughter, on years of family gatherings where nothing felt complicated. Her parents had always talked about retiring here one day, about growing old in rocking chairs on the porch, watching grandkids chase fireflies in the yard. But life had a way of rewriting plans. Her father passed before they could make that dream a reality, and after that, her mother had stopped coming as often. The house had remained, standing strong against the coastal storms, but it had become more of a relic than a retreat.

Savannah hadn't been back in years. At first, it was work that kept her away.

Then, it became easier to make excuses—to avoid the memories, the ghosts that lingered in every sun-drenched corner of this house, and, most of all, the reminder of a love she once thought would last forever.

She exhaled, rolling her shoulders back as she took in the familiar sight of the two-story home—whitewashed siding, blue shutters, and a wraparound porch that still looked exactly as she had left it. The porch swing swayed gently in the breeze, as if waiting for someone to settle into it, as if daring her to sit and let herself feel everything she had spent years ignoring.

"You're thinking too much again."

The voice pulled her out of her thoughts, and she turned to see Mallory, her best friend, standing beside the open trunk, sunglasses perched on top of her head, arms crossed with a knowing smirk.

"I'm fine," Savannah replied automatically.

Mallory arched a brow. "You stood there for a full two minutes just staring at the house. That's not 'fine.' That's emotionally avoiding something."

Savannah huffed, grabbing her bag and slinging it over her shoulder. "I don't avoid things."

Mallory let out an exaggerated laugh, shutting the trunk. "Suuure. That's why you haven't set foot here in—what? Seven years?"

"Five," Savannah corrected.

Mallory's smirk deepened. "Still too long."

Savannah sighed, brushing past her friend and heading toward the front door. "Can we just get inside before you start psychoanalyzing me?"

Mallory followed, rolling her eyes but saying nothing more.

The inside of the house smelled like salt, aged wood, and the faintest trace of something familiar—maybe the remnants of old summer candles, the kind her mother used to keep burning when guests were over. Savannah ran her fingers along the banister as they made their way inside, memories pressing in with every step. The living room looked almost untouched, the old white couch still in its place, the same seashell decorations lined along the fireplace mantel.

She swallowed.

Too many nights had been spent here, tangled up in a blanket, her legs draped over his lap, his voice murmuring low in her ear as they talked about everything and nothing at all.

She hadn't thought about him in a long time. At least, that's what she told herself. But being here made the memories feel fresh, like they were waiting just beneath the surface, eager to be revived.

Back then, he was the one everyone wanted, the one who never had to try. Charming, reckless, impossible to ignore. And yet, before she ever belonged to Trevor, before she ever fell into the safe, steady love she thought would last forever, there had been stolen looks. Fleeting moments where she wondered what if. There had been a time when his eyes lingered too long, when her heart raced a little faster around him, when it felt like something might happen between them if only she had let it. But she hadn't. And then, she met Trevor.

Trevor was the safer choice, the one who didn't come with complications. He had loved her in a way that felt solid, in a way she thought she needed. And for a while, it had been enough. Until it wasn't. Until the cracks formed, the distance grew, and the love that once felt unshakable slowly faded into something unrecognizable.

She sighed, pushing the thought away. This trip wasn't about the past—it was about unwinding, resetting, and remembering who she was before life had pulled her in a million directions.

"This place is incredible," Mallory said, spinning in a slow circle as she took it all in. "I can't believe you stayed away this long."

Savannah forced a small smile. "Yeah, well... life happened."

Mallory didn't press, which she appreciated. Instead, her friend stretched her arms above her head and grinned. "Alright, here's the plan. We drop our bags, open a bottle of wine, and then go find some trouble."

Savannah shot her a look. "Define 'trouble.'"

Mallory wiggled her brows. "Oh, you know. A little mischief, a little dancing, maybe a little harmless flirting with attractive strangers."

Savannah snorted. "You do realize we're not twenty-one anymore, right?"

Mallory waved a hand. "Speak for yourself. I fully intend to make the most of this trip. And you, my dear, are going to have fun, whether you like it or not."

Savannah wanted to argue, but part of her knew Mallory wouldn't let her. And maybe—just maybe—she didn't want to fight it this time.

She wondered, just for a fleeting second, if he was still around. But that was ridiculous. After all, they had been teenagers, caught up in the thrill of summer and possibility. Whatever had existed between them—if anything had truly existed at all—was long gone.

What she didn't know was that some things never really fade. And Wrightsville Beach had a way of pulling people back together—whether they were ready for it or not.

3

Unwritten Past

AFTER SAVANNAH AND MALLORY got settled in, unpacked their bags, and changed into something more fitting for the warm coastal air, they decided to take a drive through town. Mallory was eager to explore, taking in the charm of Wrightsville Beach for the first time, while Savannah—well, she wouldn't admit to wanting to see what, or maybe who, was still here.

The streets felt both familiar and foreign as she navigated them. The same winding roads, the same towering oak trees lining the outskirts of town, their sprawling branches forming a canopy overhead, casting shifting shadows against the pavement. The salty breeze drifted in through the open windows, bringing with it the unmistakable scents of fried seafood, warm boardwalk planks, and the faintest trace of suntan lotion lingering in the air.

Storefronts had changed. Some bore fresh coats of paint, while others had been replaced entirely, but the essence of Wrightsville Beach remained the same—unchanged, unwavering, just as she had left it.

She slowed the car as they approached the pier, a place that had once been a staple of her summers. The ice cream shop on the corner still had its bright red awning, though the sign now looked newer, shinier. The bait shop next door had undergone a facelift, its once-faded exterior now crisp and well-maintained, yet the wooden dock that stretched into the water remained untouched—weathered, sturdy, a constant in a town that had evolved in pieces.

She could still remember the late nights spent there, wrapped up in someone's hoodie, toes dipping into the cool water, laughter carried away by the wind. The scent of bonfires and salt, the sound of distant music playing from a car stereo, and the unmistakable pull of something that had once felt bigger than anything else in the world.

Then, as they turned the corner, something else caught her attention.

A name.

A sign she hadn't expected to see.

Montgomery & Associates

Consulting Services

Her fingers instinctively tightened around the steering wheel as she eased the car to a stop in front of the building. It was an old Southern-style home, the kind that had been repurposed for business without sacrificing its charm. A white wraparound porch stretched across the front, supported by thick columns that looked as if they had witnessed decades of whispered conversations and quiet confessions. The windows glowed softly from the inside, warm and inviting, and the front yard was landscaped with such precision that it was clear—this was not temporary. This was rooted. Permanent.

Her stomach twisted.

It couldn't be his.

It couldn't be the same Chase Montgomery she had known—the one who had spent his nights charming every girl in town, the one who had been as wild and unpredictable as the ocean itself.

"Holy shit."

Mallory's voice cut through the quiet, snapping Savannah out of her trance.

She turned to find her friend staring at the sign, wide-eyed.

"That's his, isn't it?" Mallory asked, though it wasn't really a question.

Savannah swallowed hard. "I don't know."

Mallory scoffed. "Don't lie to me. That's Chase Montgomery's. I remember the way you used to talk about him."

Savannah shook her head, shifting her gaze back to the building, as if looking at it long enough might make it disappear. "That was a long time ago."

"But it was real." Mallory folded her arms. "You were crazy about him."

Savannah let out a quiet laugh, one devoid of humor. "I was young."

"You were in love," Mallory corrected. "And instead, you went for the safe choice."

Savannah's chest tightened. "Trevor wasn't—"

"Trevor wasn't Chase," Mallory interjected, blunt as ever. "I've heard the stories, Sav. How your face would light up when Chase was around. How even when you were with Trevor, it was always him."

Savannah exhaled slowly, willing the memories to stay buried where they belonged. But they didn't.

She could still picture Chase—tan skin, wind-tousled hair, the mischievous grin he always wore like a second skin. She could still hear the sound of his laughter, the way he used to make everything feel effortless, weightless. He had been the kind of person you didn't just forget. The kind that lingered.

She looked back at the sign, her pulse quickening.

She had spent years convincing herself that Chase had been nothing more than a reckless infatuation, a fleeting crush on someone she had no business wanting. She had told herself that leaving had been the right choice, that choosing stability over chaos had been smart.

But standing here now, staring at proof that he had stayed, that he had built something real, something lasting in this town... it made her question everything.

"It doesn't matter now," she said finally, her voice quieter than she intended.

Mallory studied her for a long moment before sighing. "Fine. If that's what you want to tell yourself. But I have a feeling you're about to find out otherwise."

Savannah's hands tightened on the wheel as she stared out at the quiet street. The sunset bathed everything in golden light, casting an almost nostalgic glow over the town, making it feel harder to stay detached.

She wanted to believe that Chase was just another piece of her past, another name she had long since left behind.

But deep down, she knew better.

"I get it," Mallory said, her tone softer now. "You think letting him go was the right thing. That playing it safe was smart. But, Savannah, safe doesn't mean happy."

Savannah sighed, shaking her head. "Maybe some people aren't meant to be 'your person,' Mallory. Maybe they're just meant to be part of your story."

Mallory tilted her head, watching her carefully. "And what part of your story was Chase?"

Savannah hesitated. She could still remember the way his eyes lingered when he thought no one was watching, the way his voice sounded when he said her name. The way her heart had betrayed her every single time she saw him, no matter how much she told herself otherwise.

"The chapter that never got written," she finally admitted, her voice barely above a whisper.

Mallory let out a slow breath. "And you're okay with that?"

Savannah forced a small smile, though it didn't quite reach her eyes. "I don't really have a choice, do I?"

Mallory didn't push further, but the silence between them was weighted.

The sun had begun to dip lower, streaking the sky with hues of orange and pink, reflecting off the water in a way that made everything feel softer, almost dreamlike. For a moment, Savannah let herself sink into it—the familiarity, the memories, the ache of something unresolved.

Then, Mallory smirked. "Alright, serious moment over. Now, I'm starving. Where's the best place to eat around here?"

Savannah exhaled a laugh, grateful for the shift. "The Low-Tide Tavern."

Mallory raised an eyebrow. "That's the one you said was his favorite, isn't it?"

Savannah hesitated, then nodded. "Yeah."

Mallory's smirk widened. "Then that's definitely where we're going."

Savannah's heart pounded as she turned onto the road leading toward the tavern. Toward the inevitable.

Toward him.

4

Never, Yet

MEANWHILE, ON THE BACKSIDE of Wrightsville, where the sound met the shore in a quiet, undisturbed embrace, Chase Montgomery stepped out of the shower, steam curling around him like a ghost of heat. He raked a towel over his damp hair, watching his own reflection in the fogged-up mirror. His face, still sharp and defined, carried the echoes of a man who had lived a little too recklessly in his younger years—late nights, whiskey-soaked promises, and a reputation that had made him both infamous and irresistible.

But tonight wasn't about that. It wasn't about chasing another Friday night thrill, another meaningless rendezvous that left his sheets warm but his bed feeling colder than ever by morning. No, the infamous Friday Night Fling Circuit had lost its appeal. The start of tourist season meant the bars were about to be filled with out-of-towners looking for a Wrightsville Beach adventure—just as they always were.

And yet, for once, Chase wasn't interested.

Instead, he planned to head into town early, before the Low-Tide Tavern filled up with summer visitors who wanted nothing more than to hear a Southern drawl whisper something tempting in their ears. He wanted a drink, a little time to breathe before the night took on a life of its own.

He reached for his watch, clasping it around his wrist just as the sound of tires crunching over the gravel driveway reached his ears. A smirk tugged at the corner of his mouth. Right on time.

Jaxon Stone.

The two had met back when Chase was just a kid, before his family had picked up and moved to Wrightsville when he was sixteen. Jaxon had been one of the few friendships that survived the distance, the years, the inevitable shifts that came with growing up. While Chase had built his empire in coastal consulting, Jaxon had carved out a different kind of success—partner at one of the largest financial firms in the Southeast, a man who handled wealth like an artist worked a canvas.

Now, he lived in Oak Island, close enough that their occasional meetups had turned into something more regular. And though they were in entirely different industries, Jaxon was also Chase's financial advisor—the one person he trusted to keep his assets in order, his investments thriving.

A sharp knock echoed through the house just before the front door swung open.

"Why would you just walk in?"

The exasperated voice came from behind Jaxon, a playful huff of frustration that made Chase chuckle before he even stepped into the living room.

Sara.

Jaxon's wife had a way of reigning him in, balancing out his easygoing, sometimes oblivious demeanor. She was fierce in the best way, the kind of woman who could run an entire event without breaking a sweat and still manage to make you feel like you were the most important person in the room. Owning a catering business meant she was often too busy to join them on their nights out, but when she did, she made her presence known.

Jaxon held up his hands in mock surrender, a smirk pulling at his lips. "I've been coming here for years. If he was worried about it, he'd lock the damn door."

Sara rolled her eyes, stepping into the house behind him. "One day, Chase is going to have some poor girl in here, and you're going to walk in on something you *definitely* don't want to see."

Chase grinned, leaning against the counter. "Not tonight. I'm keeping things simple."

Jaxon raised a brow. "Simple? That's new for you."

Chase shrugged, grabbing a beer from the fridge and tossing one to Jaxon. "Besides, you know I don't bring them here anyway."

Sara smirked, crossing her arms. "So, no charming some unsuspecting tourist out of her sundress tonight?"

Chase chuckled, taking a sip of his beer. "Not in the mood."

Jaxon shook his head. "Well, that's a first."

Sara narrowed her eyes at him. "Wait... is this about someone specific?"

Chase didn't flinch, but he could feel the weight of Sara's gaze on him. If anyone could read through his bullshit, it was her.

"Not everything is about a woman, Sara."

She tilted her head. "Uh-huh. Sure."

Jaxon smirked and leaned against the counter. "Well, now I have to know. But first, we're grabbing dinner before drinks."

Chase arched a brow. "Since when do we do dinner first?"

"Since we have a sitter and my wife is actually free for once," Jaxon said, throwing an arm around Sara. "And you're buying, since you never eat actual meals unless someone forces you to."

Chase scoffed but didn't argue. "Fine, but we're not going anywhere fancy."

Sara clapped her hands together. "Perfect, because I want some damn good seafood."

They headed out together, piling into Chase's truck, the familiarity of their friendship settling in like an old, comfortable habit. The drive to the restaurant was filled with easy conversation, the kind that didn't require effort, the kind Chase appreciated more than he let on.

As they pulled into the parking lot, Sara glanced out the window, her eyes scanning the rustic exterior of the Low-Tide Tavern. "This place looks a lot like Tides Rising back in Oak Island," she mused. "Jaxon and I love that place. Feels like home every time we walk in."

Jaxon smirked, nudging her playfully. "That's because you charm the bartender, Mike into giving us extra hush puppies every time."

Sara shrugged with a grin. "What can I say? People like me."

Chase chuckled, shaking his head as they stepped inside.

By the time they slid into a booth at the seafood joint just off the marina, Chase found himself watching them—Jaxon and Sara—without meaning to. The way she leaned into him, how he whispered something in her ear that made her laugh. The way Jaxon rested a hand on her thigh like it was the most natural thing in the world.

Chase took a sip of his whiskey, his gaze flicking away. He didn't do that. He didn't bring women to dinner, didn't have anyone to lean into, didn't have someone who made him feel like home wasn't just a place but a person.

Sara caught him staring, her expression softening. "You ever think about it?"

Chase raised a brow. "Think about what?"

She gestured between her and Jaxon. "This. A real thing. Something steady."

Jaxon smirked. "Be careful, man. She's matchmaking again."

Chase chuckled, shaking his head. "I don't do this," he admitted, gesturing to their easy affection. "Never have."

Sara studied him for a moment before she smiled knowingly. "Never yet."

Chase didn't answer. Because for the first time in a long time, he wasn't so sure.

After a moment of silence, he exhaled and ran a hand through his hair. "You know, I've never really said this out loud before... but I think I've always wanted what you two have. Not the wild nights or the endless options—just someone who gets me. Someone to come home to."

Sara leaned in, her expression soft but knowing. "And you think that's not possible for you?"

Chase hesitated. "I don't know. Maybe I've played this role for so long that I don't even know how to be something else."

Sara shook her head with a small smile. "You and Jaxon are more alike than you think. He used to say the same thing before we got together. Thought he wasn't built for all of this. Turns out, he was wrong." She squeezed Jaxon's hand under the table before looking back at Chase. "Maybe you're wrong, too."

Chase let her words settle, staring into his glass as if it held the answers he wasn't ready to face. Because deep down, he knew—she might just be right.

He let out a dry chuckle and shook his head. "Damnit Jaxon, I know you can't get anything by this woman. If she can read me and see through my bullshit, I can only imagine how it is with you."

5

Where It Began

THE LOW-TIDE TAVERN SAT just off the water, the kind of place that smelled like salt, beer, and fried food. A place where the wooden floors creaked under years of footsteps and spilled whiskey. It was the perfect blend of local grit and coastal charm, where the regulars had their seats claimed before sundown, and the tourists got just drunk enough to believe they belonged.

As Savannah and Mallory pulled into the gravel parking lot, the warm, sticky air of Wrightsville wrapped around them like an old memory. The neon sign flickers against the twilight sky, casting a dull glow over the steady hum of music and laughter spilling from inside. The place was packed. It always was this time of year.

Savannah's grip tightened on the steering wheel for half a second before she exhaled and put the car in park.

Mallory caught the hesitation immediately. "What?"

Savannah shook her head, forcing a smirk. "Nothing. Just hasn't changed much."

Mallory arched a brow. "That's the point of coming back, isn't it? Nostalgia, a little sun, a little drinking? Maybe a little—"

"Nope." Savannah cut her off with a sharp look. "Not happening. I am not here for that."

Mallory scoffed. "Please. It's a beach town and it's you. That alone means trouble."

Savannah laughed, shaking her head, but as she stepped out of the car, she couldn't deny the way her heart clenched at the sight of the old bar. This place had history—her history. Back when she was younger, before life got complicated—before she traded spontaneous beach nights for GIS searches and real estate deals—this was where it all happened. Late-night drinks that turned into sunrise conversations. Friends that felt like family. The kind of summers that made you believe in forever.

And then, of course, there was him.

She ignored the thought as she and Mallory stepped inside, pushing through the crowd and heading straight for the hostess stand.

"Patio seating?" Savannah asked over the noise, already knowing the answer.

The hostess, a younger girl with sun-kissed skin and salt-dried curls, barely glanced up from her seating chart. "It's a wait. Ten, maybe fifteen. Bar's open, though."

Savannah glanced at Mallory, who just shrugged. "We'll wait."

The hostess scribbled something down and nodded toward the side door. "Go grab a drink. I'll come find you."

Savannah and Mallory maneuvered their way through the crowd, past groups of tourists nursing colorful cocktails, past the jukebox that had probably been broken since 2008, and finally out onto the patio.

The air was thick with summer heat, the sound of waves lapping against the dock blending with the murmur of conversation. String lights stretched overhead, casting a soft glow over the bar area, where locals and tourists alike drank, laughed, and leaned in a little too close over their beers.

They found a standing spot near the railing, Savannah settling into her chair as Mallory draped her arms over the back of hers, surveying the crowd.

"I like it," Mallory decided. "Feels... lived in."

Savannah smirked. "That's one way to put it."

Mallory stretched her legs out. "Alright, I need a drink. What do you want?"

Savannah exhaled, rubbing the condensation from the table with her fingertips. "Vodka soda."

"Classy." Mallory grinned. "Be back in a sec."

Savannah watched her disappear into the crowd before leaning back in her chair, letting the atmosphere settle around her. It felt the same but different, like returning to a house you hadn't lived in for years—familiar, but just foreign enough to keep you on edge.

A breeze rolled off the water, lifting strands of her hair as she glanced around. The patio was packed with a mix of sun-kissed locals and out-of-towners, their voices weaving into the hum of the night. A group of guys stood near the dock, laughing a little too loudly, their drinks sloshing as they gestured wildly. A couple leaned into each other near the bar, their touches lingering, their words meant only for each other.

Savannah exhaled, forcing herself to relax. The past was just that—the past. She wasn't that girl anymore, the one who had let a summer fling consume her, who had believed in reckless promises whispered under the cover of night.

She stared out at the water, watching the way the lights reflected against the gentle ripples. The ocean had a way of making everything feel smaller, reminding her that time moved forward whether she was ready or not.

"Alright, I made a friend," Mallory announced, dropping into the seat across from her and sliding a drink over. "Bartender's got a heavy pour, so drink up."

Savannah reached for the glass, grateful for the distraction. "Thanks."

Mallory took a sip of her own drink, then studied her. "So, are you going to tell me what's actually on your mind, or are we going to pretend you're just brooding for fun?"

Savannah smirked. "I don't brood."

"The fuck you don't. Especially when a certain topic—person—comes up." Mallory wiggled her eyebrows.

Savannah rolled her eyes. "It's not about him."

Mallory arched a skeptical brow. "Mmmhmm. Sure."

Savannah exhaled, tapping her fingers against her glass. "It's just weird being back. Seeing everything the same but knowing that I'm different."

Mallory softened. "Yeah, I get that. But maybe that's a good thing. Maybe it's a sign that you needed to come back, at least for a little while."

Savannah let her gaze drift back to the water. "Maybe."

They sat in silence for a moment, the background noise of the bar filling the space between them.

Then, Mallory smirked. "Okay, serious moment over. Now, let's talk about the important things—like how that guy at the bar keeps looking over here, and how you should absolutely let me play wing-woman tonight."

Savannah groaned, shaking her head. "Hard pass."

"Oh, come on." Mallory grinned, taking another sip of her drink. "I promise I'll only embarrass you a little."

Savannah laughed despite herself, the weight on her chest easing just a fraction. "I'll think about it."

Mallory raised her glass. "I'll take that as a yes."

Savannah clinked her glass against Mallory's, letting herself get lost in the moment, in the familiar rhythm of the town that had once been her entire world.

For tonight, at least, the past could wait.

Almost Was

AT THE OTHER END of the tavern, Chase nursed his beer, half-listening as Jaxon rattled off something about a new investment opportunity. He wasn't paying attention. Not really. His thoughts had drifted, restless and unsettled.

Sara was the first to notice.

"Okay, what's going on with you?" she asked, crossing her arms as she studied him.

Chase raised an eyebrow. "What are you talking about?"

Sara smirked. "You're quiet tonight. That's never a good sign."

Jaxon chuckled. "Yeah, man. You got that faraway look."

Chase exhaled, shaking his head. "It's nothing. Just... this place. Brings back memories."

Sara tilted her head. "What kind of memories?"

Chase hesitated. He traced the rim of his beer bottle with his thumb, debating how much to say. Finally, he sighed. "The kind that stick."

Jaxon leaned back, his curiosity piqued. "So, we talking about a girl?"

Chase let out a dry laugh. "Yeah. Savannah Monroe."

Jaxon let out a low whistle. "Damn. Now that is a name I haven't heard in a while."

Sara's eyes gleamed. "You liked her."

Chase shook his head. "It wasn't like that. Not really. She was with Trevor."

Sara scoffed. "And? Jaxon was with my sister, and look how we turned out."

Jaxon smirked. "She's got a point."

Chase sighed. "It's different. She wasn't just some fling."

Sara leaned in. "Then what was she?"

Chase ran a hand through his hair, exhaling slowly. "She was... the one that got away."

Sara's teasing faded, replaced with something softer. "How so?"

Chase glanced at Jaxon and Sara—the way she leaned into him, the way he looked at her like she was the best damn thing in the world. Chase cleared his throat, forcing the words out. "Because I looked at her the way Jaxon looks at you. Like she was it. Like if I had her, I wouldn't need anything else."

Sara's smile was knowing, but she didn't gloat. "Then why didn't you do something about it?"

Chase shrugged. "Timing. Choices. Life."

Jaxon took a slow sip of his drink. "And now?"

Chase chuckled, but there was no humor in it. "Now? It doesn't matter. That was years ago."

Sara arched a brow. "Then why do you still talk about her like it does?"

Chase exhaled, rubbing the back of his neck. "Because I still think about her from time to time. The what ifs. The fact that she's successful, several hours away, and probably hasn't thought about this town in years. I have no clue if she'd ever come back. But if she did..."

He trailed off, shaking his head like he was foolish for even saying it.

Sara leaned in, her voice softer now. "You'd do something about it."

Chase glanced down at his drink, rolling the bottle between his palms. He wasn't sure what he'd do. Hell, he wasn't even sure if he deserved the chance to do anything. Years had passed, and life had moved forward whether he liked it or not. But some nights, in a place like this, surrounded by memories so thick he could almost reach out and touch them, it was impossible not to wonder.

Jaxon watched him carefully, his expression unreadable. "You ever try looking her up? Social media, mutual friends? Something?"

Chase smirked, but it was a little sad around the edges. "What would be the point? I doubt she's sitting around wondering about me."

Sara shook her head. "Men are so damn clueless. If she was ever really yours, even for a moment, I promise you—she's wondered."

Chase exhaled, pressing the heel of his hand against his forehead. He wanted to believe that. Wanted to believe that in some quiet moment, in some stolen thought between business meetings or late-night drives, Savannah Monroe still thought of him.

But that wasn't how life worked. Not really.

"So what are you gonna do?" Jaxon asked after a beat.

Chase leaned back in his chair, staring out at the crowd, at the way the tavern hummed with energy, completely unaware of the war inside his head. He tapped his fingers against the table, considering his answer before he finally shrugged.

"I don't know."

Sara wasn't satisfied with that answer. "That's bullshit. If she walked in here right now, you're telling me you wouldn't say a word? Wouldn't even try?"

Chase's jaw tightened. "It's not that simple."

Sara scoffed. "It is. You either let the past stay buried, or you do something about it."

Jaxon leaned in. "What's the worst that could happen?"

Chase let out a short laugh. "You really want the list?" He ran a hand down his face. "What if she's married? What if she looks right through me like I don't exist? What if I'm just some guy she used to know?"

Jaxon shrugged. "And what if she's not?"

Silence hung between them for a beat too long. Chase didn't answer, because deep down, that was the part that scared him the most.

Because if she wasn't, if she did remember, if there was still something there—

Then he'd have to do something about it. And he wasn't sure he was ready for that kind of truth.

One Drink In

Mallory plopped back into her chair, setting Savannah's drink in front of her with a mischievous grin. She leaned forward, eyes sparkling with something that Savannah immediately knew meant trouble.

"Okay, don't look now, but there's a ridiculously hot guy sitting over by the bar with a man and a woman."

Savannah lifted a skeptical brow, fingers wrapping around the condensation-slick glass in front of her. "And you're telling me this why?"

Mallory took a slow, deliberate sip of her drink before smirking. "Because, my dear, I am deeply invested in your love life. And because... damn. He's got that whole brooding, 'I probably break hearts for fun' thing going on. You know the type—strong jaw, broad shoulders, bearded and tattooed, beer in one hand, and probably a trail of exes who still dream about him."

Savannah huffed a laugh, shaking her head. "Not interested."

Mallory groaned. "Oh, come on. Don't be that girl. It's been too long since you've had fun. And this guy? He looks like the kind of fun that ruins you for all other fun."

Savannah took a slow sip of her drink, eyes flickering toward the water instead of the bar. "I came here for a vacation, Mal. Not for—"

"A good time? A distraction? A little toe-curling, screaming-his-name-against-the-wall fun?" Mallory teased, her voice low and scandalous.

Savannah nearly choked on her drink, setting it down with a sharp clink. "Jesus Christ, Mal."

Mallory cackled, fully enjoying herself. "I'm just saying, a little fun wouldn't kill you. Besides, you always did have a thing for—"

"I don't even know what he looks like," Savannah interrupted, her tone exasperated.

Mallory grinned wickedly. "Oh, but I do. And let me tell you, he's exactly your type. Rugged. Intense. The kind of guy who looks like he could build you a house with his bare hands and then wreck you in it."

Savannah rolled her eyes, trying to ignore the warmth creeping up her neck. "Sounds exhausting."

"Sounds exhilarating," Mallory corrected. "And you need exhilarating. You need something to shake you up."

Savannah sighed, tapping a nail against the side of her glass. "I think my life is shaken up enough as it is."

Mallory tilted her head, studying her. "That what this trip is really about? Escaping the chaos?"

Savannah hesitated, then nodded. "Yeah. Something like that."

Mallory let the moment hang before nudging her foot under the table. "Fine. But just know that if you don't make a move, I might have to go introduce myself. You know, for research purposes."

Savannah groaned. "I hate you."

Mallory laughed, raising her glass. "You love me. Now, drink up. This night is just getting started."

Just as Savannah was about to respond, the hostess reappeared, a clipboard in hand and a practiced, polite smile on her face. "Ladies, your table is ready."

Mallory clapped her hands together. "Perfect timing. Come on, Savy, let's get you seated closer to this mystery man."

Savannah rolled her eyes but stood, grabbing her drink as she followed the hostess through the crowd. As they weaved between tables, Savannah was hyper-aware of her surroundings—the low hum of conversations, the occasional burst of laughter, the scent of fried seafood mingling with the salty breeze drifting in from the open patio doors.

Her heart thudded a little harder in her chest, though she refused to acknowledge why. It was just the atmosphere. The nostalgia. Nothing more.

They stepped onto the patio, the warm air wrapping around them, string lights swaying slightly with the night breeze. The hostess led them toward a table tucked in the corner, offering a perfect view of the dock and just enough privacy to escape the chaos of the main bar.

Savannah slid into her seat, exhaling slowly as Mallory took the one across from her, still grinning like she knew something Savannah didn't.

"This is nice," Savannah admitted, glancing around.

Mallory smirked. "It is. And the best part? You're in prime position to make eye contact with the hot guy by the bar."

Savannah groaned. "Would you stop?"

Mallory propped her chin in her hand, feigning innocence. "What? I'm just pointing out the obvious."

Savannah shook her head, taking a sip of her drink, trying to focus on the view rather than the possibility of some 'ridiculously hot guy' lurking nearby. She wasn't here for that. She wasn't here for any of it.

Mallory, however, was relentless.

"Okay, okay, serious question," Mallory said, swirling the ice in her glass. "When was the last time you actually had fun? I mean, real, no-strings, no-reservations fun?"

Savannah frowned. "I have fun."

Mallory shot her a look. "Binge-watching crime documentaries with a glass of wine doesn't count."

Savannah hesitated, then exhaled. "It's been a while."

"Exactly," Mallory said triumphantly. "Which is why I am officially your designated bad influence for this trip. And step one? You stop overthinking and just enjoy yourself."

Savannah smirked. "You realize you sound like a bad rom-com character, right?"

Mallory grinned. "And yet, I'm not wrong."

Savannah chuckled despite herself, the tension in her shoulders easing just slightly. Maybe Mallory had a point. Maybe it wouldn't hurt to let go just a little.

The night stretched ahead of them, full of possibility. And for the first time in a long time, Savannah considered the idea of stepping outside her comfort zone.

Mallory took another sip of her drink before scanning the patio with interest. "You know," she mused, "we could always make this more interesting."

Savannah raised a brow. "How so?"

Mallory smirked. "A game."

Savannah sighed. "I already don't like this."

"Oh, hush. It's simple," Mallory insisted. "If you can go the entire night without sneaking a peek at Mr. Brooding Hotness, I'll buy all your drinks tomorrow. But if you look—just once—you have to go talk to him."

Savannah scoffed. "That's ridiculous."

"Is it, though?" Mallory challenged. "Because you're already thinking about it."

Savannah crossed her arms. "Fine. But when I win, I'm getting the most expensive cocktails on the menu."

Mallory grinned. "Deal. Now, let's see how long you last."

Familiar Eyes

CHASE WAS MID-BITE, HIS fork hovering just inches from his mouth when the trio walked by. It wasn't unusual for him to be half-distracted while eating—after all, the Low-Tide Tavern was as much a place for people-watching as it was for good food and cold beer. But something about this particular moment made his body tense, his senses heighten like a fucking hunter in the wild.

Two women, led by the hostess, strolled past his table, their laughter soft and easy, like the sound of waves rolling in at low tide. He didn't even realize he was watching them so intently until—

"You good, man?" Jaxon's voice pulled him back to the present.

Chase blinked, forcing himself to focus, but it was too late. His attention was already hooked.

The women settled into a table on the patio, just within his periphery. He tore his gaze away, but his ears stayed tuned to the background noise, his subconscious catching every note of their conversation without meaning to.

A few minutes passed. He forced himself to engage with Jaxon and Sara, to focus on his food, but the weight in his chest wouldn't let up. Then, movement. One of the women—tall, blonde, confident as hell—rose from her chair and headed toward the bar.

Chase wasn't watching her. Not really. He was just... aware.

Until she called out. "Savy, what do you want?"

He froze.

The fork in his hand clattered against the plate, his grip loosening as his mind short-circuited. He had only ever known one person called Savy.

His heart pounded. His ocean-blue eyes immediately flicked up, scanning the restaurant with military precision, sweeping over tables, chairs, groups of tourists, trying to follow the path of the blonde's voice, trying to pinpoint exactly who she had been shouting at.

But there were too many people. Too much movement. His pulse was a fucking drumline in his ears, drowning out the rest of the noise in the restaurant.

No. No fucking way.

He leaned forward, trying to look past a cluster of customers, but all he could make out were bits and pieces—shoulders, arms, glimpses of movement. His gut twisted with something between hope and panic. It had been years. She was hours away. She had built a life somewhere else. There was no way she was here.

And then, the blonde at the bar turned, her gaze catching his.

A slow, knowing smirk spread across her lips as she lifted her hand in a casual wave. Chase tensed. His fingers curled into his palms.

She knew who he was.

He barely managed to nod back, his face an unreadable mask, but his insides were a damn hurricane. She grabbed her drinks, spun on her heel, and strode back toward her table.

Chase sat frozen as he watched her return, watched her lean in close, and whisper something to the brunette sitting across from her. And then—

Savannah.

His chest squeezed so tight he swore he forgot how to breathe.

She turned in her seat, following the blonde's gesture, and then bam. Their eyes met.

Everything stopped. The noise. The conversations. The clatter of silverware and the low hum of the bar. Nothing fucking mattered because Savannah Monroe was staring right at him.

And Chase? He was staring right the fuck back.

Her expression shifted in slow motion—recognition first, then something unreadable. Surprise? Maybe. Hesitation? Probably. But beneath all of that, buried under years and distance and things unsaid, there was something else.

Something that damn near knocked the air from his lungs.

Across the table, Sara muttered, "Holy shit."

Chase heard it distantly, but his body was no longer his own. It was reacting on instinct, his pulse hammering against his ribs, his fingers flexing against the table. His mind was working overtime, flipping through the years, piecing together every moment that had led to this.

Jaxon, always observant, leaned in slightly, eyes flicking between Chase and Savannah. "Well... that's unexpected."

Sara, however, wasn't so quiet. She nudged Chase's arm, watching him closely.

"You good?"

His jaw tightened. He couldn't take his fucking eyes off her. Savannah Monroe. Right here. In his bar. In his town. Sitting twenty mother-fucking feet away like she hadn't haunted him for years.

Sara exhaled, reading him like an open book. "Jesus, Chase," she murmured. "Your eyes just gave you away."

He forced himself to look at her, brow furrowing. "What?"

She smirked, shaking her head. "You might as well have just walked over there and announced you're still in love with her."

Chase clenched his fists under the table, dragging in a slow breath. "I never said—"

Sara cut him off with a knowing look. "You didn't have to."

His stomach was a damn wrecking ball, slamming into his ribs, but he couldn't pull his gaze away. Savannah looked different, yet exactly the same. More polished. More grown. More... untouchable.

And yet, the way she was looking at him?

It told him she was feeling every damn bit of this moment, too.

Jaxon leaned back, shaking his head with a grin. "So, what's the plan?"

Chase scoffed, his voice rough. "The plan? There is no plan."

Sara hummed, giving him a look that made it clear she didn't believe him. "Bullshit. You're a man with a plan, Chase Montgomery. You always have been."

Chase dragged a hand down his face, feeling the weight of everything. "I don't even know what I'd say to her."

Jaxon shrugged. "Start with hello."

Chase huffed out a breath, his fingers tapping against the table as his eyes drifted back to Savannah. "Yeah. Easy. Hello. After all these years. After everything. Like that's gonna fucking work."

Sara smirked, lifting her glass. "Well, the way you're looking at her? She won't be the one walking away first."

Chase swallowed hard, jaw tightening as Savannah took a slow sip of her drink, eyes never leaving his.

He was fucked.

The weight of the past pressed down on him, memories colliding with reality in a way that made his chest ache. He could almost hear her laugh, almost feel the heat of those stolen nights, the whispered conversations under starlit skies, the taste of goodbye that had never really settled.

And now, just when he thought he had buried it, just when he had convinced himself that history had been rewritten—

She was here, rewriting it all over again.

Chase leaned forward, gripping the edge of the table as if steadying himself.

Jaxon let out a low whistle. "Man, you look like you just seen a ghost."

He had.

And she was more real than ever.

Collision Course

MALLORY RETURNED TO THE table, practically bouncing into her seat, her face lit up with barely contained excitement. She set Savannah's drink down with a dramatic flourish and leaned in conspiratorially.

"Okay, check it out," she whispered, eyes gleaming, "that ridiculously hot guy sitting over there with a couple of people. And I swear to God, he just looked this way. Twice."

Savannah barely reached for her drink before she felt it—a shift in the air, a strange, unexpected tension that wrapped around her chest before she even turned around. Her fingers curled tightly around the glass, moisture from the condensation slick against her palm.

She should've ignored it. Should've rolled her eyes and laughed at Mallory's ridiculous matchmaking attempts. But something in Mallory's voice—some edge—made her pause.

And then she looked.

And everything inside her unraveled.

Chase fucking Montgomery.

Sitting there, halfway through a meal, his hands curled into fists on the table, his ocean-blue eyes locked onto her like she was the only thing in the fucking world.

Savannah's breath stalled somewhere between her chest and her mouth. The air in the tavern suddenly felt too thick, too charged with something she wasn't ready to face.

Mallory, still oblivious to the tidal wave crashing through Savannah's system, kept going. "I mean, seriously, look at him. He's like some kind of dark, brooding, life-ruining fantasy. That jawline? Those arms? Tell me you don't want to climb that man and ride him like your life depends on it."

Savannah barely heard her. The world had tilted on its axis. She was drowning in a tide she hadn't seen coming, one that dragged her back into memories she had no business reliving.

Mallory finally caught on to the fact that Savannah wasn't speaking, and wasn't moving. Her grin faltered. "Savy? What's wrong?"

Savannah's gaze remained locked onto Chase, her pulse hammering. She swallowed hard, trying to find her voice, but it came out barely above a whisper. "That's him."

Mallory frowned. "Who?"

Savannah dragged her eyes away from the past and met Mallory's. "That's Chase Montgomery."

Mallory's reaction was immediate and dramatic. She blinked rapidly and looked back at Chase, then back at Savannah. "The Chase Montgomery? Your Chase? The one you never shut up about when we first met?"

Savannah nodded once, throat too tight to speak.

Mallory's jaw nearly hit the damn table. "Wait a second. That's him? That's the guy? The one you let slip through your fingers? The one you used to stare off into the distance about like some tragic Hallmark movie heroine?"

Savannah clenched her drink. "I didn't let him go. We never got the chance to start."

Mallory made a strangled sound, flailing her hands. "Okay, no offense, but why the hell did you never mention that he was this level of hot? Jesus, Savannah. That man looks like he was built to ruin lives in the best possible way. And judging by the way he's eye-fucking you, he's about two seconds from wrecking yours all over again."

Savannah swallowed hard, her entire body taut with the weight of the moment. She could feel the burn of Chase's gaze from across the room, feel the way the years between them suddenly shrank to nothing.

Mallory leaned in, her voice dropping to a whisper. "Well, sweetheart, I think you just got your second chance. And you'd be an idiot not to take it."

Savannah dragged in a slow breath, forcing herself to tear her eyes away, but it was like trying to unhook herself from gravity. Chase had always been like this—magnetic, dangerous, a storm you saw coming but didn't have the sense to run from.

Memories came rushing back in a flood she wasn't prepared for. The way he used to look at her when he thought no one was watching. The way his fingers would brush against her skin, just for a second too long, enough to leave goosebumps in their wake. The sound of his voice when he whispered her name like it meant something. Like she meant something.

Her chest tightened. No. She wasn't going to do this. She wasn't going to fall into that old trap, let herself believe for even a second that fate had decided to give her a redo. Because that wasn't how life worked.

Savannah exhaled sharply, shaking her head. "It doesn't matter. It was a lifetime ago."

Mallory scoffed. "Yeah, well, tell that to the way you two are currently undressing each other with your eyes."

Savannah's fingers tightened around her glass. "Mallory—"

"Savannah." Mallory's tone shifted, losing its teasing edge. "Just answer me one thing. If you could go back—if you could do it over—would you?"

Savannah's heart pounded. "It's not that simple."

"But what if it is?" Mallory challenged. "What if the universe is handing you something you thought you lost forever?"

Savannah forced herself to take another sip of her drink, to steady her shaking fingers. "Then I'd have to decide if I was brave enough to take it."

Mallory smiled slowly. "Well, sweetheart, I think you're about to find out."

As if on cue, Chase shifted in his seat, his body language screaming indecision and restraint. He was fighting it—fighting the pull between them—but she saw the moment he lost the battle.

He pushed his chair back and stood, his eyes never leaving hers. The tavern around them buzzed with conversation, laughter, the clinking of glasses, but to Savannah, it was nothing more than background noise. White noise to the drumbeat of her pulse.

Mallory's eyes widened, excitement flashing across her face. "Oh my God. He's coming over here."

Savannah's stomach dropped to her feet. "Shit."

Mallory grinned, reaching for her drink and settling back comfortably. "Well, this just got interesting."

Savannah couldn't breathe. Couldn't move. Every muscle in her body had turned to stone. She wanted to look away, wanted to pretend this wasn't happening, but her eyes betrayed her, tracking his every move as he closed the distance between them.

The way he walked—it was the same. Confident. Unhurried. Like he knew exactly how much space he took up in the world. Like he owned every damn room he walked into. And now, that intensity, that presence, was coming straight for her.

Her heart slammed against her ribs.

And then, just like that, he was standing at her table.

Chase Montgomery, in the flesh. Bigger. Broader. Rougher around the edges.

Still the most dangerous man she'd ever known.

His voice, low and steady, sent a shiver down her spine. "Savannah."

And just like that, everything she thought she'd buried came rushing back to life.

10

The Edge

ACROSS THE TAVERN, CHASE hadn't moved a damn inch. His fork was still abandoned on his plate, his drink untouched, his entire body coiled tight like a spring about to snap. The weight in his chest pressed down hard, making it difficult to draw in a full breath. He wasn't sure if it was nerves, anticipation, or some wicked mix of both, but either way, he felt like he was standing on the edge of something monumental, something irreversible.

Sara, ever perceptive, arched an eyebrow and leaned in, resting her chin on her hand. "So, what exactly is your plan here?"

Chase tore his gaze away from Savannah for half a second, just long enough to scowl at her. "Plan?"

Sara rolled her eyes. "Don't play dumb. You're sitting here looking like you've just seen a ghost, but let's be real—you've thought about this moment, haven't you? What would happen if you saw her again? If you got another shot?"

Chase clenched his jaw. Of course, he had. More times than he'd ever admit. Late at night, when he let himself slip back into old memories. When he heard a song that reminded him of those stolen glances, those lingering moments that never quite turned into something more. He had wondered what it would feel like to be in front of her again, to see if time had dulled the pull between them—or if it had only sharpened it into something dangerous.

Jaxon smirked, clearly enjoying this way too much. "Gotta say, man, I've never seen you this rattled. It's kinda entertaining."

Chase exhaled sharply, running a hand through his hair. "I don't even know what the fuck I'd say."

Sara scoffed. "Oh, for God's sake. You're acting like you don't have a set of balls. Get up, walk over there, and talk to her."

Chase glared. "And say what? 'Hey, remember me? The guy you used to steal glances at before you chose the safe bet'?"

Sara's lips curled into a smirk. "That's a start. Hell, it's better than sitting here looking like you might pass out."

Jaxon chuckled. "Pretty sure that's not the worst pickup line she's ever heard."

Chase sighed, gripping the edge of the table. "You think she even wants to talk to me?"

Sara leaned in, lowering her voice. "Chase, look at her. Look at the way she's staring at you right now, like she just had the wind knocked out of her. If she didn't want to talk to you, she would've turned away by now."

Chase hesitated. His pulse was a fucking war drum in his ears, but she was right. Savannah hadn't looked away. She hadn't moved. It was like they were frozen in some suspended moment, hanging in the balance between past and present.

His fingers drummed against the table, restless, indecisive. "I don't know, Sara. It's been a long time. What if—"

"What if what?" Sara interjected, tilting her head. "What if she hates you? She doesn't. What if she's moved on? Maybe. But maybe not. What if she regrets never taking that chance? What if this is your shot?" She leaned in, her voice firm but knowing. "Since I've known you, you've never been one to back down from anything. Don't start now."

Jaxon grinned, lifting his glass in mock salute. "Worst that happens? She tells you to fuck off. But judging by the way she's looking at you... I doubt it."

Chase swallowed, exhaled, and finally pushed back his chair. His heartbeat thundered as he stood, his feet suddenly heavy as hell. Every muscle in his body felt taut, bracing for impact.

Sara grinned, watching him. "That's it, cowboy. Go get your girl."

Chase took a step, then another, each one heavier than the last. The space between him and Savannah felt impossibly far, the air thick with something too charged to name. He swore he could hear the blood pounding in his ears, drowning out the music, the chatter, everything except the sound of his own name echoing in his head—her voice, saying it the way she used to, soft and hesitant, like she knew she was playing with fire.

The years between them vanished as he walked, memories slamming into him with every breath.

Savannah standing on the dock, her hair wild in the wind, smiling at him like he was the only person in the world.

The way her fingers used to curl around the hem of her dress when she was nervous, when she was about to say something she knew she shouldn't.

The night he almost kissed her but didn't. The regret that had burned in his gut for years afterward.

Now, here she was. Right in front of him. And this time, he wasn't walking away without an answer.

As he neared, Savannah straightened in her chair, her lips parting slightly, her fingers tightening around her glass. He could see the way her chest rose and fell just a little too quickly, the way her gaze flickered with something unspoken, something just as dangerous as what was running through him.

Mallory, the ever-observant instigator, leaned back in her chair with a grin. "Oh, this is about to be good."

Chase barely registered her. He stopped just short of Savannah's table, his hands flexing at his sides, trying to suppress the storm raging inside him.

"Savannah," he said, his voice rougher than he intended.

She blinked up at him, her expression unreadable, but he caught the way her throat bobbed, the way her grip on her drink tightened like she needed something to hold onto.

"Chase," she said softly, and damn if that didn't knock the wind right out of him.

The air between them stretched tight, thick with everything unspoken. Years of silence, of missed chances, of paths that had almost crossed but never quite did.

Mallory, sensing the shift, lifted her drink to her lips. "Well, don't just stand there looking pretty, cowboy. Say something."

Chase dragged in a breath, his jaw tightening. He had no idea what the hell to say, no script to follow, no plan. Just the weight of everything he'd never said before pressing against his ribs.

So, he did the only thing that felt right.

He pulled out the chair across from Savannah and sat the hell down.

Tempting Tension

SAVANNAH BARELY HEARD WHAT Mallory was saying over the pounding in her ears. Every nerve in her body was on fire, and she wasn't even sure she was breathing properly.

This was fucking ridiculous.

She was a grown woman—accomplished, confident, in control. But right now? Right now, she felt like a damn teenager with a stomach full of nerves and no idea what to do with her hands.

Because Chase Montgomery was here.

And worse? He had noticed her.

"Fuck me," Mallory muttered, eyes locked across the bar. "He's getting up, Savannah. He's coming over."

Savannah's fingers tightened around her drink, nails pressing into the glass. "I can fucking see that, Mal," she hissed, heart slamming against her ribs.

"Jesus Christ." Mallory smirked. "I feel like I should be recording this. It's giving second-chance porn-level tension."

"Shut the fuck up," Savannah snapped, but before she could say anything else—

Chase was there.

Standing at their table. Hands in his pockets. Looking every bit like the mistake she was dying to make.

"Savannah."

Her name left his mouth like gravel—rough, deliberate, like he'd said it a thousand times in his head before now.

She lifted her chin, forcing herself to meet his gaze. "Chase."

Mallory let out a low whistle. "Well, damn."

Savannah resisted the urge to kick her under the table.

Behind Chase, a guy she didn't recognize leaned back in his chair, grinning like an instigator. "Well, this just got interesting."

Savannah's eyes flicked to him, then to the sharp-eyed blonde beside him, smirking in amusement.

Jaxon gestured to the empty seats. "C'mon," he said.

Mallory shot Savannah a look before getting up and making her way over. Chase and Savannah followed.

Once they sat, the conversation took on a life of its own.

Mallory, completely unbothered, leaned forward, eyes dragging over Chase like he was a damn five-course meal. "Chase Montgomery, you have no right being this fine. What the fuck?"

Chase barely spared her a glance, but the smirk on his lips was undeniable. "Appreciate that."

Mallory shook her head. "No, seriously. You look like someone made a lumberjack and a Greek god fuck. What kind of skincare routine do you have? Or is the universe just playing favorites?"

Jaxon barked out a laugh. "Oh, I fucking love her."

Sara smirked, tilting her head. "Glad y'all came to sit with us. This kind of chaos is best experienced up close."

Jaxon flagged down the waitress. "I'll buy the next round if you promise to either fight or fuck by the end of the night."

Mallory scoffed. "Oh, I like them."

Savannah groaned. "You're unbearable."

Jaxon grinned, looking between her and Chase. "Well? You gonna speak, or just keep eye-fucking each other?"

Mallory nudged Sara. "So, are you two a thing, or does Chase always keep gorgeous company?"

Sara snorted. "God, no." She nodded toward Jaxon. "He's pretty, but I have standards."

Jaxon gasped, pressing a hand to his chest. "You wound me."

Mallory cackled. "Oh, I'm gonna love you guys."

The conversation flowed, filled with teasing remarks, casual banter, and enough tension between Savannah and Chase to light the whole damn bar on fire. He was watching her, the same way he always had—like he was trying to figure out exactly how much space he was still allowed to take up in her world.

She hated how much she wanted him to take all of it.

Mallory lifted her drink, glancing between them. "You know, this is almost painful to watch. Just putting that out there."

Jaxon nodded. "Agreed. There's an entire war of sexual tension happening here, and we're just innocent bystanders."

Sara smirked. "I feel like we should be placing bets on how this ends."

"Yeah," Jaxon agreed. "But do we bet on a screaming match or a backseat makeout session?"

Mallory snorted. "Why not both? Do it in reverse order for a little extra drama."

Savannah groaned, pressing her fingers against her temple. "I swear to God, you're all insufferable."

Chase leaned in, his voice just for her. "You sure about that?"

She turned to him, already regretting it the moment she locked eyes with him. His gaze was steady, unreadable, but his presence? It was suffocating in the best, worst way.

Sara sighed dramatically. "Alright, alright. Enough of this foreplay. Just go talk. Somewhere else."

Jaxon clinked his beer against Chase's. "Yeah, get out of here before we start narrating your inner monologues for you."

Mallory grinned. "I can already hear it now: 'Savannah, why do I still want you? Why do I still dream about—'"

Savannah shoved her chair back with a groan. "Okay! We're leaving."

Mallory laughed, raising her drink in victory. "You're welcome."

Chase stood too, rubbing the back of his neck as he glanced at Jaxon and Sara. "Appreciate the warm welcome."

Jaxon smirked. "Anytime, Montgomery. Go do whatever it is you need to do."

Savannah rolled her eyes but led the way out of the booth, Chase following closely behind. As they moved toward the edge of the bar, Mallory called after them, "Don't do anything I wouldn't do!"

Jaxon added, "Or, better yet—do everything she would do."

Sara just sighed, sipping her drink. "Idiots. All of you."

Savannah exhaled as she and Chase stepped away from the table, the bar suddenly feeling too small, too hot, too charged. She felt the heat of his presence beside her, the awareness of how close he was settling over her like a heavy weight.

And she knew—whatever happened next wasn't something she could ignore.

12

Temptation Rising

OUTSIDE, THE AIR HIT her first—thick, salty, warm against her skin. Chase stopped near the railing, bracing his hands against the wood, staring out at the dark water like it held all the answers. The distant sound of waves crashing against the shore filled the silence between them, stretching it tight like a wire ready to snap.

Savannah exhaled, arms crossed over her chest, heart still hammering in her ribs. "What's on your mind, Montgomery?"

He let out a quiet laugh, rough around the edges. "Still call me that, huh?"

"It fits," she shot back, voice laced with snark.

At that, he turned—finally looking at her. Really looking at her. His gaze dragged over her face, slow and deliberate, like he was memorizing every inch, like he wasn't sure when or if he'd ever get to do it again. The weight of it settled low in her stomach, a deep, unwelcome ache.

"You look good, Savannah."

She swallowed, trying to ignore the way her breath stuttered. "You do too."

Silence stretched between them. Not awkward. Not empty. Just heavy with all the things they had never said. Every breath felt charged, like the air between them was alive, humming with unspoken truths neither of them were willing to say aloud.

Then Chase exhaled, rubbing a hand over his jaw. "I don't even know where to start. I wasn't expecting this. Seeing you. It just... threw me."

She nodded, fingers trailing along the railing. "Yeah. Me too."

He turned fully now, his broad shoulders tense, hands shoved into his pockets. His voice dipped lower, like he wasn't sure he wanted to ask but had to anyway. "Did you ever think about it? About us?"

Her breath caught. "Chase..."

He shook his head, his voice rough and raw. "No, let me—let me just fucking say it." His jaw worked, his frustration clear. "I spent years moving from one girl to another, acting like none of it mattered. Like I didn't care. But I did." His voice roughened. "You were the only one who ever fucking mattered."

Savannah's stomach clenched. Heat curled low and deep, twisting around something she didn't want to name.

"You were always with someone else, though." His voice dipped lower, his gaze dark, intense. "And not just anyone. Trevor."

She flinched. The name landed between them like a stone, heavy and unmovable.

"Trevor was..." She swallowed hard, shaking her head. "Safe. He was steady. He didn't make me feel like I was losing control just by looking at me."

Chase's expression darkened, his jaw flexing. "And I did?"

She let out a breath, unsteady. "You still do."

A slow exhale left him, his shoulders stiff. "Do you have any idea how fucking hard it was?" He dragged a hand through his hair, voice tight with something unspoken. "Watching you with him? Watching you smile at him the way I wanted you to smile at me?" His eyes burned into hers. "Knowing I couldn't do a damn thing about it?"

Savannah's grip tightened on the railing. "Then why didn't you say something?"

He let out a short laugh, low and bitter. "Because you were happy. Or at least, I thought you were." His voice dropped, softer now, almost broken. "And if you were happy with him, what the fuck was I supposed to do?"

Her heart pounded. She thought of Trevor, of the easy way he loved her, of the stability he gave her. But then she thought of Chase. The way he made her feel everything too much, the way he lit something inside her that she never knew how to handle.

Trevor had always been safe.

Chase has always been wildfire.

And she had been too much of a coward to walk into the flames.

Chase took a step closer, his heat pressing into her skin, and it was instant—electric. Her breath stuttered, thighs pressing together on instinct.

"Tell me something." His voice was low, intimate, wrapping around her like a hand at her throat.

She swallowed hard. "What?"

He reached up, his fingers barely brushing against the side of her arm. It was nothing. And it was everything. A shiver shot through her, heat pooling between her legs, her lips parting involuntarily.

"If I had kissed you back then—if I had grabbed you and just fucking kissed you—would you have let me?"

Her pulse slammed, her skin heating like he had set her on fire just by asking.

She should say no. Should tell him it wouldn't have mattered. That she would have still chosen Trevor. That it wouldn't have changed a damn thing.

But she didn't.

Because they both knew it would've changed everything.

She exhaled shakily, fingers flexing against the wood. "I don't know."

Something flickered in his eyes—something dark, something that made her toes curl inside her shoes.

"I do," he murmured.

A shiver ran down her spine, her body betraying her before she could think.

"Chase..." Her voice came out breathless, uneven.

"You're shaking," he said, gaze dropping to her lips before flicking back up. "Tell me to back off, and I will."

She clenched her jaw, fighting the instinct to lean into him, to let this happen.

His fingers ghosted over her forearm, not quite touching, but she felt it everywhere. Every nerve in her body screamed at her to close the space, to let herself have this—just once.

"You want to tell me to stop," he murmured, voice rough, thick with restraint. "But you won't."

She swallowed hard. "You don't know that."

His smirk was slow, devastating. "I know you, Savannah. I know every tell you have. And right now? Your pulse is racing, your breath is coming too fast, and you're gripping that railing like it's the only thing keeping you from grabbing me."

Her grip tightened on the wood, nails digging into the worn grain. She hated that he was right. Hated that he could read her so easily, like he always had.

Chase's breath fanned against her cheek as he leaned in just enough to make her dizzy. "Tell me to stop, and I swear to God, I'll walk away. But if you don't..."

She exhaled shakily, closing her eyes for half a second. She needed to end this. Needed to put space between them before she did something reckless.

But she didn't step back.

She didn't say a damn thing.

Chase let out a quiet chuckle, the sound vibrating through her, dark and knowing. "That's what I thought."

Her lashes fluttered, her breath coming sharp as he pulled back—just enough to keep her wanting, just enough to make her crave the thing she refused to ask for.

His voice was low, nearly a whisper. "I don't want this to be another what-if."

Her pulse pounded. "What are you saying?"

His lips curled, just enough to make her stomach flip. "I'm saying, Savannah Monroe, I'm not gonna let you walk away without seeing where this could go. Not this time."

Her breath hitched. He was too fucking close. But for the first time in years, she didn't want to run.

Savannah licked her lips. "And if it goes nowhere?"

Chase smirked, voice rough. "Then at least we'll finally fucking know."

She hesitated—just for a second.

Then she nodded.

13

This Time, Maybe

THE NEXT MORNING, SAVANNAH lay in bed, staring at the ceiling, last night's conversation replaying in her head like a song she couldn't turn off. Every word, every glance, every fucking breath he had taken felt like it had been burned into her memory.

Chase Montgomery.

She sighed, running a hand over her face. It was maddening, the way he had settled so easily back into her world, into her thoughts, like he had never really left. Her body still hummed from being near him, from the way his presence had wrapped around her like a slow, intoxicating fog. It wasn't just that he was familiar—it was that he still felt like something she had never been able to replace.

She hadn't expected him. Hadn't expected the way he still looked at her, like she was the only thing in the room that mattered. Hadn't expected the way her body had betrayed her the second he stepped closer, how the heat of him had wrapped around her like a drug she hadn't realized she still craved.

God, he smelled good.

That mix of fresh cedar and something deeper, darker—like worn leather and the faintest hint of smoke. The kind of scent that made her want to bury her face in his shirt and breathe him in until she was dizzy. She had stood too close, let the scent of him fill her lungs, let herself sink into it for just a moment too long. Her fingers still itched to grab the front of his shirt, to see if he felt as solid and real as he looked.

And his voice.

Low. Rough. Like he had been holding back for too long, and every word that left his lips was a battle between control and something reckless. She could still hear it, the way it had wrapped around her, teasing and coaxing, sending shivers down her spine.

"Tell me something—if I had kissed you back then, would you have let me?"

Savannah groaned, rolling onto her stomach and shoving her face into the pillow, heat spreading through her chest, pooling lower. He had no fucking right sounding like that, looking at her like that, making her feel like she was about to combust.

She'd felt drunk on him last night, her body betraying her at every turn. The way his fingers had barely brushed her arm, how her breath had stuttered, how her thighs had pressed together against the ache low in her belly.

She had wanted him.

She still wanted him.

And now? Now, she had his number.

He hadn't pushed. Hadn't demanded anything. Just slipped the piece of paper into her palm, let his fingers linger against hers a second too long, and left it up to her.

No pressure. No expectations.

Just the possibility of something.

And wasn't that the scariest part?

Savannah ran her thumb over the paper still sitting on her nightstand, tracing the numbers she had already memorized. The promise of it made her stomach twist, made something deep inside her flicker to life.

All she had to do was call.

Just one call.

One call to see if this was real.

One call to see if that fire between them could finally, finally burn.

She exhaled sharply, grabbing her phone before she could overthink it.

Before she could talk herself out of it.

Chase answered on the second ring, his voice still rough from sleep. That deep, gravelly sound that sent a jolt of warmth straight down her spine.

"Didn't think you'd actually call," he murmured, voice laced with something warm, teasing, like he was smiling through the words.

Savannah rolled onto her back, staring at the ceiling, her heart thudding against her ribs. "Neither did I."

A low chuckle rumbled through the speaker, deep and smooth. "Well, I like surprises."

"That so?" She teased.

"Mmhmm." His voice was slow, unhurried, like he was savoring the moment. "And hearing your voice first thing in the morning? Might be my favorite surprise yet."

Her stomach flipped, heat curling in her core.

Damn him.

She bit her lip, trying to keep her voice steady. "Didn't know you were so easily impressed."

"Oh, sweetheart, you underestimate yourself." His voice dropped lower, a lazy drawl wrapping around each syllable like silk. "I could listen to you talk all damn day."

A shiver ran down her spine. "You always this smooth in the morning?"

"Only when I'm talking to you."

Her breath caught. She saw a glimpse of the Chase she remembered—the one who could disarm her with a single glance, who was smooth, witty, flirty, and could leave her hanging on to just a few words. The kind of man who knew exactly what he was doing, and worse, knew exactly how to get under her skin.

"You busy today?" he asked, voice shifting—casual, but expectant, like he already knew the answer and was just waiting for her to admit it.

She hesitated. She had things to do. Errands, check in with work, a whole list of things she should be focusing on.

But none of it seemed to matter right now.

"No," she said. "I'm free."

"Good."

There was a pause, just long enough for her to imagine the slow smirk spreading across his lips.

"Then let me take you out."

Savannah felt the flutter in her chest, the anticipation prickling at the edges of her skin. "Is that an invitation or a demand?"

Chase chuckled, low and smooth. "Would it turn you on if it were a demand?"

Her breath hitched, pulse skipping a beat. "Bold question."

"Honest question." He answered smugly.

She swallowed, hating how easily he got under her skin. Hating how much she fucking loved it.

"Well, I'll let you come and pick me up. How about I text you this afternoon and let you know when to come?"

There was a beat of silence. Then his voice dipped lower, raspier, and so damn confident it sent a flush creeping up her neck.

"Careful, Savannah. You keep playing hard to get, and I might just have to make you beg."

Her stomach clenched, heat licking at the edges of her control. She opened her mouth to fire back, but nothing came out—just the sharp intake of breath that she knew he fucking heard.

His chuckle was slow, knowing. "I'll be waiting. Don't keep me waiting too long, sweetheart."

The call ended, but Savannah just lay there, staring at the phone, her heart thudding hard against her ribs.

She realized then,

She was in so much more trouble than she thought.

14

Sound of Us

MALLORY WANTED TO SHOP, and Savannah just wanted to walk around; at least that's what she told Mallory. Knowing that she was having Chase come pick her up in town, Savannah played it cool, but her heart pounded a little faster each time she checked her phone for the time. The anticipation was a slow burn, creeping into her bones with every glance at the clock, every brush of the warm evening breeze against her skin.

As the sun dipped low, Chase arrived, his truck rolling to a stop beside her. The sight of him, backlit by the golden hues of the setting sun, made her stomach flip. The moment she slid into the passenger seat, she felt it—that slow burn of something unspoken between them. The scent of leather and cedar filled the cab, mingling with something uniquely him.

They drove in silence at first, the kind that wasn't awkward, just charged. Every glance out the window, every shift in his grip on the steering wheel, every breath felt weighted, like they were on the edge of something monumental. The winding road stretched before them, shadowed by towering pines and tangled branches that wove a canopy overhead. The golden light of dusk filtered through the trees, casting long, fleeting shadows. Then, the road shifted, turning into a gravel drive that seemed to go on forever, curving through dense woodland until the trees parted like a grand reveal.

Her breath caught.

The house stood against the dusk like something out of a dream. Midnight blue, two stories, its honey-oak stained shutters framing each window like a picture. The porch wrapped around the entire structure, stately columns standing tall beneath the soft glow of lanterns that flickered in the settling twilight. The matching colored door, strong and sure, was a stark contrast to the warmth spilling from inside. It wasn't just a house—it was a home. His home.

She turned to him, her voice barely above a whisper. "This is your house?"

Chase smirked, his fingers drumming casually against the steering wheel. "Yes ma'am. It is."

Savannah swallowed, the weight of that admission settling over her. This wasn't the Chase she remembered—wild and untamed. This was something different. Something steadier. Something she wasn't sure how to define.

"What are we doing here?" she asked, a mix of anticipation and nervous energy curling in her stomach.

As the truck came to a stop, he turned, his eyes locked on hers, his voice quiet but firm. "I'm cooking dinner for you."

A flutter of surprise rippled through her.

"If that's okay with you," he added, his voice softer now. "We'll eat out by the dock."

Her heart did a strange little flip, her pulse quickening.

Inside, his home was just as breathtaking—vaulted ceilings, exposed wooden beams, and warm lighting that cast everything in a golden glow, and it's only the kitchen. It was masculine but inviting, like him. She watched as he moved effortlessly through the space, rolling up his sleeves, pouring them each a glass of wine. His movements were confident, sure, like this was just another ordinary evening. But nothing about this felt ordinary.

"You cook now?" she teased, trying to lighten the air between them.

He glanced at her, amused. "I always have."

"That's debatable." She mocked.

He handed her a glass, the corners of his mouth tugging up in a smirk. "Sit tight. Let me impress you."

She asked if she could help, his response was calm and demanding. "No, just sit there—look beautiful, and talk to me."

Her brows raised. "Well damn," she thought, heat curling low in her stomach.

"Can I at least know what you're cooking?"

Turns out, it was—Seared salmon, perfectly seasoned, a lemon-dill sauce that melted over the top. Roasted vegetables, crisp and golden, and a risotto so creamy it was almost sinful.

Once dinner was finished, Chase plated the food and asked her to grab the wine and join him out by the dock. As he pushed open the screen door, Savannah followed—only then realizing that his house sat right on the sound. The sight took her breath away.

The water stretched endlessly beyond the backyard, calm and shimmering under the last light of dusk, reflecting the sky like melted gold. A dock jutted out over the glassy surface, and at its edge, beneath a pergola wrapped in soft, flickering lanterns, a table was set for two. It was intimate, secluded, like something out of a dream.

As they sat, the sound lapped gently beneath them, the air thick with something unspoken, something more than just shared history.

The conversation started light—old memories, laughter that came easy. But then, somewhere between the lingering glances and the glow of the lanterns, it deepened.

They spoke of the past. Of regrets. Of the people who had come before.

"I didn't treat them right," Chase admitted, his voice quieter now, laced with something raw. "The women I dated. I was always looking for something that wasn't there."

Savannah studied him, noting the weight in his words, the honesty in his expression. "Something you could never find," she murmured.

His eyes met hers, holding them. "Yeah, you could say that."

Her chest tightened—because she knew exactly what he meant.

After a moment, she asked softly, "Why haven't you settled down, Montgomery?"

Chase exhaled, setting his wine glass down before reaching for her hand. There was confusion in her gaze, but she didn't pull away as he guided her toward the fire pit at the end of the dock, where chairs circled around a bed of unlit wood. He pulled one out for her before striking a match, the fire flickering to life between them.

Then he asked, "Are you ready to know?"

Something in his tone made her pulse quicken. "Yes," she whispered.

He took a breath. "People don't see this side of me, Savy. What I'm about to tell you—it's probably the most reckless thing I've ever said."

Her heart skipped at the name. She hadn't heard him call her that in years.

"Close your eyes," he said gently.

She did.

"Listen to the wind—the way it brushes against your skin," he continued. "Listen to the water drifting to shore. The way the seagrass rustles in the salt air. Now—listen to your heart. The rhythm of it. The way it moves with the tide." A pause. Then, his voice softer now—"This is my second favorite place in the world. Do you hear it?"

"Yes," she whispered, eyes still closed. "It's beautiful." When she opened them, she found him watching her. "But—what makes it your favorite place?"

Chase's expression shifted—something deeper, something unguarded. He inhaled slowly, then said, "Savannah, this place—this dock—it's the echoes of us."

Her breath hitched. "What do you mean?"

He looked out at the water for a long moment before answering. "Because of me—you, it's the Echoes of Us."

Her lips parted, but no words came.

"No matter how breathtaking this place is... it will always be my second favorite."

His fingers tightened around hers.

"My first?" A brief pause, "Well, my favorite place is wherever you are."

Savannah inhaled sharply, her heart pounding. Because for the first time in years, she realized—he wasn't just the echoes of her past.

He was the promise of something more.

Something worth taking a chance on.

Savannah tried to steady her breath, but it was impossible with Chase so close, his forehead still resting against hers, his fingers still tracing the edge of her jaw like he was memorizing her. Every touch sent a shiver through her, every breath between them thick with tension.

This wasn't supposed to happen.

And yet... it was inevitable.

She swallowed hard, pulling back just enough to meet his gaze. "Chase—"

His name was a warning. A plea. A whisper of something both fragile and unbreakable.

But he just smirked, like he knew exactly how this would play out. Like he knew she was already his, whether she admitted it or not.

"You still haven't answered my question," he murmured, running his thumb over her cheek, his voice soft but weighted with something dangerous, something consuming. "Why haven't you settled down?"

Savannah exhaled, looking past him, out at the water. Because the truth—the real truth—was something she had never spoken out loud.

Not to Trevor. Not to herself. Not to anyone.

"I stayed with Trevor because he was good to me," she confessed, her voice barely above a whisper. "Because he was easy."

Chase's jaw tensed. His fingers flexed against her skin, his body coiled like he was holding himself back. "And I was never easy."

She looked back at him then, eyes locking, something raw twisting between them, something that had never faded.

"No," she admitted, her voice uneven. "You weren't."

Silence stretched between them, thick and heavy, laced with all the things they had never said. It pressed against her ribs, settled in the spaces between every heartbeat, every inhale, every stolen moment they had let slip through their fingers.

Then Chase leaned in, his voice so quiet, so certain, it sent a shiver down her spine, "But I was yours."

Her breath caught.

Her fingers curled around the stem of her glass, gripping tighter as the moment expanded, as the air crackled between them.

"You still are." She said softly.

The words hovered in the space between them, unspoken but deafening.

And then—before she could stop it, before she could convince herself this was a mistake—his lips were on hers. It wasn't tentative. It wasn't cautious. It was everything unsaid, everything missed, everything they had both been too stubborn to admit.

Savannah gasped against his mouth, and Chase took the opportunity to deepen the kiss, his hand coming up to cradle her face, his thumb brushing against her jawline. It sent a shiver through her, the kind that made her press closer, needing more. Wanting everything.

She had kissed other men. She had thought she knew passion, had thought she understood what it felt like to be wanted.

She had been wrong.

Because this kiss—this—was something else entirely.

His lips moved against hers with purpose, with heat, with years of restraint breaking apart like waves crashing against the shore. He tasted like wine and fire, like something forbidden and fated all at once. His fingers tangled in her hair, pulling her even closer, deepening the kiss until there was nothing left between them but raw need.

By the time they broke apart, breathless and dizzy, Chase rested his forehead against hers, his smirk lazy and confident, his fingers still tangled in her hair, his other hand gripping her waist like he wasn't ready to let go. Like he never wanted to let go.

"That," he murmured, brushing his thumb over her swollen bottom lip, his voice rough with want, "was definitely worth the wait."

Savannah exhaled shakily, her heart slamming against her ribs. "Chase, I—"

She stopped, her throat tightening, the words pressing against her tongue, desperate to escape. But how did she say it? How did she tell him that he had been right all along? That no matter how far she ran, no matter how many times she tried to convince herself otherwise, she had always belonged to him?

Chase's fingers tightened around hers, his expression unreadable, but his eyes—God, his eyes—they saw straight through her. They always had.

"Say it," he whispered. Not a demand. Not a plea. Just a quiet, steady invitation.

She swallowed hard, her gaze flickering to where their hands were intertwined, where his thumb brushed slow, lazy circles against her skin like he had all the time in the world to wait for her to be brave.

She had spent years convincing herself she had made the right choice. That choosing Trevor, choosing stability, choosing the easy path had been the only way to keep herself safe.

But Chase Montgomery was never safe.

He was wild oceans and crashing waves. He was lightning in the middle of a summer storm. He was everything that made her heart race and her soul ache.

And standing here now, in the glow of the fire, his warmth wrapping around her like the tide, she realized something.

She didn't want safe anymore.

She wanted him.

She took a breath, steadied herself, and finally—finally—let the truth fall from her lips.

"I never settled down because no one was ever you."

The second the words were out, she felt Chase's breath hitch. His fingers tensed against hers, like he was holding himself back, like he needed to be sure she meant it.

But Savannah didn't look away. Didn't run. Didn't hide.

"I never chose you, Chase," she whispered, emotion thick in her throat, "because if I did, there would be no going back. You were never just someone I could love and then walk away from. You were... everything. And that scared the hell out of me."

Chase exhaled sharply, his grip tightening as he took a half step closer, his presence overwhelming, consuming.

"And now?" he asked, his voice rough, low, edged with something dangerous.

Savannah's heart pounded, but for the first time in years, she wasn't afraid of it.

She lifted her chin, met his gaze head-on, and gave him the only answer that had ever been true.

"Now—I'm ready to take the chance."

A slow, knowing smirk curved his lips. "Are you?"

She let out a breathy laugh. "I am."

That was all he needed.

Because in the next second, Chase pulled her against him, crashing his lips to hers in a way that told her—no more running, no more regrets, no more what-ifs.

This time, she was his.

And this time, she wasn't letting go.

15

Mallory Knows Best

LATER THAT NIGHT, DURING the drive back into town, Chase was dropping Savannah off. She couldn't help but steal glances at him from time to time. The way the dash lights illuminated his stormy, gravel-colored eyes. The way the passing streetlights traced over his tattoos like whispered secrets against his skin. She was coming undone, entangled in Chase Montgomery in a way she hadn't expected.

Every shift of his hands on the wheel sent a slow curl of heat through her. He drove with the same quiet confidence he had always carried, the same ease that made her stomach flutter. The space between them felt small, electric. Her skin tingled, overly aware of the way the air crackled with something unspoken, something charged. Every second in the truck felt like the build-up before a storm.

As his truck rolled to a stop in front of the Monroe house, he turned to her, his expression unreadable yet intent. The air in the cab felt heavier, warmer, wrapping around them like a cocoon. His voice was low, rough, and sent shivers down her spine. "Savannah, I don't know how long you're in town for, but I want to take advantage of this. I want to spend as much time with you as I can. All the things we should have experienced first, together—I want to do them with you."

Savannah's heart slammed against her ribs, her lips curling into a slow, teasing smile. "I'm in town for two weeks," she admitted, her voice softer now. "And, Chase—I'd like that too. Can I call you tomorrow?"

She didn't give him a chance to answer before she leaned across the console, her fingers sliding up the back of his neck as she pulled him in. His lips met hers instantly, the kiss slow but deep, consuming her in a way that sent a pulse of heat down her spine. He tasted like whiskey and something inherently him—wild and steady all at once. His fingers curled into the fabric of her shirt, like he wanted to pull her closer but was holding himself back. The restraint in it, the promise, made her ache in ways she hadn't expected.

When she finally stepped out of the truck, she turned to watch him drive away, her pulse still hammering in her throat. The warmth of his lips still lingered, tingling against her own like a ghost of something unfinished.

When she walked into the house, Mallory was waiting in the living room, arms crossed, an empty wine glass in her lap.

"Since when does car-shares drive diesels?" Mallory asked, her brows raised.

Savannah frowned, kicking off her shoes. "What?"

"I heard a vehicle in the driveway and looked out the window. I expected to see a small car or an SUV. Instead, I saw a gorgeous, lifted 2500 that did not have a glowing sign in the windshield."

Savannah narrowed her eyes. "Since when do you know trucks?"

Mallory scoffed. "Honey, we live in Asheville. Remember?" She grinned, "You can't go anywhere without smelling that burnt diesel."

Savannah sighed, already knowing where this was going. "Okay, fine. I went on a date with Chase."

Mallory's mouth dropped open. "You did what!?" she screeched, nearly knocking over her wine glass.

Savannah barely had a second to brace herself before Mallory's face transformed, equal parts shock and excitement. "Bitch, what the fuck?! Where did he take you?"

Savannah hesitated, then sat down beside her, tucking her legs under herself. "His house."

Mallory's brows shot up. "His house?"

Savannah nodded. "Yeah. It's on the sound. The most beautiful house I've ever seen—midnight blue, honey-oak shutters, a wraparound porch. It was like something out of a dream."

Mallory stared at her, stunned. "Oh, he's serious about you."

Savannah swallowed, her fingers fidgeting with the hem of her sweater. "You think?"

Mallory rolled her eyes. "Savy, men like him, don't just take women to their homes like that—especially not a home like his. He's showing you his world."

Savannah chewed on her lip. "We had dinner on the dock. He cooked. And not just any meal—he put effort into it. Seared salmon, risotto so creamy it melted in your mouth, roasted vegetables with just the right amount of crisp. There were lanterns, a firepit—the whole thing felt like something out of a movie."

Mallory let out a low whistle. "Jesus. That man is trying to ruin you for anyone else."

Savannah laughed softly, shaking her head. "It felt like that."

Mallory smirked. "Tell me he at least let you help."

Savannah grinned. "Nope. He told me to sit there, look beautiful, and talk to him. Said he wanted to impress me."

Mallory threw her head back with a laugh. "Oh, he's good. And what did you two talk about?"

Savannah exhaled, her fingers tracing invisible patterns on the table. "Everything. Life, dreams, regrets... old relationships."

Mallory sobered a little, tilting her head. "Did he mention Trevor?"

Savannah hesitated, then nodded. "Yeah. He did."

Mallory leaned in, curiosity flickering across her face. "And?"

Savannah exhaled, fingers tightening around her glass. "He said he hated watching me with him. That every girl he was with was just him trying to forget me. And that it never worked."

Mallory's expression softened. "Damn."

"Yeah."

A beat of silence.

Then Mallory waggled her brows. "So—did you fuck?"

Savannah groaned. "Jesus, Mal."

Mallory shrugged. "I mean, c'mon! I can practically see you dripping, from here. Plus— he's got big dick energy, and the sexual tension between you two has been cooking for years. I thought for sure you'd finally do something about it."

Savannah bit her lip, hesitating.

Mallory's eyes widened. "Holy shit. You did—"

Savannah cut her off. "No! We didn't fuck. But we—kissed."

Mallory clutched her chest. "Oh, thank God. If you had left that date without at least making out, I was going to fight you."

Savannah shook her head, laughing. "It wasn't just a kiss, Mal. It was—*everything*."

Mallory's grin faded slightly, her voice softer. "Yeah?"

Savannah nodded, staring at her hands. "It was years of waiting, of missing him, of wondering what it would've been like if we had just... gone for it back then. And then suddenly, it wasn't a question anymore. He kissed me like he'd been waiting his whole life for it."

Mallory exhaled, shaking her head. "Damn. That's some movie shit right there."

Savannah smiled, her heart still racing at the memory. "It felt like one."

Mallory smirked. "And did he?" Lifting her arms to see if something was being left out.

Savannah exhaled. "No. He kissed me like he was ready to devour me, then stopped. Said he didn't want to rush. That he wanted to do it right."

Mallory's mouth dropped open. "Oh my God. That's—that's fucking hotter than if he had just fucked you."

Savannah laughed. "I know, right?!"

Mallory shook her head. "That man is dangerous."

Savannah's stomach flipped. "Tell me about it."

A silence settled between them, but it wasn't empty.

Then Mallory smirked. "So, are you gonna call him again?"

Savannah exhaled, gripping her phone like it held the answer.

She already knew the answer.

"Yeah," she said, her lips curving slightly. "I think I am."

16

Chasing Last-Night

THE NEXT MORNING, SAVANNAH lay in bed, her body still humming with the echoes of last night. The sheets were cool against her skin, but the air carried the warmth of something more—of Chase. The faint scent of salt and his cologne clung to her hair, a lingering whisper of his touch, his kiss, the way his voice had wrapped around her in the moonlight.

She turned onto her side, pulling the blanket tighter around her, letting the memories wash over her like the slow, rhythmic pull of the tide. His hands—God, those hands—had settled on her waist with an ownership that sent heat curling low in her belly. His breath had been warm against her neck, teasing, making her shiver with want.

And his lips—firm, insistent, reverent—had branded her.

Chase Montgomery kissed her like he was afraid she would disappear. Like she was something sacred, something he needed to memorize with his mouth, his hands, his entire body. And she let him. Because, deep down, she had never really stopped being his.

Her pulse quickened just thinking about it.

The way his fingers had traced slow circles against the back of her neck. The way he had murmured her name like a damn prayer. The way he had pulled away, just enough to rest his forehead against hers, as if he needed a second to steady himself.

He hadn't rushed her. Hadn't pushed. Hadn't let his hands wander past the boundaries they both knew they weren't ready to cross—yet.

But the hunger in his eyes was unmistakable.

She squeezed her eyes shut, breathing through the ache building deep inside her. No one had ever kissed her like that. No one had ever made her feel so seen, so wanted—so completely undone.

Sunlight streamed through the sheer curtains, casting golden stripes across the bed. The world outside felt distant, unreal, as though she were still tangled in the dream of last night. But the soft buzz of her phone on the nightstand pulled her back.

She reached for it, heart thudding, fingers unsteady.

A single message.

"Meet me at the Marina. 9:30."

A slow smile tugged at her lips, heat building in her stomach. No hesitation, no overthinking—just Chase, asking her to meet him.

And she would.

Because after last night, after the way he looked at her, touched her, kissed her like she was the only thing that had ever mattered, how could she not?

Adrenaline surged through her, waking her faster than any cup of coffee ever could. She threw back the covers, padding barefoot across the room. The cool tile of the bathroom floor sent a shiver up her spine as she turned the water on, stepping into the heat.

Steam curled around her, filling the space with warmth as she let the spray cascade over her shoulders. Her fingers traced absentmindedly over her skin, ghosting over the places where Chase had touched her, where his thumb had brushed along her jaw, where his hands had rested on her hips, steadying her as he kissed her slow, deep, and devastating.

She lathered Jasmine and sandalwood-scented shampoo into her hair, her movements slower than usual, lost in the memory of the way his voice had dropped when he whispered her name, the way his fingers had lingered at the small of her back as he pulled away—reluctant, like he hadn't wanted to leave.

By the time she stepped out, her skin was warm, her curls damp and tumbling over her shoulders in soft waves. She wrapped herself in a towel, catching her reflection in the mirror.

She looked—different.

Lighter. Brighter.

Like the weight of something she hadn't even realized she'd been carrying had finally lifted.

She took her time getting ready—denim shorts, a white linen top, sandals. Something effortless. Something that said she hadn't spent twenty minutes thinking about what to wear even though her heart was racing.

A swipe of mascara, a touch of lip balm, and she was ready.

Descending the stairs, she found Mallory in the kitchen, coffee in hand, her expression already knowing.

"You're glowing," Mallory smirked over the rim of her mug. "Something tells me that's not just from good sleep."

Savannah rolled her eyes, but she couldn't suppress the smile tugging at her lips. "Shut up."

"I won't," Mallory teased, leaning against the counter. "Not when you've spent years pretending Chase was just an old friend. And now you're practically floating down the stairs? Spill."

Savannah hesitated, chewing on her lip. "He texted. Wants me to meet him at the marina."

Mallory's grin widened. "Oh, girl. This is it, isn't it?"

Savannah inhaled deeply. "I don't know," she admitted. "But it feels... different. Good different."

She hesitated, guilt tugging at her. "I feel bad leaving you. We planned to hang out today."

Mallory waved her off, setting her coffee down. "Savy, stop. You're allowed to have this. We've been talking about him for years. And now? He's finally showing you what he's been holding onto. I'd be pissed if you didn't go."

Savannah exhaled, the tension in her chest loosening. "You're sure?"

Mallory rolled her eyes. "If you don't walk out that door in the next five minutes, I will take your place."

Relief flooded Savannah as she hugged her best friend quickly.

"You're the best."

"I know," Mallory said with a wink. "Now, go make some memories."

Savannah didn't take her car. The marina was only a few blocks away, and she wanted the walk—the crisp ocean air, the way the morning sun kissed her skin, the electric anticipation thrumming beneath her ribs.

Her mind raced with questions as she made her way down the quiet streets.

Where was this going?

Could they really do this?

Could they erase years of what-ifs and turn them into something real?

Or had last night just been a beautiful moment in time, one that would fade with the morning light?

She didn't know.

But she wanted to find out.

As she rounded the corner, the marina came into view, the gentle lapping of water against the docks filling the quiet morning air. Boats bobbed in their slips, their white hulls glistening beneath the sun. The scent of salt and fresh morning air wrapped around her, calming, centering.

And then she saw him.

Chase.

Leaning against his truck in the gravel lot, arms crossed, looking every bit the boy she had fallen for all those years ago—only now, he was a man who knew exactly what he wanted.

Her.

17

Wildfire

HER BREATH HITCHED AS she took him in—the worn Henley that stretched across his broad shoulders, the way his jeans clung to his hips, the hint of scruff along his jaw. He looked effortlessly good, but it was his eyes that got her.

Dark and knowing.

Like he had been waiting for this moment.

Waiting for her.

His lips twitched into a smirk as she approached, that familiar cocky confidence threading into his voice.

"Took you long enough. You're late, Monroe."

Savannah arched a brow. "Excuse me? You're lucky I am here at all." She teased.

Chase pushed off the truck, stepping into her space, so close she could feel the heat of him. "I've been waiting for you since the day you left, Savannah. Another ten minutes wouldn't have made a difference."

Her stomach flipped.

He reached for her hand, threading his fingers through hers, his grip firm, steady.

"Let's go," he murmured.

And just like that, Savannah knew.

She wasn't just walking into another morning.

She was walking straight into him.

Into them.

And she wasn't turning back.

They drove with the windows down, the summer air thick with salt and warmth, rolling over their skin like a lover's touch. Savannah let her hand drift outside the window, her fingers slicing through the golden morning light, the breeze carrying the scent of ocean spray and wild jasmine.

Chase sat beside her, one hand on the wheel, the other resting casually on the gearshift, his thumb tapping to a rhythm she couldn't hear. His profile was sharp in the early light—the strong cut of his jaw, the way the corners of his lips hinted at a smirk, like he knew something she didn't. Maybe he did. Maybe he had known all along that no matter how many miles or years stretched between them, she would always find her way back to him.

She stole glances when she thought he wasn't looking, but Chase had always been good at reading her.

"I can feel you staring," he murmured, not taking his eyes off the road.

Savannah smirked, shifting in her seat. "And if I am?"

His lips twitched. "Then I'll take that as a good sign."

She shook her head, but her heart was already slamming against her ribs.

The town was slowly waking up around them—surfers catching the early morning swell, joggers tracing the boardwalk, shopkeepers unlocking their doors. The sounds of life were everywhere, but Chase had something else in mind.

She noticed when he took a turn off the main road, veering away from the bustle of the beach, down a narrow road lined with towering oaks draped in Spanish moss. The further they drove, the quieter it became, the air growing heavier with the scent of pine and salt, the distant hum of waves softening into something even more peaceful.

"Where are we going?" she asked, her fingers trailing against the seam of her seat.

"You'll see," Chase said, casting her a knowing glance before turning down a dirt path.

A few minutes later, he rolled to a stop, and Savannah's breath hitched.

They were at a secluded inlet, the kind of place only locals knew. The water stretched out in perfect, glassy blue-green, reflecting the morning sun like a sheet of silk. The sand was untouched, pristine, as if waiting for them to leave the first footprints of the day. Gentle waves lapped against the shore, whispering secrets only the sea could hold.

Chase cut the engine and hopped out, grabbing a blanket and a cooler from the back of the truck. Savannah followed, watching as he led her toward the shade of a few ghost trees, their twisted branches reaching toward the sky like something out of a storybook.

"Breakfast by the water," he said simply, spreading the blanket on the soft sand.

She settled beside him, their knees brushing as he handed her a container filled with fresh fruit, croissants, and cheese. She hadn't realized how hungry she was until she took a bite, the buttery pastry melting on her tongue.

They ate in comfortable silence, the kind that was full of understanding rather than emptiness. The sound of the ocean filled the spaces between their words, the occasional call of a seabird overhead making the moment feel untouched by time.

Savannah watched as Chase leaned back on his elbows, tilting his face toward the sky, his eyes half-lidded, utterly at ease.

He looked different here—unburdened. Free.

She wanted to bottle up this version of him and keep it for herself.

"Tell me something you've never told anyone," she said suddenly, her voice softer than she intended.

Chase's eyes flicked open, his gaze locking onto hers. A beat passed before he exhaled, the tension in his shoulders melting away as he turned onto his side, propping his head up with one hand.

"I have always imagined bringing you here."

Her breath caught.

"Chase—"

"Don't say anything," he murmured, his fingers finding hers, twining them together with effortless familiarity. "Just—know that it's true."

And she did. She felt it in the way he looked at her, in the way his thumb traced lazy circles against her palm. She felt it even more when he sat up and tugged her onto his lap, his arms wrapping around her waist like she belonged there.

His lips found hers, soft and slow, tasting like salt and longing and years of waiting.

The world faded, narrowing down to just him—the heat of his skin, the press of his fingers at the small of her back, the way his heartbeat thrummed against her own.

They spent the day wrapped up in each other—walking barefoot along the shore, stealing kisses between playful splashes, laughter tangled with the drift of the tide. When he tossed her into the water, she shrieked, kicking up water that hit him square in the chest.

"Oh, you're gonna pay for that, Montgomery," she warned.

He grinned, wiping water from his face, his wet t-shirt clinging to every defined inch of him. "That so?"

She lunged at him, but he caught her with ease, spinning her in the shallows, their laughter dissolving into something quieter, something heavier, as his hands settled on her waist.

She stilled, her fingers grazing his jaw, her breath catching at the intensity in his gaze.

"You're dangerous," she murmured.

His lips curved. "To you?"

She swallowed, nodding.

Chase's grip on her tightened. "Good."

As the sun dipped lower, Chase pulled away, his eyes holding a flicker of mischief.

"Give me three minutes," he said, then disappeared around the bend.

Savannah watched him go, confusion knitting her brows. Moments later, the low rumble of an engine met her ears.

She turned just in time to see Chase pulling up in a boat.

He stepped onto the bow, holding out his hand.

"You coming, Monroe?"

Her lips parted in surprise, but she didn't hesitate. She took his hand, letting him pull her onto the boat, the warmth of his palm sending a shiver through her.

He guided them away from the shore, taking them where the inlet stretched wide and seemed endless. The boat rocked gently as he killed the engine, the silence between them thick with something unsaid.

"This is my favorite time of day for this spot," he admitted, his arm wrapping around her waist.

She tilted her head up at him. "Why?"

His eyes held something deep, something reverent.

"Because it's yours." He said softly, as if he was unsure if he should say it.

Her breath caught. "What do you mean?"

"Turn around and look," he said.

She did. And what she saw stole the air from her lungs.

There, just beyond the bend, sat the midnight blue house on the hill. The dock where everything had changed.

Her chest tightened.

"Last night, when I told you about the Echoes of Us... this was part of it." His fingers brushed against her cheek. "I told myself if I ever got another chance with you, I'd give you everything you deserve."

She swallowed hard, tears pricking her eyes.

"You deserve the ocean and the shore, Savannah." He kissed her temple. "But this is the best I can do."

A tear slipped down her cheek, and Chase wiped it away with his thumb, his touch achingly tender.

"I think I get it now," she whispered.

He smiled, pressing a lingering kiss to the top of her head.

"I knew you would."

As the sky deepened, she curled into him, the stars blinking awake above them.

He pulled out a blanket, wrapping it around both of them as they sat on the bow, watching the sky melt into twilight.

Savannah traced the inked patterns along his forearm, the warmth of his body seeping into hers, the steady rhythm of his breath grounding her in the moment.

"You know," she murmured, "I wish we could stay like this forever."

Chase's fingers skimmed her jaw, tilting her chin up until their eyes met. "We can."

Her breath hitched at the weight of those words, at the way his gaze darkened with something more, something deeper.

But before she could speak, he kissed her—slow and unhurried, his lips moving over hers with a tenderness that made her heart ache.

It wasn't rushed. It wasn't desperate.

It was something infinitely more dangerous.

It was a promise.

She knew this wasn't just a rekindled spark.

It was a wildfire.

And she was already burning.

18

Weight of Wanting

THAT NIGHT, AFTER HOURS on the water, they found themselves back at his place, standing on the dock under a blanket of stars. The sound stretched endlessly before them, black as ink, the water barely rippling against the wooden posts. The lanterns along the railing flickered softly, casting golden light against the dark, making everything feel impossibly intimate.

The air between them was thick with something unspoken, something electric. Chase stood close, his body a wall of warmth, his scent—salt, cedar, and something uniquely him—wrapping around her, making her dizzy.

Savannah shivered, though the night wasn't cold.

It was him.

All him.

Chase's gaze was heavy, lingering, his jaw tight as he studied her. He reached for her slowly, his fingers brushing over her wrist, then sliding up the inside of her forearm, leaving a trail of fire in their wake.

That touch undid her.

She inhaled sharply, tilting her chin up, her lips parting slightly—an invitation, a challenge, a plea. Chase took it without hesitation.

He pulled her in, capturing her lips in a way that made the rest of the world disappear.

His kiss wasn't tentative. It wasn't careful. It was consuming, deep, filled with the kind of hunger that spoke of years lost, of time wasted, of second chances finally seized. His hands gripped her waist, pulling her closer, fitting her body against his like he had been made to hold her. Savannah melted, her fingers threading into his hair, fisting the strands as if letting go meant losing everything.

She knew then—this wasn't just a fling. It wasn't just two people rekindling an old spark.

This was something deeper. Something undeniable.

And it terrified her just as much as it thrilled her.

Savannah didn't think—she just reacted.

She climbed onto his lap, her knees straddling his hips, her dress riding up as she settled against him. Chase let out a low, almost guttural groan, his grip on her tightening like he was holding onto the last thread of his control. His hands spanned her thighs, warm and rough, his fingers pressing into her skin as if he needed to anchor himself.

"Jesus, Savannah—" His voice was hoarse, strained.

She leaned in, pressing her forehead against his, her breath mingling with his. "You started it," she murmured, a teasing lilt in her voice, though her own heart was hammering, her body thrumming with the need for more.

His chest rose and fell beneath her hands, his restraint evident in the way his muscles tensed beneath his shirt.

"Not like this," he said, his voice like gravel, full of need and something else.

Her stomach flipped. "What do you mean?"

Chase exhaled slowly, his forehead still resting against hers. His hands settled at her waist, thumbs tracing slow, deliberate circles against her skin, soothing and torturous all at once.

"I want this," he admitted. "God, do I want this. But not here. Not like this."

Confusion flickered across her face, but before she could say anything, he lifted one hand, threading his fingers through her hair, untangling the strands that had caught in the sea breeze. His touch was achingly tender, reverent in a way that sent heat pooling in her belly.

"You're not just another night, Savannah," he murmured, his lips ghosting over the corner of her mouth. "You're not just someone I'm going to fuck."

Her breath caught. The blunt honesty of his words sent a sharp, sweet ache through her chest.

"I want to do this right," he continued, his fingers brushing along her jaw, his thumb tracing the curve of her cheek. "You deserve more than rushed kisses on a dock and a night that feels too good to be real in the morning."

Savannah swallowed hard, her hands still fisted in the fabric of his shirt. Her body was screaming in protest, every nerve ending on high alert, aching for him, for more.

But her heart?

Her heart whispered that he was right.

This wasn't something fleeting. This wasn't something she could wake up from and pretend hadn't meant everything.

And that terrified her.

"Chase—" she started, but she didn't know what to say.

He leaned in, brushing his lips over hers once more—slow, lingering, filled with the promise of something worth waiting for. He kissed her like he was telling her a secret, like he was sealing something between them, something irrevocable.

Then, with an exhale that sounded like it physically pained him, he pulled back.

His forehead pressed against hers for a second longer, their breaths mingling, their bodies still tangled, before he finally eased her off his lap.

"Come on," he murmured, standing and holding out a hand to help her up. "I'm taking you home."

Savannah hesitated.

She could still feel the heat of him, still taste him on her lips, still hear the way his voice had cracked just slightly when he said her name. And God, she didn't want to leave.

But this was Chase. The boy she had wanted for years. The man who was still standing in front of her, offering her something real.

So, she took his hand.

Let him guide her off the dock, back toward the house, back toward the truck.

The ride home was quiet, but it wasn't empty.

Chase kept one hand on the wheel, the other resting on the console, close enough that she could reach for him, lace her fingers through his, feel the steady warmth of his palm against hers.

She almost did.

Almost.

When he pulled up in front of the Monroe house, the streetlights cast long shadows, the world still and quiet around them. He shifted into park but didn't move to open her door. Instead, he turned toward her, his gaze roaming her face like he was memorizing her all over again.

Savannah bit her lip. "You sure you don't want to come inside?" she teased, though her voice was softer than she intended.

Chase let out a low chuckle, shaking his head. "You're trying to kill me, aren't you?"

She grinned. "Maybe just a little."

His eyes darkened, his fingers brushing against her thigh. "Oh, Savannah. You have no idea what you're doing to me."

She shivered, but before she could respond, he leaned in, pressing one last kiss to her lips—slow and deep, stealing whatever breath she had left.

Then he pulled back, his thumb tracing along her jawline before he exhaled and nodded toward the house. "Go. Before I change my mind."

Savannah smirked, opening the door, but just before she stepped out, she turned back to him, her voice playful, teasing. "Sweet dreams, Montgomery."

Chase's smirk turned downright sinful.

"Oh, they will be," he murmured. "And they'll all be about you."

Her stomach flipped, heat rushing to her cheeks, but before she could let him see just how much his words affected her, she closed the door and walked inside.

But she didn't stop smiling.

Not once.

19

Chasing Forever

Mallory's Reaction

SAVANNAH BARELY MADE IT three steps into the house before Mallory was on her.

Her best friend was perched on the couch, a glass of wine in hand despite the late hour, her eyes sharp and way too knowing. The moment Savannah stepped through the door, Mallory arched an eyebrow, her lips parting in anticipation.

"Oh my God." Mallory sat up straighter, setting her wine down with a thunk. "You did it, didn't you?"

Savannah let out a breathless laugh, kicking off her sandals before collapsing onto the couch beside her. "No."

Mallory blinked, her brows furrowing. "No?"

Savannah let her head fall back against the cushions, her limbs still tingling, her mind still replaying every second of the night—the way Chase had looked at her, touched her, kissed her. But she didn't regret stopping. She didn't regret the way it had ended. Not one bit.

"No," she repeated, turning her head to face Mallory.

Mallory looked appalled. "I don't understand. The sexual tension between you two is enough to fuel a small country. Are you seriously telling me you didn't—?"

Savannah groaned, pressing her hands over her face. "Trust me. I wanted to. He wanted to. But Chase..." She exhaled sharply, her stomach flipping just at the memory of his words. "He wants to do it right."

Mallory's jaw dropped. "He stopped? Voluntarily?"

Savannah nodded.

Mallory's head fell back against the couch, her eyes squeezed shut. "I hate you."

Savannah burst out laughing, but Mallory wasn't finished.

"I mean, I love you, I do," she continued, waving a hand dramatically. "But God, Sav. Where the hell do I find a man who stops himself because he respects me too much to rush it? Like, do I need to go put in a request with the universe? Light some candles? Do a damn séance?"

Savannah smirked, nudging her with her foot. "Get in line."

Mallory groaned, grabbing a throw pillow and smacking Savannah with it. "No, seriously. You have to tell me everything. And I mean everything."

Savannah grinned, biting her lip as warmth spread through her chest. "Where do I even start?"

"Start with the second you saw him. And don't leave out a damn thing."

Savannah tucked her legs under her, fingers trailing over the seam of the couch as she started talking.

"So when I get to the marina, he hands me this coffee like he just knows exactly how I take it, and then he tells me to get in his truck. No explanation, nothing. Just 'you're late, Monroe." She smiles. Then he says "I've been waiting for you since the day you left, Savannah. Another ten minutes wouldn't have made a difference."

Mallory throws her hands up. "What the actual fuck? He just—what? That's some Nicholas Sparks-level shit right there. Are you kidding me?"

Savannah snorted. "So we drive, and instead of taking me to the usual spots, he pulls up at this little hidden inlet—one of those places that only locals know about. There's no one around. Just the water, the sand, and us."

Mallory's eyes widened, leaning forward like she was absorbing every word. "Romantic as hell. And?"

Savannah smiled, remembering how the morning air had felt cool against her skin, how Chase had moved with ease, spreading out the blanket, pulling out a cooler.

"He had breakfast packed."

Mallory gasped. "Tell me he made it himself."

Savannah bit her lip, tilting her head. "I'm pretty sure he did."

Mallory smacked the couch. "I hate you."

Savannah laughed, shaking her head. "We sat there, eating, talking, just being, you know? Then came the boat."

"What boat?" Mallory scoffed.

Savannah's heart skipped a beat just thinking about it. "God, Mal, it was perfect."

Mallory clutched her pillow, ready to combust. "I want to fucking know, tell me."

Savannah exhaled, tucking her feet under her. "So after breakfast, we spent the whole day together. Just us. No distractions, no rushing. And then, when the sun started going down, he tells me to wait while he goes to grab something. Next thing I know, I hear the low rumble of an engine, and there he is, pulling up in a boat."

Mallory gasped dramatically, gripping Savannah's arm. "No. No."

Savannah nodded, smiling. "He just stood there, holding out his hand, and said, 'You coming, Monroe?'"

Mallory groaned. "That's it. I'm dead."

Savannah laughed. "So I get on the boat, and he takes me out to this little cove where the water stretches for miles. There were these tiny sandbanks covered in seagrass, and the sky—God, the sky was melting into golds and pinks. And we just sat there, watching the sun go down, wrapped in a blanket, his arm around me like he was claiming the moment."

Mallory exhaled, pressing a hand to her heart. "Savannah Monroe, if you don't kiss that man senseless the next time you see him, I will physically fight you."

Savannah chuckled, but then her voice softened. "That's not even the best part."

Mallory's eyes went wide. "There's more?"

Savannah nodded. "At one point, he just looks at me and says, 'This is my favorite time of day for this spot.'"

Mallory blinked. "And?"

Savannah swallowed. "I asked him why. And he just looked at me and said, 'Because it's yours.'"

Mallory shot up. "What in the actual hell?!"

Savannah laughed. "He pointed toward the shore, and I realized where we were. Right in front of his house. Where everything started. And then he said it again—he meant it, Mal. He told me I deserve the ocean and the shore, and this was the best he could do."

Mallory slapped a hand over her mouth. "I swear to God, Savannah, you better marry this man, or I will."

Savannah laughed, warmth creeping up her neck. "It was the way he said it, Mal. Like he'd been carrying those words around for years."

Mallory groaned, collapsing onto the couch. "No. I can't. This is unreal. This man is writing poetry with his damn existence."

Savannah sighed, her heart full. "It was... everything."

Mallory fell back against the cushions. "This is some Christmas movie-level romance, and I'm losing my mind. Savy, I don't think you get it. This isn't just a guy you like. This is it. This is the story that people dream about."

Savannah laughed, shaking her head, but her chest tightened at the truth of it. Because Chase meant it. Every damn word.

And for the first time, she let herself believe it.

Because Mallory was right.

This was it.

And Savannah was finally ready to let herself have it.

Later that night, Savannah nestles beneath the cool sheets, staring at the ceiling, her heart still tangled in the aftermath of Chase Montgomery.

It wasn't just his words that clung to her—it was his touch, his scent, the way his voice had wrapped around her like a warm tide pulling her under. She closed her eyes, letting the memories settle over her, slow and sweet like honey dripping from a spoon.

She could still feel the ghost of his hands on her waist, the way he had held her like she was something fragile and fierce all at once. The way his thumb had traced slow, reverent circles against her hip, as if memorizing her, grounding himself in her presence.

The way his lips had lingered at her temple before he'd whispered, *Not tonight. Not like this.*

And the way she had felt those words, deeper than just her skin.

Her breath wavered, her pulse uneven as she turned onto her side, staring at the phone on her nightstand. The screen was dark, but she didn't need it to see the message forming in her mind.

She bit her lip, reaching for it, fingers hovering over the keyboard.

Was it too much? Too soon?

Would it make her seem needy?

She groaned, pressing the phone to her forehead, exhaling sharply. She hated overthinking. She had spent years pushing her emotions down, keeping them locked behind logic and caution.

But Chase wasn't someone you guarded yourself against. He was the kind of man you fell for without a parachute, knowing the landing would be worth it.

She couldn't play games with him. Didn't want to.

Her fingers found the keys before her brain could catch up, her heart hammering with each word.

Savannah: I know you're probably asleep, but I just wanted to say—thank you. For tonight. For stopping. For proving you're not just some guy who wants to add another name to a list. It meant more to me than I can explain. And I can't stop thinking about you. Sweet dreams, Montgomery.

She hovered over the send button, hesitating for a single, breathless second before pressing it.

The moment it was sent, she let the phone fall to her chest, staring at the ceiling, her nerves tangled with something warm and unfamiliar.

This wasn't just about attraction. This wasn't just about chemistry.

This wasn't just about the way he kissed her like he had waited a lifetime to do it.

This was *more*.

And for the first time, she let herself feel it.

Let herself want it.

Maybe this wasn't just about wanting Chase.

Maybe she was already falling for him.

Her phone vibrated, the sound slicing through the quiet.

Her breath hitched as she grabbed it, her pulse a drumbeat against her ribs.

Chase: *I wasn't asleep.*

Her stomach flipped, her fingers tightening around the phone.

Chase: I've been lying here, thinking about you. Thinking about how hard it was to walk away tonight. How I almost didn't.

Her heart stuttered.

Chase: You deserve more, Savannah. You deserve every damn thing this could be. And I'm going to prove it to you.

Savannah swallowed, her body burning from just the words.

Chase: Sweet dreams, Monroe. You're the last thing on my mind tonight.

She inhaled sharply, her fingers curling into the sheets.

Oh, she was *so* gone for this man.

20

Distraction

The Next Morning

Chase Montgomery had never been good at patience.

Hell, he had spent most of his life moving—pushing forward, chasing the next goal, making shit happen. But this?

This waiting game?

It was fucking brutal.

He sat at his desk, staring at the spreadsheet on his laptop, but none of it registered. His fingers hovered over the keyboard, motionless. His coffee sat untouched, long since gone cold. The numbers and reports blurred, white noise against the only thing occupying his mind.

Savannah Monroe.

Jesus Christ. Last night had wrecked him. Every single part of him.

The way she had felt in his arms—warm, soft, fitting against him like she belonged there. The way she had kissed him back—not just with heat, not just with hunger, but with something more. The way she had looked at him when he pulled back, when he told her he wanted to do it right.

He groaned, dragging a rough hand over his jaw, fingers gripping his beard. It had been the hardest thing he had ever done—stopping. Telling her no. Pacing his damn breathing when everything in him had been screaming to keep going, to keep taking.

And yet, he didn't regret a damn thing.

Because that look in her eyes?

The mix of shock, understanding, something deep and aching?

That had made it worth it.

He turned in his chair, gazing out the window of his office. The town was waking up—surfers out catching early waves, runners dotting the boardwalk, fishermen prepping their boats before the heat of the day set in. The hum of Wrightsville Beach easing into the morning routine.

And somewhere out there, she was waking up too.

Maybe she was still tangled in her sheets, her curls a mess against her pillow, her skin carrying the faint scent of salt air. Maybe she was staring at her ceiling, biting her lip, thinking about him.

A muscle jumped in his jaw.

Chase had spent half the night tossing and turning, running through every second of their time together. How her breath had hitched when he kissed her slow. How her fingers had tightened in his hair. How her voice had trembled when she whispered his name.

Stopping felt like going to war with himself.

The Distraction

Fifteen minutes later, Chase was still staring at the same damn screen, the spreadsheet glaring back at him like it knew he wasn't worth a damn at work today. His coffee sat untouched, his mind still stuck on her.

Then—

"Dude."

Chase blinked, looking up as Nate, his project manager and longtime friend, leaned lazily against the doorframe, arms crossed, looking entirely too amused for Chase's liking.

"You've been staring at the same damn screen for twenty minutes." Nate smirked, nodding at the neglected coffee. "Who's the girl?"

Chase exhaled sharply, rubbing his hand down his face. "What makes you think it's a girl?"

Nate scoffed. "Because I've known you for years. You don't get this distracted unless it involves baseball or a woman. And last I checked, you weren't swinging a bat this morning."

Chase rolled his eyes, but the corner of his mouth twitched. "You're an idiot."

"Sure am." Nate pushed off the doorframe, stepping further inside. "But I'm right, aren't I?"

Chase hesitated. Then, with a heavy sigh, he leaned back in his chair, his fingers drumming against the desk. "Yeah. Yeah, You are."

Nate whistled low, dropping into the chair across from him. "Damn. It's that serious?"

Chase didn't answer immediately. Instead, he let his gaze drop to his phone again, to the words that had been on repeat in his mind since the moment he read them.

It always been serious.

Even when she left. Even when he convinced himself to move on.

Even when he knew deep down—there was never going to be another Savannah Monroe.

Nate studied him, rubbing his jaw. "You look wrecked, man."

Chase smirked, shaking his head. "You have no idea."

Nate laughed. "Oh, I think I do. That's the look of a man who had the night of his life, but somehow didn't get laid."

Chase huffed out a laugh, shaking his head. "You're not wrong."

Nate blinked. "Wait. Seriously?" He leaned in, eyes wide. "You had her in your arms, you wanted her, she wanted you, and you didn't—" He stopped, shaking his head like he was personally offended. "Who the fuck are you?"

Chase let out a dry laugh, rubbing the back of his neck. "Trust me, I wanted to. More than I can even explain." His jaw tightened. "But she's not just anyone."

Nate studied him for a beat, then let out a low whistle. "Shit." He leaned back, crossing his arms. "Well, I'll be damned. The Chase Montgomery I know would've never had that much self-control."

Chase smirked, shaking his head. "Yeah, well... this isn't just about me." His voice dropped slightly, his expression softening. "She deserves more than that."

Nate let out a slow breath, nodding in understanding. "Damn, man. You've got it bad."

Chase didn't even bother denying it.

Nate laughed, shaking his head as he pushed up from his chair. "Well, whoever she is, she's got you all twisted up. And honestly? I like seeing you like this. It's entertaining as hell."

Chase shot him a dry look. "Get the fuck out of my office!"

Nate grinned, backing toward the door. "Fine, fine. But if you start writing poetry in that damn notebook of yours, I need to be the first to mock you for it."

Chase groaned. "I don't write poetry."

Nate snorted. "Sure, you don't."

With a heckle, he disappeared down the hall, leaving Chase alone once again.

As soon as the office was quiet, Chase let out a slow breath, his gaze dropping back to his phone, his fingers hovering over the keyboard.

He wanted to text her. Needed to. Wanted to hear her voice, see her, touch her. But he told her to wait.

And if Chase Montgomery was going to do this?

He was going to do it right.

With a sigh, he tucked his phone into his pocket, picked up his coffee, and forced himself to focus.

Because tonight?

Tonight, he was going to see her again.

And he had every intention of showing her that waiting?

Was going to be worth it.

21

The Invitation

Unraveling Savannah

And Chase Montgomery was to blame.

She had never been the kind of woman to wait for anything. She made decisions. She moved forward. She never lingered on what-ifs and almosts. But Chase?

He was making her wait.

And it was driving her absolutely insane.

Sitting cross-legged on the couch, her phone gripped between her fingers, Savannah stared at the screen, rereading his message for what had to be the twentieth time that morning, her pulse hammering in her ears.

Chase: I meant what I said. You deserve more than a stolen moment on a dock. You deserve everything. I'm going to give you that. Just wait.

Her breath hitched.

Wait?

How the hell was she supposed to wait when every inch of her body was still burning from his touch, from his lips, from the way his voice had wrapped around her like a damn sin?

And worse?

He knew what he was doing to her.

The man was a menace. A beautiful, smug, self-controlled menace.

Her phone buzzed again.

Chase: Dinner at my place tonight. Bring Mallory. Nate will be there. 7:30.

A pause.

Then—

Chase: No excuses, Monroe.

Savannah smirked, fingers already moving over the keyboard.

Savannah: Bossy.

Chase: And yet, you're still reading my messages like they're your new favorite sin.

Her breath caught.

Oh, he was good.

Savannah: Cocky much?

Chase: Not cocky. Confident. There's a difference.

Savannah: Mm. Debatable.

Chase: You want to debate it?

A slow heat curled in her stomach.

Savannah: Depends. How good are you at convincing a woman to change her mind?

The response came instantly.

Chase: Monroe, I don't need to convince you of anything.

Her thighs pressed together.

Jesus Christ.

Savannah let a few seconds pass before she typed her next message, wanting to make him wait—make him feel the burn for once.

Savannah: Is that so?

Chase: I don't have to convince you, because you're already picturing it.

Her fingers trembled slightly over the keyboard.

Chase: You're already thinking about the way my hands felt on you. About the way I kissed you slow just to hear that little sound you make when you want more.

Her breath hitched.

Chase: You're thinking about how my hands felt in your hair. How I could've pulled you under me, pinned your wrists above your head, taken my time tasting every damn inch of you.

Oh, hell.

Savannah clenched the phone in her grip, heat pooling in her belly.

He was not playing fair.

Savannah: You seem very sure of yourself, Montgomery.

Chase: Not sure of myself, sweetheart.

A pause.

Chase: Sure of you.

Her pulse slammed against her ribs.

And then, just when she was about to tell him exactly how infuriating he was, another message came through.

Chase: But like I said… you deserve more than a stolen moment on a dock.

Her stomach clenched.

Damn him.

Damn him and his restraint.

Savannah: You're a dangerous man, Chase Montgomery.

Chase: And you, Savannah Monroe, are going to love every second of it.

Savannah bit her lip, staring at the screen.

She was so screwed.

And she couldn't fucking wait.

Malory's Interrogation

Across the room, Mallory, who had been watching her like a hawk, let out a dramatic groan, flopping onto the couch with a loud sigh.

"If you don't tell me what that man just texted you, I swear to God, Savannah, I will physically wrestle that phone from your hands and launch it into the ocean."

Savannah glanced up, arching a brow. "You do realize I have a passcode, right?"

Mallory narrowed her eyes. "And you do realize I will figure it out just to expose all the filthy, flirty little messages Chase Montgomery has been sending you?"

Savannah snorted, shaking her head. "He invited us to dinner."

Mallory perked up instantly. "Us? As in me too?"

"Yep." Savannah tossed her phone onto the coffee table. "Apparently, his coworker Nate is going to be there, and Chase thought you two should meet."

Mallory's smirk was instant. "Oh, I like the sound of that. The man clearly has good taste."

Savannah rolled her eyes, but she couldn't stop the warmth from blooming in her chest.

"So, you're in?" she asked, already knowing the answer.

Mallory scoffed, tossing her curls over her shoulder. "Are you kidding? If Chase Montgomery is cooking, I wouldn't miss it."

Savannah let out a soft laugh, shaking her head.

But beneath the amusement, beneath the teasing, there was something deeper curling low in her stomach.

Because tonight, she was going to Chase's house.

Again.

And there would be no dock between them this time.

No space.

No distractions.

Just him.

And she had a feeling she wouldn't survive the night without giving in.

22

Table for Four

SAVANNAH MONROE WAS SCREWED. Not in the literal sense, unfortunately. But in the utterly done for, completely gone, absolutely ruined by Chase Montgomery sense.

And judging by Mallory's reaction the moment they pulled up to his house, she wasn't far behind.

They barely made it up the porch steps before Mallory let out a long, slow whistle, tilting her head back to take it all in. "Okay, this man is officially trying to ruin my standards. This is gorgeous."

Savannah hadn't taken the time to truly appreciate it before, but now, standing beside her best friend, she saw it through fresh eyes. The house was effortlessly masculine—coastal yet strong, with deep blue siding, crisp honey trim, and windows glowing with soft golden light. The porch stretched wide, lined with weathered rocking chairs that seemed to whisper of slow mornings and late-night conversations.

Mallory elbowed her. "Tell me this man doesn't own candles. If he does, I'm dead. I will die on this doorstep."

Savannah rolled her eyes. "You're so dramatic."

"I am aware," Mallory said solemnly, "but that doesn't answer my question."

Before Savannah could respond, the front door swung open.

And there he was.

Chase stood barefoot in the doorway, wearing dark jeans and a fitted navy Henley that clung in all the right places. His hair was slightly tousled, as if he'd run his fingers through it while cooking, and the sight of him sent a fresh wave of warmth rolling through Savannah's stomach.

"Ladies," he drawled, his deep voice laced with amusement as his gaze locked onto Savannah's with a slow-burning intensity that made her breath catch.

Mallory cleared her throat. "Hey, Chase. Do you own candles?"

Chase blinked, taken aback. "Uh—yeah?"

Mallory groaned, pressing a hand to her chest. "I knew it. You're killing me."

Savannah laughed as Chase smirked, stepping aside. "Come on in. Nate's already raiding my whiskey stash."

They followed him inside, and the moment Mallory stepped through the door, she gasped so loudly Savannah thought she might need medical attention.

"Oh. My. God."

Savannah turned, watching as Mallory spun in a slow circle, eyes wide in awe.

"Savy, look at this place," she breathed. "This is some ripped-out-of-a-magazine, dream-home shit. What the hell?"

And honestly? Mallory wasn't wrong.

Savannah had only really seen the kitchen before, but now, standing in the open living room, it was like stepping into something unreal. The walls were a warm, muted gray, complemented by navy and deep walnut wood. A massive stone fireplace stretched from floor to ceiling, its hearth flickering with soft light. A plush, oversized sectional faced it—the kind of couch that invited sinking in for hours. Across the room, glass doors opened onto a patio where string lights twinkled like stars against the night.

Mallory turned to Chase, pointing an accusing finger. "How dare you."

Chase lifted an amused brow. "How dare I what?"

"Be this good-looking and have impeccable taste? It's infuriating." She spun on Savannah. "You've never been in this house?"

Savannah shook her head, still a little overwhelmed.

Mallory placed a hand on her hip. "Montgomery. Tour. Now."

Chase chuckled, shaking his head. "Go ahead. Look around."

Savannah hesitated. "You sure?"

His gaze flickered with something unreadable. "Yeah. Go on, Monroe."

That was all Mallory needed to hear before she practically dragged Savannah down the hallway, flinging doors open with reckless enthusiasm.

The dining room was elegant yet inviting—rich wood, low-hanging pendant lights, and a table large enough to fit eight comfortably.

"Imagine Sunday dinners here," Mallory muttered. "I'd move in."

Savannah laughed as they continued upstairs, moving from one beautifully designed space to another until they reached a closed door at the end of the hall.

Mallory shot her a look. "Is this his room?"

Savannah shrugged. "How would I know? First time in the house, remember?"

Mallory rolled her eyes before Savannah reached for the rustic doorknob, twisting it open.

Mallory gasped, grabbing Savannah's arm in dramatic horror.

The bedroom was nothing short of breathtaking.

Deep navy walls. Dark gray bedding. Floor-to-ceiling windows that framed the water like a living painting. The bed was massive—king-sized, with a rough-hewn wooden headboard that looked like something handcrafted. It was the kind of space that felt private—untouchable.

Mallory smirked, tilting her head. "Soooo... this is where the magic almost happened, huh?"

Savannah's cheeks burned. "Shut up."

Mallory ignored her, stepping inside and spinning slowly in place. "Oh, I hate him. This is too good. I wonder how many women have been in this bed?" She flopped onto it, bouncing once.

Savannah wrinkled her nose, not particularly wanting to dwell on that thought. Instead, she pointed toward the massive walk-in shower. Dark tile. A rainfall showerhead. And—of course—candles lined up neatly on the built-in shelf.

Mallory groaned so loudly it was almost comical. "Oh my God. He has candles in the bathroom."

Savannah slapped a hand over her face.

Mallory turned, hands on her hips, deadly serious. "Savy, if you don't sleep with this man, I will."

Savannah burst out laughing, shaking her head as Chase's voice rang from the kitchen.

"You two done snooping?"

Mallory grinned. "We're coming!" She smirked at Savannah, wiggling her brows. "You lucky bitch."

Savannah just smiled, warmth curling in her chest. "Yeah."

She knew.

They returned to the kitchen, where Nate—who was tall, broad-shouldered, and undeniably good-looking—was leaning against the counter, swirling a glass of bourbon.

When he saw Mallory, he grinned. "Well, damn. Chase didn't tell me you were gorgeous."

Mallory tilted her head, smirking. "And you must be Nate."

"Guilty." He extended his glass. "Want a drink?"

She took it without hesitation, taking a slow sip. "Depends. What are we drinking to?"

Nate's smirk widened. "To distractions worth wanting?"

Mallory's gaze flickered to Savannah briefly before she looked back at Nate, her lips curving in amusement. "I'll drink to that."

Chase leaned down, his breath hot against Savannah's ear. "Should we be worried about them?"

Savannah tilted her head, pretending to think. "Eh. Let them have their fun."

Chase chuckled, but there was something in his eyes that made her stomach flip. Something dark. Something heated.

"So," she said, trying to act casual. "What's on the menu, Chef Montgomery?"

Chase smirked, stepping back toward the stove. "Steak, grilled asparagus, and roasted potatoes."

Savannah raised an eyebrow. "Fancy."

He shrugged, grabbing a bottle of wine and pouring them each a glass. "You deserve a real meal."

She took the glass, their fingers brushing, and the simple touch sent a spark racing up her spine.

Mallory and Nate were already deep in conversation at the kitchen island, their flirting practically sizzling in the air.

Chase leaned against the counter, watching Savannah as he took a sip of his wine. "Come here."

Her breath caught at the command in his voice.

She stepped closer, and he reached for her, his fingers trailing lightly along her hip before settling at her waist.

"You're staring," she murmured.

"You're beautiful," he countered, his voice husky.

Her heart pounded. "Are you always this smooth?"

Chase smirked. "Only when it comes to you."

Savannah exhaled slowly, shaking her head. "You really don't fight fair, do you?"

Chase tilted his head, his lips hovering just above hers.

"Nope."

And God help her—she loved it.

23

Before Me

DINNER WAS PERFECT. MAYBE too perfect.

The steak was cooked to absolute perfection—juicy, tender, seared to just the right temperature. The wine flowed freely, loosening their inhibitions but never crossing into excess. The conversation was effortless, filled with easy laughter and teasing banter.

And yet, Savannah Monroe could barely focus on a damn thing.

Because every few minutes, Chase's fingers would graze hers when he reached for his glass, each touch sending a delicious shiver up her spine. His voice would dip just a little lower whenever he leaned in close, like he knew what it did to her. And then there was the way he watched her—like she was the only person in the room, like he was committing her every reaction to memory, like he was waiting for something.

Like he was waiting for her.

Meanwhile, Mallory and Nate were deep in their own world, their banter so charged it might as well have been foreplay at this point.

"I'm sorry," Mallory argued, leaning back in her chair, waving her wine glass dramatically. "But pineapple on pizza is a crime. You might as well dump sugar on spaghetti."

Nate scoffed, shaking his head in disbelief. "You're so wrong, it actually hurts. The sweet with the salty? It's god-tier."

Mallory made a face. "I should have known you were one of those people."

Nate smirked, taking a slow sip of his whiskey. "What? You can't handle a little risk in your life?"

Mallory arched a brow. "I love risk, but I don't go around committing war crimes against pizza."

Chase chuckled, cutting into his steak. "I hate to agree with him, but he's got a point."

Mallory gasped, looking personally offended. "Not you too! Savannah, back me up here."

Savannah blinked, dragging herself out of her thoughts. "Huh?"

And that's when she felt it—Chase's knee brushing against hers under the table.

A simple touch. Barely there. But her skin burned from it.

She had been distracted—not by the conversation, not even by the delicious meal, but by Mallory's comment earlier.

How many women have been in his bed?

Savannah had laughed it off at the time, but now, as she sat in his home, drank his wine, felt his leg pressed against hers, she couldn't stop thinking about it.

How many?

How many women had he carried upstairs, tangled in his sheets, made soundless with pleasure?

The thought made her stomach twist.

She hated that it bothered her.

Because she wasn't that girl. The insecure one. The one who asked about numbers.

But fuck if she didn't care.

She snuck a glance at Chase, who was leaning back in his chair, his fingers tapping idly against his glass.

If he noticed how quiet she'd gotten, he didn't say anything.

But he felt it.

She could tell.

By the time 10:30 PM rolled around, Nate stretched with a long sigh, smirking as he set his empty glass down. "Alright, as much as I'd love to keep watching you two make heart eyes at each other, I gotta head out."

Mallory pouted dramatically, but Nate just grinned, slipping his phone from his pocket. "Don't worry, sweetheart. You're not getting rid of me that easily."

She rolled her eyes but still handed him her phone to put in his number, her lips curving slightly as she glanced at him beneath her lashes.

Savannah barely registered them saying goodbye. Barely noticed Mallory's sly wink before heading toward the door.

Because she wasn't ready to leave.

Not yet.

And he wasn't ready for her to leave, either.

Chase leaned against the counter, arms crossed over his chest, watching her. "You wanna stay a while longer?"

Savannah hesitated for half a second before nodding. "Yeah. I kinda want a movie night."

Chase's smirk was slow, lazy. "I can do that."

Mallory paused in the doorway, glancing over her shoulder, her eyes filled with mischief. "You sure you don't want me to stay? Keep things PG?"

Savannah shot her a look. "Goodbye, Mallory."

Mallory grinned. "Make good choices, Monroe."

Then she was gone.

And suddenly, it was just the two of them.

Chase pushed off the counter, stepping closer. "I'll clean up, then we can start something."

Savannah chewed on her lip, hesitating.

Then, before she could second-guess herself, she spoke. "Hey, um... would it be okay if I took a shower first? I know I'll probably fall asleep before the movie's over."

His lips twitched slightly. "Yeah. Of course."

And then, before she could walk away, his fingers brushed against her arm. Just the faintest touch. But it sent a shockwave of heat through her, so quick and potent she almost stumbled.

His voice dipped lower, teasing. "Need anything? A t-shirt? A warm towel?"

Savannah swallowed hard. "I—I'm good."

His smirk deepened, his gaze knowing. "Mmm."

Damn him.

With one last glance, she turned and headed upstairs, her heart pounding in her chest.

Because she was alone.

In his house.

With him downstairs.

And all she could think about was whether she'd actually make it through that movie...

Or if she'd finally, finally stop waiting.

The second Savannah stepped into Chase's bathroom, she knew immediately—it was him.

Everything about it screamed Chase.

Dark walls, deep navy towels, sleek black fixtures. The kind of sharp, understated elegance that felt effortless. But what caught her attention wasn't the perfectly designed space.

It was the bathtub.

A claw-footed soaking tub sat against the far wall, positioned beneath a massive window overlooking the sound. It was stunning, bathed in the soft glow of the moon, the water outside stretching endlessly into the night.

Her fingers traced absently along the cool porcelain edge, her pulse a slow, steady hum.

She could imagine it—him in here, steam curling around his body, head tipped back, eyes closed.

She swallowed hard.

Jesus.

Forcing herself to move, she turned the shower on, hot water rushing to drown out her thoughts. Steam curled around her, wrapping her in warmth as she stepped inside, letting the spray wash over her skin.

But it didn't wash away the thoughts.

Because Mallory's words still wouldn't leave her the hell alone.

"How many women have been in his bed?"

Savannah squeezed her eyes shut, pressing her palms against the cool tile.

She hated that the question had rooted itself in her brain. Hated that she cared.

But she did.

Because Chase Montgomery wasn't a saint.

He was a man who could have anyone. A man women probably threw themselves at.

And yet...

He was waiting for her.

Why?

Her heart slammed against her ribs.

Was she really different? Or just the latest challenge?

Savannah exhaled sharply, running her fingers through her hair, trying to force the thoughts away.

She wasn't going to drive herself crazy.

Not tonight.

24

Holding Back

By the time she came downstairs, the air between them was already charged.

Chase had showered in the downstairs bath, fresh and clean, but there was nothing calm about the way he sat on the couch, watching her.

And fuck, he looked too good.

His damp hair curled slightly, the ends clinging to the skin at the nape of his neck, a few stray drops of water sliding down to disappear beneath the thin, white tank stretched across his broad chest. The dim lighting cast flickering shadows over the ridges of his sharp jaw, the dark scruff shadowing his face in a way that made her want to run her tongue over it. The deep ink of his tattoos contrasted against golden, tanned skin, every muscle thick, defined, flexing beneath her stare.

And those damn gray shorts.

Loose and low on his hips, just enough to be dangerous.

There was no mistaking the etched bulge of his cock beneath the fabric. A sign of what she could have.

And yet, he sat there like a man completely in control. As if his body wasn't betraying him. As if his self-control wasn't wearing dangerously thin.

Savannah had stolen one of his t-shirts from the laundry room before coming downstairs—soft, white, oversized, barely skimming the tops of her thighs. That was it. No leggings. No pajama shorts.

Just his shirt. And her.

The air thickened as his gaze flicked over her, slow and unhurried, drinking in bare legs, damp curls, the outline of her nipples beneath thin cotton.

"Feel better?" His voice was deep, husky, a slow drag of heat over her skin.

Savannah swallowed, feeling something tight coil in her belly. "Yeah." She said quickly.

He patted the space beside him, but she saw it—the clench of his jaw, the way his fingers twitched slightly, the way his thighs tensed.

Still, she sat.

Right beside him.

She tucked one leg under her, curling against his chest like she belonged there. His scent surrounded her—clean, crisp, masculine—and when his arm draped lazily over the back of the couch, his fingers tracing absentmindedly along her shoulder, her pulse skipped.

The movie started.

Savannah wasn't watching. She was feeling.

Her fingers traced his tattoos without thinking, outlining the swirls of ink that curved over his forearm, the intricate lines that wrapped up his bicep, disappearing beneath his tank. His skin was warm, firm beneath her touch, and she wondered what it would feel like to trace every inch of him.

Chase inhaled slowly, his chest rising and falling beneath her hand.

"You keep doing that, sweetheart," he murmured, voice thick, low, dangerous, "and we're not gonna make it through this movie."

A shiver curled down her spine.

She smirked.

Still, something in her thoughts lingered, gnawed at her. So she asked.

"Can I ask you a question?"

Chase turned slightly, fingers still stroking along her back. "Yeah. Shoot."

She hesitated, then exhaled. "Do you promise to be honest with me?"

His brows furrowed. "Of course."

She finally forced the words out.

"How many women have been in your bed?"

Chase stilled.

She saw it—the way his jaw ticked, his lips parted slightly, his fingers tensed against her waist.

But he didn't hesitate.

"None."

Savannah's breath caught. "None?"

His hand slid to her cheek, his thumb brushing lightly over her skin. His voice dropped low, deep, raw.

"The Echoes of Us—this house, this space, my bed—it's yours." He tilted her chin, forcing her to look at him, to feel the weight of his words.

"I've never brought a woman here. Never even considered it." His voice turned rougher. "If you hadn't come back, my bed would have only ever held me."

She didn't breathe.

Didn't blink.

Because fuck.

Fuck.

The weight of those words wrecked her.

Chase had been waiting for her.

And she wasn't going to waste another second.

A slow, shuddering breath escaped Savannah's lips before she lunged forward, crashing into him, her hands fisting his tank top, tearing him into her mouth.

Hard. Desperate. Raw.

Chase growled, low and guttural, the sound vibrating through her like an electric current. His hands found her, possessive and rough, gripping her like she was the only thing keeping him tethered to the last fragile thread of his control.

His fingers slid into her damp hair, yanking just enough to send a wicked, delicious thrill cascading down her spine, a silent command that told her exactly who was in charge.

And God, she loved it.

He kissed her like a man on the edge of fucking insanity—like he'd been starving for her, like he had every intention of devouring her whole.

And fuck, she wanted to be consumed.

Savannah moaned, the sound swallowed by the heat of his mouth, her fingers clawing at his shirt before she yanked it over his head, baring all of him.

Hard muscle. Taut skin. Ink stretched over every ridge and curve.

Her nails scraped down his chest, and Chase hissed, his head tipping back for a split second before he claimed her again, lips rough, punishing, insatiable.

His tongue teased at the seam of her lips, and she opened for him, moaning into his mouth when he took what he wanted, deepening the kiss until she felt lightheaded, dizzy with the taste of him.

Savannah straddled his lap without thinking, her bare thighs sliding over his, her knees pressing into the couch cushions on either side of his hips, her body molding to his in the most sinful way possible.

And then she moved.

Slow. Deliberate. Dangerous.

A deep, ragged curse ripped from his lips as she rolled her hips, a slow, torturous grind that had her seeing stars before he even touched her the way she needed him to.

Jesus.

He was so damn hard, and his gray athletic shorts left nothing to the imagi-nation—every thick, rigid inch of him pressed up against the heat between her thighs, making her gasp.

Chase gripped her waist—hard, his fingers digging in, bruising, claiming, his control fucking unraveling—

"Fuck, Savannah—" His voice was wrecked, hoarse, pure sin and fire. His hands dragged up her back, slow and deliberate, teasing, taunting, promising. "You have no idea what you're doing to me."

Her head fell back, her breath stuttering as his mouth ravaged her throat, his stubble scraping, marking, branding.

His teeth grazed her pulse point, sharp enough to leave a mark, and she fucking whimpered—actually whimpered—as heat pooled low, white-hot, unbearable.

A needy little moan slipped from her lips as she rocked against him again, a silent, desperate plea for more.

And fuck, she felt him.

Every. Fucking. Inch.

Thick, heavy, so fucking hard it was almost criminal—pressing firmly against her petals, against the place she wanted him most.

Her head spun. Her body burned. And God, she needed more.

"I think I have a pretty good idea," she gasped, her fingers tangling in his hair, tugging just enough to make him groan against her skin.

Chase's hands tightened on her ass, his breathing uneven, rough, jagged.

He wanted her.

She knew it.

But he was still holding back. And she was done waiting. She leaned in, her lips brushing just against his ear, her voice dropping into something dark, something dangerous.

"Stop fucking holding back."

Chase exhaled sharply, the sound ripped from somewhere deep, primal. His grip tightened, fingers flexing against her hips like he was holding himself back by a thread.

"There's a side of me you don't want to see," he warned, his voice rough, raw, dark with something dangerous. "Because once I go there—once I claim you—you won't fucking remember who you were before me."

A shiver raked down Savannah's spine, heat pooling low and deep. She didn't want to be careful. Didn't want him to hold back. Her nails dragged down his chest, slow, deliberate, teasing the beast lurking beneath his skin. "Then stop fighting it."

His jaw ticked, a muscle flexing, his restraint razor-thin. "You don't get it, Savannah." His hands slid up her sides, possessive, firm, making her pulse hammer. "I won't stop. I'll ruin you for anyone else. You'll be mine."

Her breath caught, her body already answering him before her lips did. She tilted her chin, eyes locked on his, daring, pleading.

"I already am."

Something inside him snapped.

25

Possession

With a guttural growl, Chase flipped her onto her back, pinning her against the couch cushions, his body wrapping hers in like he was staking his claim.

His mouth crashed into hers, consuming, taking, his kiss a declaration of everything he'd been holding back. His hands roamed with wild possession—gripping, palming, sliding under her shirt to claim every inch of bare skin he could find.

Savannah arched against him, a moan slipping past her lips as his teeth scraped down her throat, sending a wicked thrill straight to her core. His hands flexed against her, pressing into her hips, his hold tight like he was barely restraining himself.

"Damn it, Savannah," he rasped, grinding against her, the solid heat of him making her gasp. "You're gonna fucking kill me."

She grinned breathlessly, fingers twisting into his tank top, yanking it up and forcing him to sit back just enough to let her strip it off.

And damn.

Chase Montgomery was built for sin.

All corded muscle and carved lines, skin stretched tight over raw strength, every inch of him looking like he was sculpted for destruction. The tattoos licking up his biceps, the sharp cut of his abs leading lower—everything about him was temptation wrapped in flesh.

Savannah didn't wait. Didn't think. She sat up, her hands dragging over his chest, nails scratching lightly down his abdomen, feeling the way his muscles jumped beneath her touch. Chase's breath hitched, his fists clenching against the cushions like he was trying to anchor himself. His gaze burned into hers, dark and heavy, daring her to keep going.

So she did.

Her lips pressed to his collarbone, her tongue gliding against his skin before she dragged it lower, slow, deliberate, mapping a path down his chest, teasing over every ridge and dip of his body. She reached his waistline, where his abs tensed, his breath stuttered, and the thick, undeniable proof of what was restrained beneath his shorts.

She swallowed, her pulse pounding, her fingers ghosting over the hard outline of him, feeling the heat radiating through the thin material, the unmistakable proof of just how much he wanted her.

Chase let out a ragged curse, his jaw clenching so tight she thought he might break. His head tipped back against the couch for a moment before his gaze snapped back to hers, pupils blown, hands flexing at his sides like he was seconds from grabbing her, flipping her over, and fucking her world up completely.

But he waited. Because he wanted to see what she'd do next. Holding his stare, she hooked her fingers into the waistband of his shorts, tugging them down in one smooth, deliberate motion.

Her breath staggered, while seeing him. All of him.—Heavy. Thick. Hard as sin. Savannah swallowed, her mouth flooding, her pulse thrumming at the sheer size of his cock.

And Chase?

Chase let out a shaky exhale, his head pressing back against the couch once more, his hands gripping the fabric beneath him like he was seconds away from losing his fucking mind. "Fuck," he rasped, his voice torn, his eyes burning as he watched her.

Savannah held his gaze, her lips curling into a smirk as she wrapped her hands around his shaft, her touch deliberate—teasing. She parted her lips, letting his cock slide into her mouth, and he snapped. "Fuck—" ripped from his throat, his head snapping back against the couch, his fingers flexing into the fabric like she had just stolen his fucking soul.

One of her hands slid up, tracing the hard ridges of his abs while the other wrapped around him, firm and in synch with her mouth.

"Damn, Savannah..." His voice was wrecked, barely holding together. His muscles tightened beneath her hands, his thighs tensing as her tongue dragged along his length, slow and fucking deliberate.

She knew exactly what she was doing.

She hollowed her cheeks, lifted her tongue, taking him deeper, savoring the weight of his throbbing—cock on her tongue, feeling the way his body shuddered beneath her.

He was losing it. She could feel it. The way his breath tripped. The way his abs flexed so hard each time she she took him.

She worked him over, slow and twisted, dragging her tongue, pressuring his balls, setting a rhythm that had his entire body trembling.

Chase's hands twitched, like he wanted to grab her. Like he was fighting every instinct to take control. To claim her.

But he didn't. Not yet. He let her play, let her tease, let her fucking ruin him as she set a slow, torturous rhythm, dragging her tongue along the thick vein that pulsed against her lips.

His chest heaved, his abs flexing hard beneath her nails as she dug into him, holding him in place as she worked him over, her tongue sliding, her lips sucking, her every move calculated.

His control was slipping. Fraying at the edges. And she fucking loved it. She pulled back just enough to glance up at him, her lips wet, swollen, a wicked smile playing at the corners. "You're shaking, Montgomery," she taunted, voice a teasing purr. "Can't handle it?"

His growl was raw, sinful. His darkened gaze locked onto hers.

"You want me to show you how to handle it?" he echoed, his voice rough, edged with warning.

Her mouth wrapped around him again, her tongue— circling his throbbing-cock. She threw him a wink while watching the way his body tensed, how his chest heaved, how his muscles jumped beneath her touch.

"I want to hear you say it," he rasped, his voice dripping with challenge. "Ask me to! Beg me to show you.!

His control was gone, restraint hanging by a fucking thread, but he still needed her to give him the green light.

And she did.

She took him deep and moaned around him, teasing, her lips dragging over him slow, deep—

That was it. That was all it took. Chase snapped.

He jumps up. His hand snapped to the back of her head, fingers twisting into her hair, forcing her to take more, to take it faster.

"Is this what you wanted? Is this what you fucking wanted?" His voice, graveled. "You wanted this side of me?"

Her answer? Obvious and so fucking deliberate— She wraps her arms around his waist, pulls him in and takes him even deeper.

Chase's grip tightened in her hair, yanking her head back just enough to expose the delicate curve of her throat. His breath was ragged, his body taut with need, but his control—his dominance—was absolute.

"You want me to stop holding back?" he growled, his voice nothing but gravel and heat against her skin. "Then listen, Savannah. From this moment on, you're mine."

He could feel the soft slide of his cock against the hollow of her throat, the heat of her breath sending fire licking down his spine. His grip in her hair tightened, just enough to make her whimper, just enough to remind her exactly who was in control.

"Fuck, Savannah," he groaned, his body shaking beneath her. "You keep doing that, and I'm gonna make damn sure you never forget who you belong to."

Her lips parted, her eyes dark, dazed, pleading.

He looks down at her. Slowly pulls out of her mouth and grabs her cheek while one hand is still on the back of her head.. Is this what you wanted? Tell me to stop, and I will. But if you keep going–you will never be the same.

"Prove it." She said while opening her mouth again.

She dragged her nails over his thighs, working him harder, faster, letting him feel just how much she loved making him fall apart.

His breath hitched, his grip tightening, his entire body coiling like a predator about to strike—

And then suddenly, he was moving.

Fast. Violent. Possessive.

In one fluid motion, Chase grabbed her, flipped her onto the couch, and caged her in, his big hands pinning her wrists above her head as his mouth crashed into hers.

She moaned against his lips, the taste of him still on her tongue, the heat between them scorching, dangerous, too fucking much—

And yet, not enough.

Chase's grip on her thighs was absolute—unyielding, dominant, pure fucking control.

He didn't rush. Didn't fumble. Didn't hesitate.

Because she wasn't just his for the taking—she was his to claim.

"You think you can tease me like that?" His voice was a low, dangerous growl against her lips, his breath hot, thick with dominance. His teeth scraped her bottom lip, punishing, possessive, before his hands dragged down her body, pushing her thighs apart, spreading her open like she was made for him.

Savannah's breath hitched. "Maybe."

The smirk he gave her was lethal. "Then I guess it's my turn, sweetheart."

She barely had time to register the shift before his mouth was on her throat, biting, sucking, marking. His hands held her down, fingers pressing into her skin, pinning her open beneath him. She wasn't going anywhere.

And fuck, she didn't want to.

"You're already this wet?" His voice was all gravel and heat, fingers sliding beneath her shorts, teasing, barely touching, driving her insane. He pressed against her—firm, taunting—making her shudder beneath him.

"Just from sucking my cock?"

She whimpered, hips bucking, needing more, needing everything. Her hand slipped free, reaching down, fingers curling around his cock, desperate to guide him in.

Chase snatched her wrist, pinning it above her head, his body pressing her deeper into the cushions, keeping her trapped. Keeping her exactly where he wanted.

His gaze was lethal, burning straight through her. "I didn't say you could do that, Monroe."

What the fuck. Why did just hearing him say that make her clench around nothing? Her body arched again, helpless against the heat surging through her veins.

His lips dragged along her jaw, slow, deliberate, the sharp graze of his teeth making her gasp. "You wanted this." His fingers stroked over her, pushing deeper, harder, but never enough. "You begged for it."

Savannah's nails bit into his skin, thighs trembling, her body completely his.

"Give it to me," she breathed, voice wrecked, desperate.

Chase growled, the sound dark, feral, vibrating against her throat.

"I'll give it to you," he gritted out. "Be a good fucking girl. Lay there and take it."

His fingers found her clit, teasing, tormenting, before plunging two fingers deep, stretching, curling, commanding.

She gasped, her back arching, moans spilling from her lips—raw, unfiltered.

He owned her.

His mouth crashed into hers, his tongue forcing past her lips as he fucked her with his fingers, each motion precise, punishing, deliberate.

His free hand slid up her body, gripping her throat, holding her exactly where he wanted her. His forehead pressed against hers, his voice low, wicked, dangerous—

"Is this what you wanted?"

Savannah sobbed out a moan, her body tightening, her pulse racing.

Chase smirked, his fingers relentless. "You want me to keep going?"

"Give it to me," she shouted, the words ripped from her chest.

His control shattered.

Chase's fingers hit her G-spot with precision, each come here motion faster, harder, more relentless. His touch was ruthless, demanding, leaving no room for restraint.

The slick sound of his fingers moving inside her, the desperate drag of her hand gripping his arm, the raw, unfiltered moans spilling from her lips—it was all too much.

Every sharp stroke sent her closer. Sent her spiraling. Savannah writhed, shaking, breaking, the pleasure overwhelming, devastating.

"Good girl. That's it, baby." Chase's voice was a rasp, his breath ragged, his grip tightening. "Let go. Give it to me."

She shattered.

Her body exploded, a violent, uncontrollable release tearing through her as she gasped his name, her legs trembling, her fingers clawing into his skin.

Chase didn't stop. Didn't slow.

He took.

And then—

26

Claiming

WITH A POOL, NOW on the hardwood floor. Chase devours her, his tongue grazing her swollen clit. Each pass is a different pressure with ruthless precision, with pure fucking ownership.

His grip on her thighs tightened, keeping her exactly where he wanted her, keeping her spread, trembling, falling apart for him.

She had no control.

He had her pinned. Open. Completely at his mercy.

And fuck, he knew it.

She arched, shuddered, her nails clawing at his shoulders, at his scalp, her thighs shaking as his tongue delved deeper, his mouth moving against her like he was fucking addicted to her.

Her pulse pounded, her body tightening, her breath coming in ragged, uneven gasps—

And then—

Chase pulled back.

Her eyes flew open, her body screaming for more, her pulse thundering, the loss of him leaving her aching, desperate, wrecked.

But before she could protest, before she could beg him to finish what he started—

He moved.

Fast. Possessive. Unstoppable.

One second she was flat on her back, legs spread for him, his mouth devouring her like a fucking feast—

And the next?

He had her off the couch, lifting her like a prize he had every intention of claiming again.

Her breath hitched, a strangled gasp leaving her throat as his hands gripped the back of her thighs, holding her in place, keeping her flush against his chest.

"Chase—"Her voice broke, but he shut her up with a kiss so brutal, so deep, so fucking consuming, it obliterated every thought in her head.

His lips were hot, his beard was dripping, his hands everywhere, gripping, claiming, commanding.

Savannah wrapped her legs around him, her finger tangling into his hair, her body shaking as he carried her effortlessly up the stairs.

He wasn't rushing.

He was taking his time.

Because this?

This was his moment.

His to control.

His to command.

His to make sure she never forgot.

Savannah's breath was shredded, her chest rising and falling against his, her body pressed to his bare skin, melting into him, desperate for more.

"You think you can just tease me like that?" Chase's voice was low, rough, dark, his lips brushing against her jaw as he climbed the stairs.

She gasped, her fingers clenching against his shoulders, her core pulsing as he took another step, his grip tightening under her thighs, pressing her harder against him.

"You thought you could get me on my knees?" His breath was hot, dangerous, his mouth grazing the shell of her ear.

She shivered, tightening her hold on him, her pulse pounding, aching, fucking starving for him.

"You thought you could take control?"

His teeth dragged over her pulse, and she whimpered, feeling the promise behind every word.

But then—

Then he reached the bedroom.

And fuck—

Savannah barely had time to register where they were before Chase threw her onto the bed, his body following instantly, pinning her down, his weight pressing her deep into the mattress.

Her breath was heavy, her skin flushed, her body aching for him—

But she wasn't the only one.

Chase's control was gone, obliterated the second he had her beneath him, open, waiting, fucking desperate.

His hands gripped her thighs, spreading her wide, exposing her completely, and Savannah swore she felt the air shift, the heat between them turning unbearable, suffocating, and so fucking consuming.

She felt him.

Heavy. Thick. Hard as sin.

Laying against her waistline, pressing into her skin, the proof of exactly how much he needed her making her pulse throb between her legs.

Savannah's breath hitched, her hand sliding down, reaching for him, wrapping around the solid, stiff length of him, stroking slow, teasing, her grip firm, demanding.

Chase groaned, a deep, guttural sound, his head dropping for a second as his hips jerked into her touch—

But then—

He grabbed her wrist, pulling her hand away, pinning it to the mattress beside her head.

Her lips parted, eyes wide, begging, silently pleading for him, for all of him.

Her legs shifted beneath him, her body arching, wordlessly offering herself to him in a way that had him fucking shaking with restraint.

Savannah's gaze dropped between them, seeing the size of him, the sheer thickness pressing against her, and fuck—

Her head threw back, her fingers fisting the sheets, her breath stuttering out of her lungs as Chase aligned himself—

And then?

Then he slid in.

Deep. Hard. Completely, fucking stretching her.

A choked gasp left her throat, her back arching violently, her body clenching around him, her thighs tightening against his hips as he filled her in a way she'd never been filled before.

She felt wrecked already, utterly claimed, but Chase?

He wasn't done.

His hands tightened on her hips, holding her down, keeping her in place, right where he wanted her, his jaw clenched so fucking tight he looked ready to break.

His eyes burned into hers, dark, possessive, devouring.

Savannah swallowed, her pulse pounding, her body trembling beneath him.

And then his voice—
Low. Feral. Uncontrollable.
"You're mine now, Monroe."
And then?
Then he fucking proved it.

27

A Breath Away

SAVANNAH STIRRED, A DEEP, satisfied ache settling into her bones, the weight of exhaustion keeping her limbs heavy, languid, utterly spent.

Every inch of her body hummed, muscles deliciously sore from where he had held her down, lifted her up, taken her apart piece by piece, only to put her back together in ways she never knew she needed.

She sighed against the pillow, her fingers curling into the soft fabric.

It wasn't just any pillow.

It was his.

His scent still clung to it—warm, masculine, a mix of salt air, faint cologne, and the heady, intoxicating smell of sex that still lingered in the air around her.

Savannah turned onto her side, breathing it in, letting the memories crash into her all at once.

The way he looked at her. The way he touched her. The way he wrecked her like he had no intention of leaving her whole.

A slow pulse ignited between her thighs.

She swallowed, her fingers grazing over the empty space beside her.

The sheets were still warm, rumpled, a mess of tangled limbs and restless, desperate hands.

But the bed was empty.

Savannah's eyes fluttered open, sunlight spilling through the wide windows, streaking golden light across the room.

The view outside was breathtaking—the sound stretched out in front of her, seagrass waving lazily in the breeze. But none of it mattered.

Because Chase wasn't there.

Her stomach tightened.

Did he regret it?

The thought was suffocating, unwelcome.

She pushed herself up onto her elbows, taking in the wreckage of their night together.

Her clothes were still scattered across the floor—her shorts were nowhere to be found, his shirt tossed haphazardly near the dresser, like he had been too impatient to wait even a second longer.

Her lips curled slightly.

Last night had been... everything.

The kind of night that burned itself into your skin.

And now?

Now she had to face the morning after.

She shoved back the covers, her body still buzzing with the remnants of his touch, of his mouth, of the way he had whispered filthy things against her skin while burying himself inside her.

Savannah bit her lip and grabbed the first thing she could find—his Henley from yesterday—slipping it over her bare skin. The fabric swallowed her whole, the sleeves falling below her elbow, but it smelled like him.

She padded toward the door, heart hammering, listening for any sign of him.

And then—

The faint sound of movement downstairs.

She exhaled.

He's still here.

Relief curled through her, followed immediately by something far more dangerous—anticipation.

Savannah descended the stairs slowly, the scent of coffee and something buttery and rich wafting through the air.

And then she saw him.

Chase—Standing in the kitchen. Barefoot. Shirtless.

Wearing only a pair of gray athletic shorts that hung far too low on his hips.

Her thighs clenched at the sight.

His back was to her, the muscles shifting effortlessly as he flipped something in the pan. The tattoos lining his arms and shoulders looked obscene in the morning light, stretching over his broad, sculpted frame like something sinful.

Savannah's breath caught.

No man should look that good in the morning.

She crossed her arms, leaning against the doorway, a slow smirk moving on her lips.

"So you cook after you fuck a woman senseless?"

Chase froze for half a second, spatula poised mid-air before he let out a low, knowing chuckle.

"Only for the ones who make me lose my fucking mind."

Her stomach flipped. Her breath hitched. Her body betrayed her.

Because that's what she was to him? A woman who made him lose control?

Before she could overthink it, he turned.

His gaze swept over her, slow, possessive, taking in the oversized shirt hanging loose around her frame, her bare legs peeking out from beneath the hem, her hair a wild mess from where his fingers had tangled into it the night before.

His jaw tightened.

His eyes darkened.

"Come here, Monroe."

A shiver rolled down her spine at the way his voice dropped, deep and gravelly.

She smirked. "Or what?"

His expression shifted.

Something wicked, dangerous, borderline feral flashed behind his eyes.

"Or I'll come get you myself."

Her breath stalled.

This man. This mother fucking man.

She loved pushing him, loved seeing how close she could get him to snapping. So she didn't move.

She just tilted her head, squinting, watching him, challenging him.

His nostrils flared. "Alright, then." Before she could react, Chase was on her, his hands gripping her thighs, lifting her off the ground effortlessly, throwing her over his shoulder like she weighed nothing.

She shrieked, laughing as he carried her toward the counter, his fingers squeezing her ass through the thin fabric of his shirt.

"Chase—put me down!" she squealed, breathless, her heart slamming against her ribs.

"You had your chance, Monroe," he growled, setting her down on the cold marble countertop, his body trapping her in place, caging her in.

Her pulse hammered as he leaned in, his mouth a breath away from hers, his hands trailing up her bare thighs, sliding under his shirt, gripping her hips like he owned them.

His voice was low, deep, a threat wrapped in a promise.

"Good morning, Darlin'."

Savannah's breath hitched, her fingers curling into the hard muscles of his biceps.

Fuck.

Everything about him was too much, yet never enough.

"Morning," she whispered back, tilting her chin, brushing her lips against his—just enough to tease.

Chase's hands tightened, his fingers digging into her skin, his body tensing, his control hanging by a thread.

"Chase," she whispered, her fingers trailing over the ridges of his abs, the sharp cut of his obliques disappearing beneath the band of his shorts.

He groaned, the sound low and wrecked, and fuck, she loved it.

She licked her lips, watching as his gaze dropped to her mouth, his control hanging by a damn thread.

"You keep looking at me like that," he muttered, voice thick, gravelly, his fingers flexing against her thighs, "and I won't be responsible for what happens next."

Savannah smirked, loving the tension, loving how close she could push him to losing it completely.

She dragged her fingers lower, tracing the sharp V of his hips, feeling his muscles jump beneath her touch.

"Maybe that's what I want," she murmured, her breath fanning over his lips.

Chase snapped.

His hands slid up, gripping her waist, pulling her flush against him, his body slotting between her legs, the heat of him pressing into her exactly where she needed it most.

She gasped, her hands fisting into his hair, holding on as his mouth crashed into hers, all heat and reckless, raw need.

The kiss was a promise, a threat, a fucking warning all at once.

Savannah whimpered as he took control, as his tongue slid against hers, as his teeth nipped at her bottom lip before soothing the bite with a slow, filthy kiss.

His hands were everywhere, mapping her, learning her, owning her.

She arched into him, her body grinding against his, and Chase let out a deep, gravelly sound, his grip tightening.

"Fucking hell, Savannah," he rasped, his forehead dropping to hers, his breathing uneven, raspy.

Her nails scraped down his back, her own breath coming in sharp little gasps, her body thrumming with need.

But Chase suddenly froze, his hands stilling against her skin.

She blinked, heart pounding, stomach flipping when he pulled back just enough to meet her gaze.

There was something different in his eyes.

Something fierce. Something real.

He exhaled sharply, like he was trying to regain control of himself, and then he smirked, grazing his hands where her shorts should be, pressing one last slow, deep kiss to her lips before pulling away.

"You're a fucking menace," he muttered, stepping back, his fingers lingering on her thighs for just a second longer than necessary.

Savannah's breath hitched, her lips still swollen, her body still burning for him.

She frowned. What the hell was he doing?

"What—?"

Chase grinned, running a hand through his hair, looking too damn smug for someone who had just turned her into a mess of need.

"Breakfast first," he said, turning back to the stove, grabbing the spatula like he hadn't just obliterated her in the span of five minutes.

Savannah gasped at him.

"Are you serious?"

He chuckled, flipping whatever the hell was in the pan, like he wasn't rock hard and one touch away from completely losing his shit again.

"Starving," he said simply.

Savannah's jaw tightened, her pulse pounding.

"You're impossible," she muttered, hopping off the counter.

She adjusted his shirt on her body, crossing her arms, glaring at him as he plated their food.

Chase barely glanced at her, just reached for a cup of coffee, taking a long, slow sip before turning back around, his eyes sparkling with amusement.

"Something wrong, Monroe?"

She narrowed her eyes.

She could play this game too.

Savannah tilted her head, stepped closer—close enough that he could feel the heat of her against him, close enough that she knew it would drive him crazy.

Then, she leaned in, her lips grazing the shell of his ear.

"Nothing at all," she whispered, her fingers ghosting over the chiseled bulge from his shorts, feeling the way his muscles tensed beneath her touch.

Then she pulled back just as quickly, grabbing her plate and heading toward the table like she hadn't just mind fucked his entire existence.

Chase cursed under his breath, his jaw clenching as he watched her.

And Savannah?

She just smirked, taking a slow, satisfied bite of food.

Game. On.

28

Game On

Savannah chewed her bite of food slowly, deliberately, watching Chase as he took a sip of his coffee, the muscles in his jaw clenching hard as hell.

He was trying to play it cool, but she saw the tension in his body.

The way his fingers gripped the handle of his mug a little too tight.

The way his eyes darkened every time her bare legs shifted, teasing, taunting.

The way his chest rose and fell, controlled, measured—like he was holding something back.

Good.

Because if Chase Montgomery thought he was the only one who could play this game, he was dead fucking wrong.

She hummed, tilting her head slightly, swinging one leg over the other, letting the oversized Henley she was wearing slide just a little higher on her thighs. "So—what's the plan for today?"

Chase exhaled slowly, setting his coffee down before leaning against the counter, his arms crossing over his chest, his tattooed forearms flexing as he did.

And fuck.

He was so damn unfair to look at.

"What do you mean?" he asked, his voice low, easy, but filled with warning.

Savannah took another slow bite, letting the fork linger at her lips just a second longer than necessary. "Well, since you're starving and all," she teased, "I assume you had a full itinerary planned before you—got distracted."

His eyes flickered dangerously. "Monroe—"

She smirked, cutting another bite of food, completely ignoring the silent warning in his tone.

Chase was watching her like a predator, his eyes locked on her mouth, on her throat, on the way she shifted slightly in her chair, teasing, taunting.

He rolled his shoulders back, exhaling hard. "I do have things to do today," he muttered.

"Oh, really?" Savannah feigned curiosity, licking a single drop of syrup from the corner of her lips, knowing full well he was watching every goddamn movement. "Like what?"

Chase's jaw ticked, his patience visibly thinning, but his voice stayed smooth, steady, dangerous.

"Like making sure you don't get away with this shit, sweetheart."

Savannah grinned, popping another bite of food into her mouth.

"Oh, I'm sorry," she mused. "Am I making things difficult for you?"

Chase didn't blink.

Didn't flinch.

Didn't even move.

Until suddenly, he did.

Fast. Decisive. Fucking ruthless.

Before she could react, he was on her, his chair scraping against the floor as he stalked toward her, dragging her plate away, his hands gripping the sides of her chair, caging her in.

Her breath mocked, her pulse pounding, but she refused to look away.

"I hope you enjoyed that little show, Monroe," Chase murmured, his lips barely a breath from hers.

Savannah swallowed hard, her fingers tightening around the edge of the table.

He leaned in, so close their noses brushed, his voice a low, lethal whisper.

"Because you just started something you won't be able to finish."

Her stomach flipped, anticipation curling low in her gut.

But she wasn't about to let him see that.

She tilted her chin up, keeping her smirk firmly in place. "We'll see about that."

Chase chuckled, dark and dangerous. "Oh, sweetheart. You have no fucking idea what you've done."

And just like that?

The game was officially on.

The First Move

Savannah pushed back in her chair, stretching out like she wasn't a second away from losing herself, like she wasn't soaked just from the way he looked at her.

She yawned, feigning innocence as she stood, making a show of adjusting his Henley, letting it slide just a little more off her shoulder, exposing just enough skin.

Chase's gaze dragged down her body, his expression shifting to something dark, wicked, unreadable.

She padded toward the sink, her bare feet silent on the hardwood, and reached for a glass, filling it with water.

And then?

She drank.

Slowly.

She let her throat move, let the cold water slip past her lips, her eyes flicking to Chase's just in time to catch the way his fingers flexed at his sides.

Good.

She set the glass down, brushed past him, letting her fingers graze over his stomach, feeling the tight, hard muscles that are normally hidden beneath a shirt.

She felt his sharp inhale, heard the way his breathing caught, but she didn't stop.

Didn't give him the satisfaction of a second glance.

She headed toward the stairs, tossing over her shoulder, "I'm gonna shower."

Silence.

Thick. Heavy. Stifling.

Then—

Chase's voice, low and fucking lethal:

"I wouldn't do that if I were you."

Savannah paused at the bottom of the stairs, looking back at him. "Why not?"

His jaw clenched, his body so fucking tense, like he was seconds away from pouncing.

She watched the way his fingers drummed against the countertop, how his nostrils flared just slightly.

He was right on the edge.

One step away from snapping.

She tilted her head, smiling sweetly. "Afraid of a little hot water, Montgomery?"

Chase exhaled, slow and controlled, shaking his head with pure amusement.

But his eyes?

Fucking deadly.

"Oh, sweetheart," he murmured, his voice soft, smooth, but absolutely terrifying.

Savannah barely had time to process it—

Because in one sharp movement, Chase launched forward, gripping the back of her thighs and lifting her off the fucking ground.

She yelped, gasping as he carried her straight up the stairs, his grip unforgiving, possessive, claiming.

"Chase—"

"You wanted to play, Monroe?" His voice vibrated through her, his breath hot against her neck as he took the stairs two at a time.

Her stomach flipped, heat pooling between her legs, her body throbbing against him.

"Now?" He reached the top of the stairs, pushing open the bedroom door with his shoulder, his body pinned against hers, pressing her into the chilled wall.

His eyes burned into hers, his hands gripping her thighs, his chest heaving, his restraint hanging by the fucking seams.

"Now, I'm gonna make sure you understand exactly what you started."

Savannah swallowed hard, her body melting against his.

But she wouldn't back down.

Wouldn't let him win so easily.

So she smirked, trailing a single finger over his chest, her lips brushing his ear.

"Then don't keep me waiting."

Savannah's breath was ragged, her back pressed against the cool wall, her thighs wrapped tight around Chase's waist.

His grip was brutal, his hands digging into her skin, his body so damn close she could feel every thick, hard inch of him through his shorts.

And God help her—

She wanted him to snap.

She wanted him to lose every ounce of control he was barely hanging onto.

But Chase?

Chase was a cruel, ruthless man.

He dragged his lips down her throat, his tongue teasing, his teeth nipping just enough to make her shudder.

His fingers skated up her thighs, pushing beneath his Henley that she still wore, his hands roaming, claiming, burning.

Her pulse pounded, her nails raking over his back, her hips grinding against him without a second thought.

"How wet are you?" He whispered as he reached down to feel.

She let out a slight moan. She was losing herself, spiraling, falling so damn fast—

And then—

Then he stopped.

Savannah let out a frustrated whimper, her chest heaving as Chase suddenly backed off, his hands leaving her like she was on fire.

She blinked, disoriented, confused, throbbing for more.

"What the—"

Chase exhaled hard, rolling his shoulders back, his hands clenching at his sides, his jaw so fucking tight it looked like he was about to break his own control in half.

But he didn't.

He just... stepped back.

Savannah's stomach dropped, her body screaming in protest, throbbing for him, for his hands, his mouth, his body—

Instead, Chase ran a hand through his already wild hair, his chest still rising and falling, his restraint so fucking fragile it was almost painful to witness.

Then?

He smirked.

And that cocky, self-satisfied expression had her blood boiling.

"Go shower, Monroe," he said, voice gravelly, thick with amusement.

Savannah scowled at him, her body still pinned to the wall, burning, pulsing, desperate for him to fucking finish what he started.

Her lips parted. "Are you—"

He tilted his head, stepping away completely, putting space between them, crossing his arms over his chest like he wasn't the very reason she was about to combust on the spot.

His next words?

Pure, evil cruelty.

"I need to go clean up the kitchen."

Savannah's jaw dropped.

Her brain barely processed the words because no fucking way was he doing this to her.

She clenched her fists, pushing off the wall, eyes narrowing. "Are you serious?"

Chase grinned, and God help her, she wanted to wipe that smirk right off his perfect, gorgeous fucking face.

She crossed her arms, glaring. "You just—" She huffed, flustered, annoyed, burning. "You just did all that—just to leave me hanging?"

His grin widened. "As you can see, I'm the one hanging" he said with a wink.

Fucking bastard.

"You started this, sweetheart," he mused, tilting his head, running a lazy, appreciative gaze down her body like he wasn't just as tortured as she was.

Savannah inhaled sharply, narrowing her gaze.

"You're such a smug asshole," she gritted out, shifting on her feet, still flushed and aching and desperate for relief.

Chase chuckled, shaking his head, completely unbothered.

Then, the final nail in her coffin:

He leaned in, just enough to brush his lips against her ear, his hands gripping her hips again—

But instead of giving her what she wanted, what she needed, what he damn well knew she was begging for—

He murmured:

"Enjoy your shower, Monroe."

And then?

He fucking walked away.

Savannah gasped, her entire body betraying her, her legs shaking with need, her breath coming too fast, too uneven, too wrecked for a man who had just abandoned her in this state.

She whipped around, watching as he disappeared down the hallway like he hadn't just ruined her life.

The sound of silverware clinking in the kitchen only infuriated her further.

"Son of a bitch," she muttered under her breath, running her hands through her hair.

Her pulse hammered, her body still on fire, still aching, still throbbing for him.

She stared at the into the bathroom, then at the empty hallway, then back at the bathroom.

She was going to kill him.
She was going to make him pay.
Game. Fucking. On.

29

Game Over

THE ENTIRE TIME SAVANNAH was in the shower, her mind was racing.

How the hell was she going to get back at Chase for what he just did?

For leaving her like that, desperate, on the edge of complete oblivion—only to walk away and clean the damn kitchen like he hadn't just fucked her mind?

The arrogance. The cruelty. The absolute nerve.

She had been seconds away from unraveling for him, from falling apart completely, and he had just walked away.

She clenched her jaw, letting the hot water cascade over her, but no amount of heat could burn away the frustration still pooling in her stomach.

No, she needed payback.

And then?

It hit her.

She knew exactly what she was going to do.

A slow, wicked smirk curled at her lips as she finished her shower, dried off, and slipped into absolutely nothing but a towel, securing it loosely around her chest.

Time to play.

Savannah descended the stairs like she had all the time in the world—calm, composed, completely unbothered. Every step was deliberate, a slow, teasing display of confidence as she wrapped herself tighter in the towel, making sure it barely skimmed mid-thigh.

Chase was just leaving the kitchen, arms crossed over that annoyingly perfect chest, his weight shifted lazily onto one foot like he had all the patience in the world. His eyes tracked her descent, that signature smirk of his curving at the edges, like he knew something she didn't.

Like he thought he still had the upper hand.

Cocky bastard.

She stopped just inches away from him, the air crackling between them. The scent of her still-warm skin, fresh from the shower, mingled with the remnants of whatever damn cologne he wore—something rich, something masculine, something that made her want to lose her mind.

She tilted her head, playing it smooth. "Did you get everything done, Montgomery?"

His brows lifted slightly, his smirk deepening like he saw straight through her act. "Yeah, sweetheart. Everything's cleaned up and put away."

Savannah hummed, slow and sweet, letting her eyes drop deliberately, dragging her gaze down his torso. Her focus barely skimmed over the cut of his abs, the deep V disappearing beneath those loose gray sweatpants before she flicked her attention back up, meeting his gaze with a slow, satisfied smile.

"Good," she said, voice syrupy smooth. "I'm so glad you were able to handle that."

Chase's smirk turned downright sinful. "Me too."

Then—

Without warning, his hand snapped out, landing a sharp, solid smack against her ass.

Savannah gasped, her body jolting at the impact, a sharp sting blooming across her skin, heat surging so fast she forgot how to breathe for a second. Her fingers curled into her towel, her spine going rigid, but before she could even process the damn audacity—

He just kept walking.

Up the stairs.

Like nothing happened.

Like he hadn't just set her entire body on fire with one ruthless, punishing slap.

He didn't look back.

Didn't check to see her reaction.

Didn't wait for retaliation.

Just walked away, slow and easy, all broad shoulders and rolling muscle, like the cocky motherfucker he was, leaving her standing there—stunned, seething, and undeniably wrecked.

Savannah pressed her lips together, inhaling sharply as her pulse throbbed in places it shouldn't. Her skin still tingled, burning from where his palm had landed, from where the heat of him still lingered.

Focus. Stick to the plan. He doesn't get to win this one.

By the time Chase made it to the bathroom, he was already stripping off his shorts, completely unbothered, his movements slow, methodical. He tossed them into the hamper, stretching slightly, muscles flexing as he grabbed a towel from the closet, tossing it onto the counter.

The shower turned on with a low hiss, steam curling through the air, thickening with each passing second.

He laid his fresh clothes on the bed, not rushing, not thinking—because Savannah was downstairs.

He had a few minutes to himself.

He stepped into the shower, the hot water pounding against his shoulders, muscles relaxing as he ran a hand through his damp hair, exhaling for what felt like the first time since she'd started her little game at breakfast.

The past hour had been torture—her teasing smirks, the way she'd dragged her fingertips across his skin like she wasn't fucking with him, like she wasn't already winning.

And now?

Now, he had space.

Now, he could breathe.

He reached for the shampoo, lathering it into his hair, closing his eyes as the heat eased the tension in his body.

And then—

He heard it.

The faint sound of the TV turning on downstairs.

Good.

She was occupied.

Which meant he could take his time, clean himself up, clear his fucking head.

He worked the shampoo through his hair, fingers dragging over his scalp, muscles finally unwinding, every inch of him sinking into the bliss of solitude.

Until—

Until he felt it.

A hand.

Small. Soft. Warm.

Gripping him.

Chase's entire body went rigid, his pulse roaring to life, his brain struggling to process what the fuck was happening—

Then?

Then he heard her.

A soft, satisfied hum.

Wicked. Knowing. Dangerous.

His eyes snapped open just in time to look down—

And fuck.

There she was.

On her knees. In the shower. Looking up at him with those big, dark eyes, the steam swirling around her like she belonged in some goddamn fantasy.

The smirk on her lips said everything.

This was payback.

And Savannah?

She was just getting started.

Chase froze, every muscle in his body going tight as a damn wire as he looked down at her.

Savannah was kneeling in front of him, her body glistening under the spray of the shower, steam curling around her like a fucking vision of sin.

But it was her eyes that really did him in.

Smug. Dark. Dangerous.

She knew exactly what she was doing.

Her fingers wrapped around him, stroking slow, teasing, her touch deliberate, unhurried—

Cruel.

Because she was playing with him.

Giving him just enough to make him burn but not enough to relieve the pressure that had been building all damn morning.

His jaw clenched hard, his hands fisting at his sides as he fought the overwhelming need to take control.

To grab her. To flip the fuckin' script. To wreck her first.

But he didn't.

He couldn't.

Because this?

This was her game now.

And fuck if that wasn't the sexiest thing he'd ever seen.

Savannah tilted her head, her nails scraping lightly against his thigh, sending a full-body shudder through him.

"Something wrong, Montgomery?" she asked, her voice sweet as honey, but dripping with challenge.

His breath came out ragged, his fingers twitching. "Savannah—"

She smirked. "You look a little—tense."

His biceps flexed, his entire body wired tight, the muscles in his stomach contracting with every slow, deliberate stroke of her hand.

"Fuck—" He cut off, his head falling back against the tile, his breath coming sharp, uneven.

She loved it.

Loved seeing him come undone.

Loved having this power over him, the same way he had over her all damn morning.

Her hand moved again, tighter, stronger, her nails scraping lightly over his skin, her lips ghosting just close enough to make him suffer.

Chase let out a deep, wrecked groan, his restraint dangling by a thread.

She could tell he was seconds from breaking.

Seconds from grabbing her, pushing her into the shower wall, giving her exactly what she'd been teasing him with.

And that's when she knew—

It was time.

Savannah licked her lips, but this wasn't hesitation.

This was her claiming her big, long, fucking prize.

She didn't ease in.

Didn't tease.

Didn't go slow.

No, the second her hands gripped his thighs for balance, she took him into her mouth in one sharp, wet, filthy motion, her tongue flattening, her lips stretching as she swallowed him deep.

Chase's curse ripped through the steam, a raw, helpless sound, his fingers slamming against the tile behind him, his entire body locking up.

"Jesus—fuck—"

Savannah didn't stop.

Didn't slow down.

Didn't give him time to breathe, think, or recover.

She hollowed her cheeks, sucking hard, dragging her nails down his tense, flexing thighs, her own thighs clenching at the sounds pouring from his lips.

She wanted him gone.

Wanted him shattered.

Wanted him to come completely undone for her.

She pulled back just enough to let him feel the drag of her tongue, flicking over the tip before she let him slide down her throat again, her nails digging into his skin as she set a brutal fucking pace.

Chase let out a choked groan, his fingers twitching, his jaw tight as hell, his hips fighting to stay still.

"Fucking hell, Savannah—"

She moaned around him, her eyes flicking up to his, and fuck—

She had never seen him like this.

His head tipped back, his throat taut, his chest rising and falling unevenly, his muscles shaking under her hands, his fingers curling into fists because he was holding back.

Trying to be good.

Trying to let her have this.

But Savannah?

She didn't want him to hold back.

She wanted him wild.

Wanted him unhinged.

Wanted him mentally, fucked.

So she fucking told him.

She pulled off him with a sharp, wet pop, her tongue dragging one long, slow lick up his length before she smirked up at him, her voice a low, dangerous whisper.

"Stop fucking fighting it, Montgomery."

His head snapped down, his eyes feral, his chest heaving.

Savannah pressed her nails into his hips, her lips hovering over him, close enough to tease, close enough to make him fucking beg.

"I want it," she murmured, her breath hot against his skin.

"I want you to fuck me like you've been dreaming about all fucking morning."

Chase cursed so viciously it sounded like a growl.

She pressed up against him, soaking wet, flushed, desperate, and reached between them, wrapping her fingers firmly around his aching length, feeling how hard, how fucking ready he was.

Her eyes locked on his, dark and dangerous, her voice a low, sultry rasp.

"I want you to release, Montgomery."

His entire body locked up, his hands tensing against her thighs, his jaw clenching so tight he looked seconds from losing every ounce of restraint he had left.

But Savannah?

She wasn't done.

She dragged his hand between her legs, letting him feel how fucking wrecked she was for him.

How wet.

How ready.

How much she needed him to let go.

Her lips brushed against his ear, and fuck, she loved how hard he shuddered at the feeling.

"You need to give it to me."

Chase groaned, wrecked, feral, his fingers flexing against her, his hips grinding into her with barely controlled restraint.

She dragged her tongue along the shell of his ear, pure fucking sin dripping from her voice.

"I want it. Deep, Hard, Rough" She moaned. "Fuck me like your life depends on it."

That was it.

That was his breaking point.

With a low, guttural curse, Chase grabbed her, lifted her, and slammed her back against the tile, his mouth crashing into hers with raw, unhinged desperation.

Savannah gasped against his lips, her nails clawing down his back, her body arching into his, grinding against him, needing him closer, deeper, harder.

Chase let out a low, possessive growl, his fingers digging into her thighs, spreading her open, his other hand tangling in her hair, tilting her head back to take everything he wanted.

"No more fucking games," he rasped against her lips, his voice rough, edged, completely destroyed.

Savannah smirked, wrapping her legs tighter around him, pulling him in exactly where she needed him most.

"No more fucking holding back."

Chase let out a sound that was half growl, half plea, his forehead dropping to hers, his body so tense, so desperate, so wrecked for her he looked seconds from coming undone.

"Savannah—"

She reached between them, gripping him, positioning him, teasing him, but not letting him inside just yet.

Her lips brushed against his, her breath hot, heavy, relentless.

"Give it to me, Chase."

And then?

He shoves it in.

Savannah's head rolls back against the tile wall. Her back sliding up and down the coarse grout lines. With each thrust, her moans get louder. Each thrust, she gets closer.

She wraps her arms around him, "Fuck, I'm coming." She shouts.

Her words sending chills across Chase's body. Exciting him more, making him thrust harder, faster.

"Release, Give it to me." She whispers as she wraps her legs around him tighter.

A low growl escapes his throat, as if he about to.

And Then—

30

BlueBalls

THE DOORBELL RANG.

Then again.

Followed by three loud, obnoxious knocks.

"Chase! I know you're home, you sexy man-bitch. Open up!"

Chase stood there, towel hanging low on his hips, completely bothered, completely hard, and still throbbing from being interrupted.

He exhaled sharply, running a hand through his wet hair, trying to reel in the absolute rage simmering beneath his skin.

Savannah was still upstairs, probably laughing her ass off, because this? This was all her fault.

The knocking grew louder.

Chase rolled his shoulders, cracking his neck like he was about to walk into a bar fight.

Then, he swung the door open.

And there stood Mallory, oversized sunglasses perched on her head, coffee in hand, grinning like she had just won the damn lottery.

She took one look at him—towel, wet hair, shirtless, still looking like sin itself—

And her smirk deepened.

"Damn, Montgomery." She whistled, tilting her head, giving him a slow once-over, her eyes not even trying to be subtle.

"Didn't know I was in for a whole-ass magic show this morning."

Chase arched a brow, completely unfazed, leaning against the doorframe like he wasn't currently standing half-naked on his front porch.

"You like what you see, Mallory?"

Mallory grinned, sipping her coffee. "I mean, I'm not mad about it."

Savannah's laughter echoed from the staircase, and Chase didn't have to turn around to know she was enjoying this way too much.

"You're a menace," he muttered, looking past Mallory like he was considering shutting the door in her face.

Mallory shrugged, still blatantly staring at his chest.

"Listen, I came here for Savannah, but this? This is a damn bonus."

"A bonus, huh?" Chase smirked, crossing his arms, making his biceps flex just to fuck with her.

Mallory narrowed her eyes at him, pointing her coffee cup in his direction. "Stop that."

"Stop what?" he asked innocently while flexing, defining his abs.

She motioned to his entire existence.

"That. Looking like a fucking romance novel cover. It's offensive."

Chase let out a low chuckle, right as Savannah stepped into view.

She was wearing one of his shirts, still damp from the shower, her bare legs peeking out from underneath, looking thoroughly ruined in the best way possible.

Mallory's eyes snapped to her, her smirk growing impossibly wider.

"Oh, well now this just got even better."

Savannah snorted, crossing her arms. "Mallory, what the hell are you doing here?"

Mallory took one slow sip of coffee, looking between the two of them like she was piecing together last night's events in high definition.

"Just checking in on my best friend. Didn't realize she was currently living in a well cast porn shoot."

Savannah bit her lip to keep from laughing, while Chase just sighed, rubbing his jaw.

"You seen enough?" he asked dryly.

Mallory took one last, blatant glance at his towel.

Then smirked.

"Not even close."

Chase let out a low, amused breath, tilting his head.

"Savannah, am I good to get dressed? Or do you think your friend here needs a minute?"

Savannah giggled, leaning into the doorway beside him, her fingers brushing against his abs like she was testing his patience.

"Oh, I don't know. Mallory? Have you gotten a good enough look?"

Mallory pursed her lips, pretending to think about it.

"Well, since you're asking—"

Chase rolled his eyes, pushing off the doorframe.

"I'm done with both of you."

He turned, heading back upstairs, but not before throwing a smirk over his shoulder.

"Don't let her steal anything."

Mallory cackled, stepping inside.

"No promises."

Savannah just grinned, shaking her head as she shut the door.

Savannah flopped onto the couch, tucking her legs underneath her as Mallory settled beside her, setting her coffee on the table with a dramatic sigh.

"So," Mallory drawled, turning to face Savannah fully, mischief practically radiating from her. "How was it?"

Savannah rolled her eyes, but the smile tugging at her lips gave her away. "Not discussing this with you."

Mallory gasped, clutching her chest. "What? But I'm your best friend! Your closest confidante! The one who—"

"—Showed up unannounced and ruined a perfectly good morning?" Savannah finished, smirking as she reached for Mallory's coffee and took a sip, ignoring the glare she received in return.

"Listen," Mallory said, flipping her hair over her shoulder, "I don't regret it. Not even a little bit. Because now I get to see you all flustered and happy, and Chase all…" She wiggled her fingers in the air, searching for the right word. "Domestic."

Savannah scoffed. "Chase is not domestic."

Mallory arched a brow, unimpressed. "Oh no? Because that man just walked up those stairs like he owns this place." She took a slow sip of her coffee, then smirked. "Oh, wait. He does own this place."

Savannah rolled her eyes. "That doesn't make him domestic."

Mallory hummed, giving her a slow once-over. "Maybe not. But judging by the way you're dressed, I'd say he owns you, too."

Savannah threw a throw pillow at her, laughing. "You're the worst."

Mallory caught it with ease, a knowing grin on her lips. "But you love me."

Savannah sighed, shaking her head as she leaned back against the couch. "Unfortunately."

A few seconds of silence passed before Mallory stretched her legs out, toeing off her shoes. "So, what's the plan for tonight?"

Savannah gave her a look. "What do you mean?"

Mallory scoffed. "Oh, come on. You're not gonna sit here all night playing house. Let's go out."

Savannah considered it. "Where?"

Mallory grinned. "Low-Tide."

Savannah smirked. "Of course you want to go to Low-Tide."

Mallory shrugged, unbothered. "It's fun, and I need fun."

Before Savannah could reply, Chase reappeared, now fully dressed in a fitted black T-shirt and jeans that only made him look more unfairly attractive. He paused at the foot of the stairs, watching the two of them with mild suspicion.

"What now?" he asked, crossing his arms.

"We're going out tonight," Mallory announced before Savannah could even open her mouth.

Chase arched a brow. "We are?"

Savannah exhaled, giving him an amused look. "Apparently."

Mallory waved a hand. "Oh, don't act like you don't want to."

Chase glanced at Savannah before sighing. "Where?"

"Low-Tide," Mallory said, beaming.

Chase narrowed his eyes slightly, like he was already regretting his decision to come downstairs. "Of course."

Savannah laughed. "It'll be fun. Maybe you can drag Nate along?"

Chase ran a hand over his jaw, thinking. "Yeah, I can do that."

Savannah stood, stretching. "And I'll make sure Chase actually follows through."

Chase smirked. "You doubt me?"

Savannah smiled, stepping close enough to press her fingers lightly against his chest. "Not at all."

Mallory made a gagging sound. "Oh my God. I swear, if you two start making heart eyes at each other, I'm leaving."

Chase chuckled, stepping back. "Wouldn't want that."

Mallory shot him a look, grabbing her coffee before standing. "Okay, I'll see you two lovebirds later." She made her way to the door, pausing long enough to glance over her shoulder.

"And Chase?"

He looked up, expectant.

Mallory grinned. "Wear something tight."

Then, she was gone.

Savannah shook her head as she shut the door, turning back to Chase, who just sighed.

"This is your fault," he muttered.

Savannah smirked, pressing a quick kiss to his jaw. "You love it."

He just sighed again, but the small smile on his lips said otherwise.

31

Palmetto Lies

THE LOW-TIDE TAVERN WAS in full swing—laughter, live music, and the scent of fried seafood mixing with the salt air drifting in through the open patio doors. The glow of neon beer signs flickered softly against the dark wood paneling, and the hum of conversation filled the space, weaving between the chords of the band playing in the corner.

At their booth, the four of them were comfortably tucked in—Savannah and Chase on one side, Nate and Mallory on the other.

It had started as casual seating, but at some point—somewhere between their first drinks and the effortless conversation—Savannah had ended up pressed against Chase's side, his thigh warm and firm against hers, his arm stretched casually along the back of the booth.

And she didn't mind.

Didn't even think about moving.

Mallory, meanwhile, was practically wrapped around her drink, laughing at whatever Nate had just said, her face bright with amusement.

"Wait, wait," she gasped, shaking her head, still giggling. "You mean to tell me that you—Nate Harper—once got kicked out of a restaurant?"

Nate groaned, scrubbing a hand down his face. "It was one time. And technically, I wasn't kicked out, I was just—strongly encouraged to leave."

Savannah raised a brow, intrigued. "What the hell did you do?"

Chase took a slow sip of his beer, smirking as if he already knew where this was going.

Nate sighed dramatically. "Listen, I may or may not have attempted to order twenty Milkshakes. All at once. During rush hour."

Mallory snorted, covering her mouth. "Why?"

"Because I was in college, drunk, and thought it was a good idea."

Chase chuckled, shaking his head. "You left out the part where you got on the counter."

Savannah nearly spit out her drink as she turned to Nate. "You what?"

Nate shot Chase a glare. "Wow. Betrayal."

Chase leaned back, his smirk widening. "I feel like it's relevant."

Savannah was laughing too hard to argue, and Mallory was nearly in tears.

"I can't believe you," Mallory managed, swiping at her eyes. "You shake'd yourself into a lifetime ban."

Nate exhaled heavily. "You know what? It was worth it."

Then Nate leaned back, stretching his arms, and said, "Well, at least I didn't knock out a groomsman at a wedding."

Savannah turned to Chase, eyes wide with amusement. "Oh, hell no. Who did you punch?"

Mallory sat up straighter, grinning. "Please tell me it was a good reason."

Nate chuckled, shaking his head. "Oh, it was. Jaxon and Sara's wedding. Chase was the best man. And let me tell you, it was legendary."

Savannah's brows lifted. "Details. Now."

Chase smirked, taking a sip of his beer before setting it down.

"One of the groomsmen was getting a little too comfortable with the bride," he explained, his tone cool, but the edge still there.

Savannah's jaw dropped. "No."

"Oh, yeah," Nate added, shaking his head. "Guy was all over her, drunk as hell, slurring about how 'Jaxon didn't deserve her.'"

Mallory gasped. "Please tell me someone handled it."

Chase grinned, tilting his beer toward himself. "Well, after Sara politely shut him down and he still didn't get the hint, I gave him one."

Savannah narrowed her eyes, smirking. "How big of a hint?"

Nate burst out laughing. "The kind where he woke up on the ground. Chase knocked his ass out cold."

Savannah's lips parted in pure admiration. "You threw hands at a wedding?"

Chase chuckled, lifting a shoulder. "Of course not, It was at the reception, but it was either that or let Jaxon do it and ruin his own wedding photos."

Mallory whistled. "Damn. I bet Sara still thanks you for that."

Chase's smirk deepened. "Every time we get together."

Savannah grinned, a warm feeling curling through her. He was loyal. Protective.

Before she could lean into him, maybe kiss him right there at the table—

A voice cut through the air.

"Well, well. Chase Montgomery."

The words dripped with confidence, the tone too familiar, too smooth, too knowing—it was obvious she knew him well.

The entire booth went quiet.

A tall, leggy blonde stood at the edge of their booth, a smirk plastered on her perfect, glossy lips. Her honey-colored hair fell in waves over bare, tanned shoulders, and her dress was a little too tight, a little too perfect.

Everything about her screamed effortlessly put together.

And completely entitled.

Savannah felt Mallory shift across from her, her best friend already sensing the shift in energy.

Meanwhile, Chase?

Chase was calm as hell.

His arm stayed stretched lazily along the back of the booth, his body still pressed against Savannah's side.

But Savannah caught it.

The tell.

The way his fingers drummed once against the wood of the table before stilling.

His only reaction.

"Jenna," Chase greeted, voice even, polite.

"So you do remember me."

Savannah felt Mallory's eyes on her, like she was waiting to see how she'd react. Nate glanced between Chase and the blonde, already assessing the situation.

Savannah didn't move.

Didn't blink.

Just—watched.

Because women like Jenna didn't just show up for no reason.

And judging by the way she was standing, the way she barely even acknowledged Savannah, Mallory, or Nate—this wasn't just a friendly catch-up.

Jenna was here for Chase.

And she wasn't subtle about it.

"I haven't seen you around lately," she said, her voice dripping with fake sweetness.

Nate grinned into his drink, clearly enjoying this way too much.

Chase just lifted his beer, taking a slow sip before answering.

"Been busy."

Jenna pouted, tilting her head. "Too busy for old friends?"

Savannah?

She just sipped her drink, waiting.

Chase didn't even hesitate. "Didn't realize we were friends."

Nate to cough into his beer, but it sounded a hell of a lot like a laugh.

But Jenna?

Jenna wasn't backing down.

She let out a light, fake laugh, shaking her head. "Still sharp. I always liked that about you."

Finally, her attention shifted—to Savannah. Like she had just now noticed her. Like she was some afterthought.

Savannah just met her gaze, unimpressed.

Jenna smiled, but there was nothing warm about it.

"And who's this?"

Savannah sipped her drink.

Didn't answer. Didn't move. Didn't bite. Because—Chase?

Chase handled it.

"This is Savannah," he said, flatly, easily, like that was all Jenna needed to know.

And for the first time, Jenna's smirk faltered.

Just for a second.

Then she recovered, her gaze flicking back to Chase.

"Huh," she mused. "I don't think I've ever seen you bring someone here before."

Savannah's stomach flipped, but she stayed still.

Jenna's smirk deepened.

"You usually just leave with them."

Savannah let out a low, slow breath.

Mallory muttered, "Oh, this is getting good."

But Chase?

Chase just laughed.

Not awkward. Not uncomfortable.

Just amused.

He leaned forward, taking another slow sip of his beer, completely unfazed.

Jenna's eyes flicked to Savannah again.

Like she had finally figured it out. Finally understood that Chase wasn't leaving with her. Wasn't entertaining her.

Because he had someone.

Savannah.

Jenna pursed her lips. "Well—it was nice catching up."

Chase smiled. "You too."

And that should have been the end of it.

But Jenna?

Jenna wasn't done.

She lingered, rolling her shoulders back, trying one more time.

"So," she said, her voice light, casual, but her eyes calculating. "You still out on Palmetto Drive?"

Savannah's stomach clenched.

Her fingers froze around her drink, her body staying completely still as she processed what Jenna had just said.

Palmetto Drive.

Jenna knew where Chase lived.

And not just vaguely. She knew the street name.

The street name of a house that no woman had ever been to.

Savannah had barely taken a breath before Mallory's eyes snapped to her.

A quick, sharp glance.

A knowing glance.

Because Chase had told Savannah that no woman had ever been inside his house.

Had never even been invited. And yet...Jenna knew Palmetto Drive.

Savannah lifted her glass, taking a slow sip, not saying a word.

Jenna watched her. Saw the reaction. Or rather, the lack of reaction.

And she smiled. Like she had finally won. Like she had finally found her opening.

Chase? Chase just shook his head, exhaling a short laugh.

Then, without a single ounce of hesitation, he turned to Savannah.

Tilted her chin up. And kissed her. Slow. Deep. Right there in front of every-one.

Jenna went stiff.

Chase pulled back, his lips barely grazing Savannah's as he smirked.

Then he turned to Jenna.

"Palmetto Drive is nowhere near my house. I just told you that so you'd leave me alone."

Silence.

Then—

Nate let out a loud, sharp laugh, his head dropping back.

Mallory covered her mouth, but her entire body shook with laughter.

Savannah? She just smirked against Chase's lips, loving every second of it.

Jenna flushed red, her jaw tightening.

"Unbelievable," she muttered, flipping her hair over her shoulder before storming off.

Chase exhaled, leaning back against the booth, taking another sip of his beer.

Mallory shook her head, still laughing. "Damn, that was satisfying."

Nate wiped a hand over his face. "Man, I gotta start keeping a list of your legendary moments."

Chase just grinned, stretching his arm back behind Savannah.

"Go ahead."

And Savannah?

She just leaned into him, smiling into her drink.

Because Jenna was gone.

And Chase?

Chase was exactly where he wanted to be.

32

Chasing Clarity

THE NIGHT AIR HUNG heavy, thick with the scent of salt and the distant hum of cicadas as Chase turned off Causeway Drive. The roar of his tires against the pavement should have been steadying, grounding, but tonight, it wasn't. His mind was too restless, too cluttered with thoughts that refused to settle. The drive home should have been simple—a straight shot down familiar roads, gravel crunching under his tires as he pulled into his driveway.

But tonight wasn't like other nights.

His grip on the wheel tightened as his mind drifted back to dinner. It had started off perfect—laughter, good food, easy conversation. Savannah had fit so effortlessly beside him, her thigh brushing his under the table, her eyes lighting up every time she laughed. He had been drowning in her, and he didn't want to come up for air.

And then?

Jenna happened.

His jaw tensed as the memory played out in his head. The way Jenna had sauntered up, full of overconfidence and expectation. The way Savannah had remained cool, collected, unshaken. The way Jenna had thrown her final jab—asking if he still lived on Palmetto Drive—and the way Savannah had gone completely still.

He exhaled sharply, rolling his shoulders as he turned onto a backroad, his headlights cutting through the thickening darkness. He wasn't even pissed—he was annoyed. Jenna had been a reminder of exactly who he used to be. A man who took what he wanted, left before the sun came up, and never—never—gave a damn about anything that lasted longer than a night.

Until now.

Until Savannah Monroe had waltzed her way back into town, wrecked his carefully laid-out existence, and made him want everything he never thought he could have.

As his truck approached his long gravel driveway, he slowed. The streetlights flickered overhead, casting long shadows across the pavement. eyes flicking to the sign standing at the entrance. His truck came to a stop as he reached the entrance to his driveway, and his eyes lifted to the sign standing at the entrance.

Whispering Echoes Drive.

He had read that sign a million times before.

Hell, he named it.

But tonight, it felt... different.

It wasn't just a name. It was a reminder.

A reminder of all that had happened.

A reminder of the memories made.

A reminder that he was running out of time.

Instead of taking the turn, he did something he hadn't done in years.

He yanked the wheel, whipping his truck around, sending gravel flying as he pointed it back toward the road.

He wasn't ready to go home.

He needed clarity.

He needed space.

He needed to think.

And he knew exactly where to do it.

Chase didn't even have to think about where he was going.

His hands knew before his brain did.

The drive was automatic—turns he had taken a thousand times before, roads that had been burned into his memory long before he even had his license.

He passed the marina where Savannah had met him two days ago.

Where she had smiled at him like he was the only man in the world.

He passed South End, where they had spent summers sneaking into the pool at the old hotel, diving under the water to muffle their laughter as the manager searched for them with a flashlight.

He passed the Monroe house, where Savannah was probably curled up on the couch with Mallory, pretending she wasn't falling just as hard as he was.

But none of it mattered.

Not when he knew exactly where he was going.

His truck came to a stop at the very edge of town, where the pavement ended and the sand began. The JP access lot was empty, the only sounds the distant crash of waves and the rustling of sea grass in the warm summer wind. He shut off the engine, letting the sudden quiet settle over him like a blanket.

Then, he stepped out.

The sand was cool beneath his boots as he walked, past the marram grass swaying in the breeze, past the old wooden fence that had long since lost its battle with the salty air. He followed the familiar path until he reached —*The Point*—where the jetties met the open water, where the beach broke apart to reveal the wide stretch of inlet, a gateway for boats to return home.

But for Chase, this was home.

This was the place that had always been his beacon.

The place he had always come when he needed to clear his head.

The Point had once been the place where the best nights happened.

Long before responsibilities, before expectations—before everything got complicated.

Back then, summer nights belonged to the locals. They'd start bonfires, drink cheap beer, tell stories that would only make sense in the haze of youth.

Chase could still see it.

Trevor leaning against a driftwood log, a beer dangling from his fingers, laughing at something that wasn't that funny. Jaxon, one of the few summers he had made it down, shaking his head at them both, the firelight catching in his grin.

And Chase?

Chase had been doing what he always did.

Flirting with a tourist, giving her just enough charm to make her think she was special, but never enough to make her believe she was staying.

Then, everything shifted.

Because that was the night he saw her.

Savannah Monroe, walking down the dunes like she belonged to them.

She hadn't been trying to get his attention. She hadn't even noticed him at first. But Chase?

Chase had felt everything stop.

The fire, the music, the people—it all blurred.

Because Savannah had stepped into his world, and nothing had been the same since.

And now?

Now, years later, he was standing in the exact same place.

And everything was different.

Because she wasn't just some girl from his past.

She was the only person who had ever made him feel like staying.

Chase exhaled sharply, dragging a hand through his hair as he took a few steps forward, past the weight of old memories, past the ghost of who he used to be. He sat down on a driftwood log, his boots digging into the damp sand as he exhaled sharply. His body felt tense, restless, but his mind was worse.

Because he had let himself get too caught up, too comfortable, too convinced that they had time.

They didn't.

Savannah was leaving in eight days.

Eight.

That's all he had left.

A week and a damn day before she packed up and drove away, taking every single piece of him with her.

And the thought damn near destroyed him.

Because he wasn't sure if he could survive it.

Chase had never needed anyone.

Had never let himself.

But Savannah?

She was different.

She was the only thing in his life that had ever felt permanent.

And now, he was about to lose her.

The wind picked up, sending a slow rustle through the sea grass as he clenched his jaw, his mind already running through every single scenario.

Every single way he could convince her to stay.

He had to try.

Because losing her wasn't an option.

And if he had to burn every bridge, rewrite every rule, and take every risk just to make sure she didn't leave?

Then he damn well would.

Because Savannah Monroe wasn't just part of his past.

She was his future.

And now?

He just had to make her see it.

33

Finding Everything

CHASE DECIDED TO TAKE the rest of the week off from work.

It wasn't something he did often. Hell, he never did it. He had built his life around routine, around discipline—knowing where he needed to be, when he needed to be there, and exactly how much time it would take to get things done.

Structure. Order. Control.

That was who Chase Montgomery was.

At least, it had been.

Until Savannah Monroe walked back into his life.

She was the opposite of predictable. The opposite of safe. And for a man who had spent his entire life making sure things stayed manageable, she was a walking contradiction to everything he thought he wanted.

And yet, he wanted her more than he had ever wanted anything.

So for the first time in as long as he could remember, he ignored his responsibilities. Turned off his phone. Told his team to handle shit without him.

And just like that?

He was free.

Free to spend every second chasing her, memorizing the way she laughed, the way she looked at him when she thought he wasn't paying attention. Free to kiss her whenever he felt like it, touch her whenever he needed to, hold her for no other reason than because he could.

For once in his life, he wasn't thinking ahead. Wasn't calculating, wasn't planning.

He was just living.

And what he wanted?

Was her.

All of her.

Every damn moment he could steal before she left.

It started with a question.

"Wanna get lost with me?"

Savannah had been sitting cross-legged on his porch, her legs tucked beneath her, the morning air crisp against her skin as she cradled a steaming cup of coffee. She was wearing his Henley, the sleeves hanging loose past her wrists, and Chase had never seen anything look better on her. The fabric swallowed her in the most effortless way, and the sight sent something warm curling in his chest.

She glanced up, her gaze lazy, her lips quirking at the edges. "Define lost."

Chase leaned against the doorframe, grinning in that way that always made her stomach flip. "No maps. No plans. Just us and the road."

Savannah bit her lip, pretending to consider the offer, even though she already knew her answer.

Because truthfully? She wanted nothing more than to get lost with Chase Montgomery. With a slow stretch, she slid on her sunglasses, the golden morning sun catching the messy waves of her hair as she stood. "Let's go."

That was how it started—the adventure neither of them knew they needed.

Some mornings, they flipped a coin at every intersection, letting fate decide whether to turn left or right. Other times, Savannah would pull out a worn road atlas she found in Chase's glove compartment, close her eyes, and point to a random spot on the map. That was their destination.

Chase loved the unpredictability of it, the thrill of winding down roads they'd never been on before, discovering places they weren't supposed to find.

Savannah loved the feeling of freedom, the idea that for once in her life, she wasn't on a timeline—that she didn't have to be anywhere but here, beside him.

And somehow, in the middle of chasing nothing, they found everything.

One afternoon, they drove until the pavement turned into cobblestone, the streets narrowing into a charming coastal town tucked near a marina. It was the kind of place that smelled like fresh salt air and old memories, where the locals sat on their porches, watching the world pass by with easy smiles and slow sips of iced tea.

Chase rolled down the windows, letting the warm breeze fill the truck.

"You ever been here?" Savannah asked, watching as a group of kids raced past on their bikes, their laughter echoing against the brick-lined streets.

Chase shook his head. "Nope. But it feels like a place I should've been."

She hummed in agreement, her gaze sweeping across the pastel-colored buildings, the weathered shop signs, the golden retriever lounging outside of a coffee shop like he owned the place. It was quiet, peaceful—the kind of town that felt like it belonged in a novel.

And then, she saw it. An old bookstore, sandwiched between a coffee shop and a fishing supply store. The front windows were filled with towers of hardcovers, their spines faded from the sun, and the hand-painted wooden sign above the door creaked softly in the breeze.

Savannah's eyes lit up. Chase noticed the way she stilled, the way her fingers reached for the door handle before she even realized she was moving.

"You wanna go in, don't you?" he smirked, already knowing the answer.

Savannah turned to face him, her grin so wide it made his chest ache. She didn't even reply before she practically skipped through the door.

Inside, the scent of ink and parchment wrapped around her like a second skin.

The store was small, but in the way that made it feel intimate, the kind of place that held secrets in its pages. The walls were lined with floor-to-ceiling bookshelves, bending slightly under the weight of forgotten stories. A dusty chandelier hung in the center, its light dim, casting a warm glow over the wooden floorboards. There was no order to the books—no genre labels, no alphabetized system, just stacks and stacks of stories waiting to be found.

Savannah's fingers brushed over the spines, whispering their titles under her breath, her lips parting slightly as she soaked in the sheer magic of the place.

Chase? He hadn't so much as glanced at a book. He just stood there, leaning against a nearby shelf, watching her. The way her fingers skimmed the edges of pages like they were something fragile, something worth treasuring. The way her eyes softened when she found a well-worn paperback, its spine cracked from a hundred lifetimes of love.

She turned toward him, eyes alight with something he couldn't quite place. "You know, the guest room on the first floor would make a great study," she said, her voice filled with quiet excitement. "The natural light from the bay windows overlooking the sound, the warm oak shelves already built in—I can picture it—rows and rows of books, a little nook under the window to sit and read. God, that would be perfect."

Chase chuckled, shaking his head. "A library? In my house? I don't even read."

She tilted her head, smiling. "Maybe you just haven't found the right book yet."

Something about the way she stood there—bathed in the soft glow of dim bookstore lighting, a novel cradled to her chest like something sacred—stirred something in him. He had never seen her like this. So at home. So completely in her element.

"You look like you belong here," he murmured, the words slipping out quieter than he intended. Savannah stilled, fingers resting on the spine of a novel before she turned to face him fully.

A slow smile spread across her lips, warm and knowing. "Books are my love language."

Something in Chase's chest tightened. He stepped forward, closing the space between them, his fingers reaching out to tuck a loose strand of hair behind her ear.

His touch lingered.

His gaze dropped to her lips. "Good to know," he said softly.

Savannah swallowed, her pulse hammering in her throat.

She had never had someone memorize her like this.

They stayed in that bookstore for over an hour. Savannah got lost in forgotten paperbacks, poetry collections, and hardcovers with yellowed pages while Chase wandered, picking up the occasional book just to watch her light up when she recognized the title.

At one point, she handed him a leather-bound novel with no cover image, just the title scrawled across the front.

"What's this?" he asked, flipping through the pages.

"One of my favorites," she admitted, watching him closely.

Chase smirked. "Are you testing me, Monroe?"

She tilted her head. "Maybe."

He chuckled, slipping the book under his arm. "Then I guess I should buy it."

Savannah blinked, surprised. "You're actually gonna read it?"

Chase shrugged, that easy smirk still on his lips. "Guess you'll have to stick around long enough to find out."

Her heart skipped. There was something in the way he said it, something that made her forget, just for a moment, that she was leaving soon.

That this—whatever this was—had an expiration date.

Savannah looked at him, this man who had never belonged to anyone.

And suddenly?

She wanted him to belong to her.

They left the bookstore with a small stack of novels and two cups of coffee from the shop next door. Chase drove while Savannah sat in the passenger seat, her bare feet resting on the dashboard, flipping through the pages of her new book.

"You're actually gonna read while I drive?" Chase teased, glancing over.

She smirked, tilting the book just enough for him to see the text. "You should be honored. I don't let just anyone distract me from my books."

Chase laughed, reaching over to squeeze her thigh. "I'll take it."

And as they drove down the open road, chasing nothing but time, Savannah realized something terrifying.

She wasn't just getting lost in the adventure.

She was getting lost in him.

And she didn't want to be found.

34

Almost Forever

THE DAYS SLIPPED THROUGH their fingers like grains of sand—each one falling faster than the last, slipping away before they had the chance to hold on.

Too fast. Too fleeting.

Time was cruel, relentless, dragging when you wanted it to pass, but racing when all Savannah wanted was for it to slow, to stop, to freeze in place and let her stay here, wrapped in him, wrapped in this.

But time didn't listen.

Time didn't care.

It never did.

Three days.

Three days until she had to pack up and leave Wrightsville Beach. Three days until she'd return to Asheville, to the life she had built, the life she had always been so sure of.

But now?

Now, that life felt hollow.

Three days until Chase would wake up alone.

Three days until she wouldn't be wrapped in his arms at night, listening to the slow, steady rhythm of his breath, feeling the warmth of his body curled around hers, safe in a way she hadn't even realized she craved.

Three days until she would step into her car, drive away, and leave this behind.

Leave him behind.

Neither of them acknowledged it out loud.

Saying it would make it too real, too final.

So instead, they let the silence swallow the truth.

They pretended.

They made those three days count.

They kissed longer.

Held tighter.

Fucked like the world was ending—like the walls were caving in, like the moment their bodies parted, everything would crumble.

And maybe it would.

Maybe this—whatever this was—wasn't something she could just walk away from without taking pieces of him with her.

They memorized every second before it was gone.

Every touch. Every sound. Every look that said what neither of them dared to say out loud.

They stole every moment, savored them, tucked them away in the deepest parts of their memories like a secret they weren't ready to share with the world.

And every evening, when the sun bled across the horizon, they found themselves back at the dock.

It had become theirs—their sanctuary, untouched by the outside world, protected from the inevitability waiting just beyond the tide.

Here, time didn't feel as heavy.

Here, they could breathe.

Here, they could ignore the fact that the sun would rise in three days and she would leave and Chase would wake up without her beside him.

The water stretched before them, endless and calm, the kind of calm that mocked the storm unraveling inside her.

Some nights, they sat side by side, sharing a bottle of wine, their voices hushed, lost in conversation that didn't involve what came next.

Other nights, Savannah sat between his legs, resting against his chest, wrapped in the kind of warmth she was already mourning.

And tonight?

Tonight was one of those nights.

Chase's arms were draped around her, his hands resting against her stomach as he pressed a slow, lingering kiss against her shoulder, his lips dragging just enough to make her shiver.

She closed her eyes, exhaling softly, committing the feeling of him—all of him—to memory.

The scent of salt and faded cologne clinging to his skin.

The slow, steady rise and fall of his chest against her back.

The rough drag of his fingertips over the bare skin beneath her shirt, like he needed to feel her.

Like if he held on tight enough, maybe she wouldn't slip through his fingers like the days already had.

Savannah traced small patterns over his forearm, swallowing against the knot in her throat.

She didn't want to break the silence.

Didn't want to break the spell.

But the words still came, quiet and aching.

"You ever think about leaving?" she murmured, staring out at the horizon, watching the sky darken.

Chase didn't answer right away.

His chin rested lightly against her temple, his arms tightening around her in a way that made her chest ache.

Then, in a voice so quiet it almost got lost in the sound of the waves, he said, "I used to."

Her breath caught.

Savannah turned her head just slightly, just enough to see the profile of his face, the sharp cut of his jaw, the way his throat worked around whatever he wasn't saying.

"And now?" she asked, barely above a whisper.

He didn't look at her.

Didn't shift.

Didn't move.

His fingers brushed slow, lazy circles over her hip, like he was thinking, really thinking.

Then, finally, his voice steady, sure—

"Now, I don't know. Some things are worth staying for."

Savannah's throat went tight.

Her heart twisted painfully inside her chest, the kind of ache that shouldn't hurt but did.

She didn't ask what he meant.

She didn't have to.

Because she felt it.

In the way he held her, like she was already slipping away.

In the way he kissed her, slow and deep, like he was trying to make her stay.

In the way his body moved against hers, desperate and unrelenting, as if memorizing her all over again, knowing that soon, she wouldn't be his to touch anymore.

Her hands slid up his chest, her lips brushing against his in a kiss that held everything she wasn't ready to say aloud.

Chase groaned softly, pulling her closer, his fingers tangling in her hair, his heartbeat pounding beneath her palm.

She felt it then.

The weight of something more.

Something terrifying.

Something real.

She wanted to tell him.

Wanted to whisper those three words against his lips.

Wanted to stay.

But she was leaving.

And this?

This was temporary.

At least, that's what she kept telling herself.

But it didn't feel temporary when Chase gripped her waist and pulled her into his lap, his arms locking around her as his forehead pressed against hers.

It didn't feel temporary when he kissed her like she was the only thing keeping him grounded.

It didn't feel temporary when her fingers shook against his skin, her body pleading with him to hold her together when she was already falling apart.

It didn't feel temporary at all.

And that was the most terrifying part of all.

Because three days weren't enough.

Three lifetimes wouldn't be enough.

But time didn't care.

Time never cared.

And in three days, time would rip them apart.

Later that night, they stayed on the dock longer than usual. The wine was gone, but neither of them wanted to move. The evening air was cool against their skin, the gentle sway of the water beneath them the only sound, but it wasn't silence. It was the space between words, the space where everything they couldn't say hung heavy in the night.

Savannah was stretched out on her back, her head resting in Chase's lap as he absently ran his fingers through her hair. His touch was steady, grounding, like it was the only thing keeping the world from spinning too fast. The sky above them was an infinite canvas, a sea of stars stretching farther than either of them could see. It felt like it would never end, just like this moment—the perfect stillness of time, just before it slipped away.

She broke the quiet with a question, her voice soft and laced with a vulnerability that she could no longer hide. "Where do you see yourself in ten years?"

Chase let out a low breath, his fingers stilling in her hair for a moment as he considered the weight of the question. "I don't know," he said, his voice rough, as though it hadn't been something he'd thought about in a long time. "I used to think I did. Used to think I'd be running the company, living alone in some fancy house by the water, doing whatever the hell I wanted."

Savannah turned her head slightly, her gaze drifting up to meet his. She saw the quiet ache in his eyes, the uncertainty that had only just begun to surface. "And now?" she asked, her heart beating faster, feeling the shift in the air.

His fingers stilled in her hair, the space between them filled with something unspoken. He didn't look away from her, his gaze unwavering. "Now," he said, voice steady but raw, "I can't picture any of it without you in it."

Her heart stuttered. The words hit her harder than she expected, crashing through the walls she had carefully built around herself.

Her lips parted, but the words wouldn't come out—not the ones she needed to say, not the ones that were suddenly too real to voice. She could feel the weight of the moment settling between them, like the stars above had suddenly grown too close.

"Do you mean that?" she whispered, her voice thick with emotion she wasn't sure she could control.

Chase's gaze never wavered, steady, unwavering, as though the truth was written on his face, in every line of his expression. "Yeah. I do."

The words seemed to hang in the air, wrapped in the quiet of the night. Savannah's chest ached, and she lifted a hand, brushing her fingers along his jaw. The touch was slow, deliberate, as though she was memorizing every inch of him, committing the feel of his skin, the roughness of his stubble, to memory. She wanted to capture him like this—under the soft glow of the moon, when the world felt small and the distance between them felt nonexistent.

"What about you?" Chase asked, his voice softer now, more careful. It was the sound of someone opening up, someone testing the waters to see how much of themselves they could expose. "What do you want?"

Savannah exhaled slowly, the weight of the question pressing down on her. It wasn't something she'd ever really allowed herself to think about, not like this. She closed her eyes for a moment, letting the cool breeze sweep over her skin before answering.

"I used to think I wanted to move to a big city," she admitted, her fingers trailing lightly down his forearm, the sensation of his warmth seeping into her. "To have a high-rise apartment, a busy career, a life full of excitement."

Chase's brows furrowed slightly, as though he were trying to read the words between hers. "And now?"

Her fingers trailed down to his hand, where she rested them, as though it were the most natural thing in the world. The weight of his hand, the simple warmth of his skin against hers, felt like an anchor, holding her steady when the ground beneath her feet felt like it was shifting.

"Now," she said, her voice soft but sure, "I think—I just want someone to come home to."

The words hung in the air, and for a long moment, neither of them spoke. There was no need. The vulnerability in the space between them was all they needed to understand. Chase didn't speak, but his grip on her hand tightened, his fingers closing around hers like a promise, like a vow, like something real.

In that moment, Savannah knew. She knew, with a certainty that shook her to her core, that this—him—was her home. That the place she was meant to be wasn't some city or fancy apartment or career. It wasn't the life she had thought she wanted. It was right here, in the space between them, under the stars, with Chase's hand in hers.

And in that stillness, as the night wrapped itself around them, she knew that wherever life took her next, no matter how far apart they might be, a part of her would always be here, with him.

She was already home.

And it was him.

35

Forever, Last Night

THE NIGHT BEFORE SHE was supposed to leave, Savannah couldn't stop shaking.

It wasn't from the cold.

It wasn't from fear.

It was from him.

From the way Chase was looking at her, from the way his hands traced over her skin like he was afraid to forget what she felt like. Like he was afraid to forget her.

The air in the room was thick, heavy, charged with something neither of them could ignore.

A storm waiting to break.

A levee ready to crumble.

Chase sat on the edge of the bed, his bare chest illuminated by the soft golden glow of the bedside lamp. Shadows flickered over the sharp edges of his jaw, the muscles in his shoulders, the way his chest rose and fell in uneven breaths.

His hair was slightly tousled, wild from where he had run his fingers through it too many times—like he was trying to grasp something just out of reach.

Like he was trying to hold onto something already slipping through his fingers.

Savannah stood in front of him, wearing nothing but his t-shirt, the hem brushing against her thighs.

Her hands were trembling.

Her heart was pounding.

She had spent the last two weeks convincing herself this wasn't real.

That it was temporary.

That when she left Wrightsville Beach, she could simply pack this up, tuck it away in some safe, quiet place inside her, and move on.

But standing there, staring at the man who had somehow become everything, she knew she had been lying to herself.

This was real.

He was real.

And tomorrow?

Tomorrow, she was leaving.

Her chest ached, her throat tightened, but not from nerves. Not from fear. From the devastating realization that this wasn't just a summer fling.

This was love.

The kind of love that wrecks you in the best way.

The kind of love that makes you believe in things you swore you never would.

The kind of love that echoes when they aren't around.

The kind of love that stays.

She swallowed hard, stepping between his knees. Chase's hands found her hips instantly, his touch firm, grounding, like he needed to hold onto her just as much as she needed to be held.

His breath was warm against her skin, his lips just inches from hers, but he didn't close the distance.

Neither of them did.

They just stayed there, suspended in the kind of silence that could break a person.

Her fingers trembled as she lifted them to his face, tracing the strong lines of his jaw, the roughness of his stubble, the tension locked in his muscles.

She wanted to memorize him.

Every feature. Every curve. Every breath. Because soon, she would have to live with only the memory of this.

"Savannah—"

His voice was low, hoarse, like he was on the verge of breaking.

She swallowed, her fingers tightening on his skin.

"I don't want to go," she whispered, the words slipping out before she could stop them. Bare. Vulnerable. True.

Chase's grip on her hips tightened just slightly, like he wanted to pull her closer but knew he couldn't hold her here forever. His eyes burned into hers, dark and full of something undeniable, inescapable.

"Then don't," he said, so simply, so easily.

Like it was the most obvious thing in the world.

Like it was that easy.

A single tear slid down her cheek, and Chase caught it with his thumb, brushing it away before cupping her face.

He kissed her then.

Soft. Slow. Deep.

Like he was trying to tell her everything he couldn't say.

Like he was begging her to hear him, to feel him, to understand that this was real.

Savannah let out a soft, shaky breath, her fingers sliding into his hair, holding onto him like she could keep this moment frozen in time.

Because tomorrow,

Tomorrow would come.

It always did.

And this?

This was the last night.

Her last chance to let herself feel it all.

Her last chance to tell him the truth.

Her last chance to stop pretending she wasn't in love with him.

Her breath shook against his lips.

"Chase…"

Her heart raced as she finally said the words.

"I love you."

Chase froze.

His hands went still.

His body tensed, his breath catching, his eyes darkening with something she couldn't name.

She didn't blink.

Didn't breathe.

She just waited.

Waited for him to say something.

Waited for him to understand what she had just given him.

And when he finally moved, when he finally exhaled, it came out ragged, wrecked, like she had just shattered something inside him.

"Say it again," he murmured, his fingers sliding into her hair, holding her to him like he needed to hear it again.

Her chest tightened.

Her lips brushed his.

"I love you."

Chase let out a sound that was somewhere between a groan and a prayer, his lips crashing into hers.

And this time?

It was different.

Because this wasn't just desperate.

It wasn't rushed.

It wasn't temporary.

This was love.

Raw. Unstoppable. Unbreakable.

His hands slid up her back, his fingers gripping at the fabric of his shirt on her body, pulling it over her head, leaving her bare beneath him.

Savannah let out a soft gasp as his lips traveled down her neck, over her collarbone, along every inch of skin like he was worshipping her.

His hands traced slow, reverent paths over her body, learning, memorizing, claiming.

She had never felt so seen, so wanted, so cherished.

This wasn't just touch.

This was love.

This was a promise.

Chase hovered over her, his forehead pressed to hers, his breath uneven, his body shaking with restraint.

His hand cupped her cheek, his thumb brushing over her lips, his eyes so full of something it stole the air from her lungs.

"I love you too, Savannah," he whispered.

Her heart stopped.

Then it soared.

And when he finally moved inside her, when their bodies joined in a slow, aching rhythm, it was different than it had ever been before.

This wasn't just passion.

This wasn't just desire.

This was two souls finding each other in the dark.

His name fell from her lips in a breathless whisper.

His hands gripped her like she was the only thing anchoring him to the world.

They moved together, slow and deep, like they had all the time in the world.

Like tomorrow wasn't waiting.

Like this wasn't the end.

Chase pressed his forehead to hers, his lips barely touching hers as he whispered,

"You were never supposed to be temporary."

Savannah's chest tightened, a tear slipping down her cheek, but he caught it with his lips.

"Then don't let me be."

His answer was a kiss.

A slow, deep, aching kiss that sealed the promise they were both too scared to say aloud.

And when they finally shattered together, when they came undone in the kind of way that couldn't be undone, Savannah knew—

She wasn't just leaving a place.

She was leaving her heart behind.

And it belonged to him.

36

Unsaid

SAVANNAH WOKE TO THE warmth of Chase's body pressed against hers, his arm draped lazily over her waist, his steady breath fanning against the back of her neck.

For a fleeting moment—a beautiful, cruel moment—she let herself forget.

She let herself pretend.

Pretend that this was just another morning wrapped up in him, tangled in sheets that smelled like him, like them. Pretend that when the sun crept higher in the sky, when the world outside their little bubble stirred awake, she wouldn't have to leave.

But pretending didn't stop time.

The weight of it settled over her like a storm cloud, thick and suffocating, pressing down on her chest until she could barely breathe.

Her stomach twisted, the sharp pang of reality cutting through the illusion, shattering the fragile what if she had dared to hold onto for just a little while longer.

Today.

Today, she was leaving.

She squeezed her eyes shut, willing the moment to last longer, to stretch time, to trap them in this bed forever. If she didn't move, if she didn't acknowledge it, maybe the universe would grant her mercy and let this morning continue indefinitely.

And for just a little while longer, she could let herself believe this wasn't the last time she'd wake up beside him.

But reality had never been kind.

She shifted just slightly, and immediately, Chase stirred behind her. His arm tensed around her waist, his body pressing closer, as if—even in sleep—he knew.

As if some part of him could feel her slipping away.

His lips brushed against her bare shoulder, warm, lingering, the softest graze of his mouth over her skin before he murmured in a sleep-roughened voice,

"Stay."

Savannah froze.

Her breath caught, her fingers tightening around the sheets.

Chase never asked for anything.

Not like this.

Not raw and bare and aching.

Her heart clenched, her pulse a slow, painful thud against her ribs as she stared at the wall, as she tried to hold herself together when every part of her was already breaking.

She wanted to say yes.

God, she wanted to say yes.

But she couldn't.

Because if she let herself believe—even for a second—that staying was an option, she wouldn't be strong enough to leave.

And she had to.

Didn't she?

Savannah turned in his arms, shifting until she was facing him, until she could take in every inch of him.

His dark hair, mussed from sleep, the sleepy weight in his deep green eyes, the rough stubble shadowing his jaw, the way his lips parted slightly as he blinked at her.

God, he was beautiful.

And she was breaking.

Chase reached up, his fingers tucking a strand of her hair behind her ear, his touch unbearably gentle.

"I meant it," he murmured, his voice gravelly and raw.

"Stay with me, Savannah."

Tears burned the backs of her eyes, but she squeezed them shut, willing them away.

She couldn't do this.

She couldn't.

Her throat tightened, the ache so sharp it stole her breath.

"Chase..."

His brows furrowed.

And he knew.

He knew she wasn't going to give him the answer he wanted.

He knew she was still planning to walk away.

His jaw tightened, his hand flexing against her hip, his body going rigid for a fraction of a second—

But he didn't argue.

Didn't beg.

Didn't demand.

Instead—he kissed her.

And it was different.

It wasn't teasing.

It wasn't playful.

It wasn't rushed or frantic or driven by desperate need.

This was slow.

Unyielding.

A kiss meant to destroy her.

A kiss meant to break her.

His hands slid over her back, pulling her closer, closer, holding onto her like she was the only thing keeping him from falling apart.

She kissed him back just as fiercely, poured everything into it—every unspoken word, every aching plea, every bit of love she was too scared to say aloud.

But no matter how hard she tried,

No matter how much she gave,

It wasn't enough.

It would never be enough.

And when she pulled away, when she whispered the words that tore her apart, she hated herself.

"I can't."

Chase exhaled sharply, his grip on her tightening like he was trying to hold on, to keep her here.

But he didn't argue.

Didn't say anything at all.

And that—

That was worse.

Because she could feel what he wasn't saying.

And it fucking hurt.

His fingers flexed against her waist, his forehead pressing against hers for just a beat, just long enough for her to hear the uneven hitch of his breath, just long enough for her to feel the weight of everything hanging between them.

His lips brushed over hers once, twice—soft, slow, like he was trying to memorize the shape of them, the taste of her, the feel of her before she was gone.

Her chest ached.

Her ribs ached.

Her soul ached.

"Tell me I won't forget this," he murmured, his voice so quiet it was barely a whisper, barely anything at all.

Savannah's throat tightened as she cupped his face, her thumbs skimming over the rough stubble of his jaw, memorizing him the way he was memorizing her.

"You won't," she whispered.

And she wasn't sure if she was saying it for him—

Or for herself.

Because how do you forget something like this?

How do you walk away from something that feels like it's carved into your bones, something that lives inside of you?

How do you leave when your heart is still here?

She swallowed back the sob threatening to escape and pressed one last kiss to his lips.

And when she finally pulled away,

When she finally sat up,

When she finally forced herself out of the bed and away from him,

She didn't look back.

Because if she did,

She wouldn't go at all.

37

Almost Gone

By mid-afternoon, she was back at the Monroe house, standing in the middle of her bedroom, staring at the suitcase that felt like a death sentence.

The room smelled the same. Looked the same. Felt the same.

But she didn't.

Savannah had packed and unpacked twice already, like somehow dragging out the process would change something. Like maybe if she just kept stalling, the universe would intervene.

But it wouldn't.

No matter how much she tried to delay it, time kept moving forward, shoving her closer and closer to the inevitable.

And God, it hurt.

Mallory sat on the edge of the bed, arms crossed, watching her with an expression that wasn't just concern anymore. It was frustration.

It was rage.

"You don't have to do this."

Savannah sighed, pressing her fingers to her temples. "Yes, I do."

Mallory shot up from the bed so fast it made Savannah jump.

"Why?"

The word cracked in the air between them, full of desperation, full of something frantic and pleading.

Savannah turned to face her, and the sheer intensity in Mallory's eyes made her stomach twist.

Because she didn't have an answer.

Because this was never supposed to be permanent.

Because what if this wasn't real?

Because what if it was?

She inhaled sharply, shaking her head, trying to convince herself. "Because it's temporary."

Mallory scoffed, her arms flying into the air as she paced the room, exhaling in disgusted disbelief. "Bullshit."

Savannah flinched.

"You think I don't see it?" Mallory snapped, whirling on her, eyes blazing. "You think I haven't been watching you fall for him every damn day?"

Savannah's throat tightened. "Mallory, please—"

"No." Mallory's voice cracked, the fight between them suddenly so much more than an argument. "You love him, Savannah. And don't you dare try to lie to me."

Savannah's chest caved.

Her vision blurred.

Because fuck.

She couldn't lie.

Not to Mallory. Not when she had spent the last few weeks seeing everything Savannah refused to admit to herself.

Mallory's breaths were uneven, her eyes pleading now, her voice shaking with the weight of what was slipping through her fingers. "You love him." She stepped closer, softer now, more broken than angry. "And you're gonna leave him?"

Savannah swallowed hard, wrapping her arms around herself. "It's not that simple."

Mallory let out a bitter laugh, shaking her head. "Actually, it is."

Savannah squeezed her eyes shut, hating how much this hurt.

Hating how much it was tearing her apart.

"He's everything I ever wanted," she admitted, her voice barely above a whisper. "And that's exactly why I have to go."

Mallory blinked. Her expression twisted. "Do you hear yourself?"

Savannah did.

And it sounded awful.

But what if she stayed and it wasn't enough? What if she stayed and he regretted it? What if she stayed and this thing between them burned out just as quickly as it ignited?

And worse—

What if she stayed, and he was everything she ever wanted, and she lost him anyway?

What if she couldn't survive that?

Savannah turned back toward her suitcase, pressing her trembling fingers to the lid, trying to breathe through the ache clawing at her ribs, trying to force herself to move.

Mallory was watching her, her shoulders rising and falling as she struggled to keep her voice even, struggled to hold herself together. Then, finally—

She sighed, pressing the heels of her hands to her eyes.

She wasn't mad anymore.

She was hurt.

She was watching her best friend ruin herself in real-time, and she was powerless to stop it.

Mallory inhaled deeply, letting the anger seep out of her before she softened. Before she tried again. Because this wasn't just Savannah running.

It was Savannah terrified of letting herself have something real for once.

And if anyone knew her well enough to see through the bullshit, it was Mallory.

She sat back down on the bed, the mattress dipping under her weight. This time, there was no frustration, no venom in her voice. Just quiet understanding.

"Vannah—" she started, her voice gentle now. "You're leaving because you're scared. But have you stopped for even a second to think about what happens if you stay?"

Savannah pressed her lips together, arms tightening around herself.

Mallory nudged her knee, coaxing, pushing. "What if it does work out?" she asked, voice full of something desperate and hopeful. "What if he is everything you ever wanted? What if this isn't just a summer thing, but the start of something you didn't even realize you were missing?"

Savannah let out a shaky breath. "And what if it's not?"

Mallory sighed. "Then at least you tried." She searched her face, her own eyes glistening now. "At least you gave it a chance instead of running before you even let yourself find out."

She leaned forward, voice soft, like she was trying to hold her together before she shattered completely. "I've never seen you like this before, Sav. I've never seen you look at someone the way you look at him. I've never seen him look at anyone the way he looks at you."

Savannah closed her eyes for a beat, her heart squeezing in her chest because she knew.

She knew.

Chase looked at her like she was it for him. Like she was the only thing that made sense in his world.

And she was about to walk away from that.

"Do you really think you're going to go back to Asheville and pretend none of this happened?" Mallory's voice pulled her back. "You think you're going to go back to your old life and just be fine without him?"

Savannah turned away, blinking hard, trying to hold herself together.

Mallory exhaled, reaching out to grip her hands, forcing her to look at her. "Babe, love isn't safe. It's messy, and terrifying, and it asks you to take risks. But it's also the best thing you'll ever have."

She squeezed her hands tighter, her voice breaking. "And you—you have a chance at it with Chase. A real one. And I don't think you're going to forgive yourself if you walk away."

Savannah swallowed past the lump in her throat, her entire body trembling because deep down, she knew Mallory was right.

She knew leaving was going to destroy her just as much as it was going to destroy Chase.

But she had spent so long convincing herself that love wasn't something she could trust, that it was fleeting, conditional, breakable—

How was she supposed to suddenly believe that this time would be different?

That Chase was different?

Mallory squeezed her hands one last time, sensing the war raging inside her. "Stay, Savannah."

Her voice cracked with emotion. "Stay for him. Stay for yourself. Stay because maybe, just maybe, you've finally found the thing that makes this place home."

Savannah opened her mouth.

No words came.

Because she wanted to.

God, she wanted to.

But she didn't know if she could.

38

Whispered Echoes

THE DRIVE TO CHASE'S house was suffocating in its silence. The weight of what she was about to do sat heavy in her chest, pressing down like an iron fist, making it impossible to breathe. She couldn't speak. Couldn't find the words. Couldn't think past the ache splitting her ribs apart. Mallory, to her credit, didn't push. She didn't tell her to turn the car around, didn't beg her to change her mind. But Savannah could feel it, the quiet tension vibrating off her best friend, the barely concealed frustration in the way her hands gripped the steering wheel a little too tight.

Savannah stared out the window, trying to memorize every stretch of road, every flickering streetlamp, every curve and crack and dip in the pavement. She tried to take it all in, to hold it inside of her, to somehow make it enough. Because soon, it would be gone. Soon, this place—this town that had only ever been a temporary escape—would be in her past.

But none of it mattered. None of it meant anything. Not without him.

Chase.

The man who had wrecked her. The man she had fallen for in the most unexpected, beautiful, earth-shattering way. The man she was about to leave.

Mallory pulled into his driveway, the familiar crunch of gravel beneath the tires making Savannah's stomach twist violently. She clenched her fingers in her lap, nails digging into her palms as her gaze lifted to the house—the house that had once been just another home on the water, just another piece of scenery.

But now?

Now it was him. And he was there.

Sitting on the dock, his back to them, staring at the water like it held the answers he was searching for.

Savannah's heart lurched.

Mallory cut the engine, but neither of them moved right away. The air inside the car was thick, suffocating, pressing down on Savannah until she couldn't breathe.

Mallory finally turned, her voice softer now.

"I don't have to tell you that you're making the biggest mistake of your life, do I?"

Savannah swallowed hard, blinking against the stinging behind her eyes.

"I already know."

Mallory exhaled, nodding once before slipping out of the car. "I'll talk to him first."

Savannah sat frozen as she watched her best friend make her way down the dock, her breath catching in her throat when Mallory dropped down beside Chase, nudging his knee with hers. He didn't look at her, didn't react, but even from here, Savannah could see the tension radiating off of him, could feel the weight of it in the air between them.

Savannah couldn't hear them.

Didn't need to.

She knew Mallory. Knew what she was saying. Knew she was telling him that she had tried. Knew she was telling him that Savannah was leaving anyway. And then—Mallory stood.

Looked back once.

Then walked back toward the car.

"It's your turn," she murmured, her voice laced with something defeated before she slipped into the driver's seat.

Savannah forced herself to move, forced herself to take the steps that led her toward him, toward an ending she didn't know how to survive. She heard the way her footsteps hit the dock, soft but hesitant, like a heartbeat slowing before stopping completely.

Chase still didn't move.

Not until she was right beside him.

Only then did he tilt his head slightly, his gaze heavy when it met hers.

"One last visit, huh?"

Savannah sat beside him, their shoulders nearly touching, and turned toward the horizon. She wished she had the words to make this hurt less. But there were no words. No comfort. No way to fix what she had already broken. "I didn't want to leave without seeing you."

Chase huffed out a humorless laugh, shaking his head.

"That's the problem, Monroe. You shouldn't be leaving at all."

Her chest caved.

She turned her head, finding him already watching her.

"You're really going," he murmured.

Her breath hitched. "Yeah."

Something flickered in his eyes, something dark and final. And then, she watched it happen. Watched the spark in him—the spark that had always been there, the one that had drawn her in, held her captive—begin to fade. She watched as he broke.

His hands flexed on his knees, and for a moment, she thought he might reach for her, might pull her into him and beg her to stay.

But he didn't.

Instead, he turned his gaze back to the water, his voice barely above a whisper.

"If you leave..." He exhaled slowly, dragging a hand through his hair, his jaw clenching tight. "I might as well burn this whole fucking place to the ground."

Her breath caught. "Chase—"

"Because, Monroe," he contin ued, his voice wrecked, "your echoes will haunt me."

Tears burned her eyes, but she blinked them back, refusing to let them fall. Her fingers trembled against the wood beneath her. Chase let out a slow, measured breath, but when he spoke again, his voice was different—softer, quieter, raw in a way that sliced through her.

"I love you."

It wasn't desperate. It wasn't rushed. It wasn't even a plea. It was a truth. A simple, undeniable truth that shattered her into a thousand unfixable pieces. A broken sound slipped from her lips, her heart felt like it was being ripped straight from her chest.

"Please don't do this," she whispered.

He turned toward her, wrecked and undone. "Why not?"

Because if she stayed, she wouldn't be able to leave. Because if she left, she would never be whole again.

She forced herself to stand.

Chase followed, his hands clenched into fists at his sides, his voice softer now, but somehow more desperate. "Don't go."

Her throat closed.

She wanted to stay.

God, she wanted to stay.

But the fear—the unknown—it was too much.

So she reached for him instead, cupping his face in her hands, memorizing every sharp angle, every line, every inch of him. He closed his eyes, leaning into her touch like it was the last thing keeping him tethered to this earth. Because it was. And then, she kissed him.

Slow.

Lingering.

A kiss that should have been enough.

But it wasn't.

And when she pulled away, when she took a step back, her heart cracked straight down the middle.

Chase's eyes were heavy, his chest rising and falling unevenly as he searched her face for something—anything—that might make sense of this.

But there was nothing.

Only heartbreak.

Only goodbye.

He stepped back.

Nodded once.

Then, with a voice so raw it shattered her, he whispered—

"Take care, Monroe."

And then?

He turned.

Walked back toward the dock.

Didn't look back.

Didn't stop.

Didn't fight her anymore.

Savannah stood there, watching him go, breaking.

The second Savannah made it back to the car, she squared her shoulders, inhaled sharply, and forced the burning behind her eyes to stay put. She wouldn't cry. Not yet. Not now. Not while she still felt the heat of his lips against hers, not while his voice still echoed in her mind, raw and wrecked.

She yanked the car door open and climbed into the passenger seat, gripping her knees with trembling hands. Mallory didn't say a word. She simply exhaled softly, turning the key in the ignition as the engine rumbled to life.

The tires crunched against the gravel as they pulled away from the dock, from him, from everything. Savannah pressed her lips together, blinking rapidly, willing herself to keep it together.

It wasn't until they reached the end of the drive that she broke.

Because that's when she saw it.

The sign.

Whispering Echoes Drive.

The name he had chosen. The name that had always been just a name—until now.

Now, it was them.

Her breath hitched, her fingers clenching into the fabric of her jeans as the first tear slipped down her cheek. And once it started, there was no stopping it.

The dam shattered.

She bit her lip, but the sob tore through her anyway, her body shaking as she crumpled forward, her forehead pressing against her hands.

Mallory glanced over, her own expression tight with pain.

"Oh, sweetheart..." she whispered.

Savannah shook her head, squeezing her eyes shut, drowning in it.

She could still feel him.

Still hear him.

Take care, Monroe.

Like she was just someone. Like they hadn't just loved each other.

At that moment, she knew.

She done this. She had just broken Chase Montgomery.

And she had destroyed herself in the process.

39

Chasing Echoes

Day One

THE FIRST THING HE noticed when he woke up was that the bed still smelled like her.

Her scent lingered, woven into the fabric of his sheets, soaked into his motherfucking skin.

Vanilla and salt and something else—something indescribable, something that was just Savannah. It was everywhere, trapped in the fibers of his pillowcase, clinging to the worn cotton of the sheets, floating in the air around him.

And God, it was fucking torture.

Because every time he breathed in, every time he shifted even the slightest bit, it felt like she was still there. Like if he just rolled over, reached across the bed, his fingers would find the smooth, warm skin of her waist, the dip of her spine. Like if he opened his eyes, he would see her, curled up beside him, her blonde hair fanned out over his pillow, her breath slow and even, her lips parted just slightly.

But when he finally forced his eyes open, she wasn't there.

Just empty sheets.

Just a cold bed.

Just a hollow, aching void where she should be.

Chase lay there, unmoving, staring at the ceiling, his arms spread wide across the bed like maybe—just maybe—if he reached far enough, she would still be there. That if he stayed still, if he refused to move, refused to acknowledge that this was real, the universe might take pity on him and give him one more second with her.

One more moment.

One more breath.

But he wasn't that fucking lucky.

The weight in his chest was unbearable, pressing down like something tangible, like a fist clenching around his ribs, squeezing until his breath came in slow, uneven drags.

He closed his eyes again.

Maybe if he fell back asleep, he could dream of her.

Maybe if he stayed like this, he wouldn't have to remember that she was gone.

And nothing—fucking nothing—was the same.

Day Two

The quiet was unbearable.

It filled every room, settled into every crack and corner, thick and suffocating, pressing against his skin like a weight he couldn't shake.

Chase had never been the kind of man who needed noise, but now?

Now, the silence was deafening.

No sound of her bare feet padding across the hardwood floors. No soft hum of her voice in the morning as she made coffee, as she stole sips of his before he could even take a damn drink. No laughter from the bathroom when she thought he wasn't listening. No distant sound of the old radio she liked to turn on while she got ready.

Just nothing.

Just the dull, empty echo of a house that felt less like a home and more like a fucking mausoleum.

He got up, dragging his hands down his face, the weight in his chest heavier than it had been the night before. It was a different kind of exhaustion—one that settled deep, one that made even breathing feel like too much effort.

And then he saw it.

Her shirt.

His fucking Henley, the one she had worn so perfectly, draped over the hamper like a silent reminder of what he'd lost.

He stared at it, his breathing uneven, his fists clenching at his sides.

It wasn't just the shirt.

It was everything.

The coffee cup in the sink, the one she had used more than her own.

The bobby pin on the bathroom counter, sitting there like a goddamn ghost.

The half-burned candle on the kitchen counter, the one she had insisted smelled like home, the scent of warm amber and vanilla still lingering in the air.

The book on his nightstand, still dog-eared to the page she had stopped reading the night before she left.

She was gone.

But her echoes were haunting him.

Still no word.

Still no text.

Still nothing.

By noon, he couldn't take it anymore. He grabbed his truck keys and left, driving aimlessly through town, past all the places that reminded him of her.

The marina, where she had met him that first day, looking like a fucking dream.

The bookstore, where she had traced her fingers over the spines of novels like they held the answers to the universe.

The coffee shop, where she had stolen sips of his drink, smirking when he pretended to be pissed.

The beach, where she had walked beside him in the moonlight, the waves lapping at her ankles, her hand wrapped so tightly around his that it felt like she never wanted to let go.

Everywhere he went, she was there.

But in reality?

She was nowhere.

Day Three

He stayed at the dock all day.

Didn't eat.

Didn't sleep.

Just sat there, staring at the water, listening to the waves as they crashed against the pilings.

She should have been here. She belonged here.

Chase leaned forward, resting his forearms on his knees, dragging a hand through his already disheveled hair.

He had told her he loved her. Had bared his fucking soul to her. Had given her everything.

And still—she left.

His jaw locked, his throat burned, his entire body coiled tight.

He had never felt like this before. Not when loved ones passed. Not when he had lost friends.

Because this wasn't just heartbreak.

This was fucking devastation.

And the worst part?

She was the only one who could fix it.

Still no word.

Still nothing.

Day Four

The knock on his door came mid-afternoon.

Chase barely moved.

He had been in the same spot for hours, staring blankly at the floor, the weight of exhaustion pressing down on him like a lead blanket.

He didn't want company.

Didn't want to talk. Didn't want to fucking exist in this moment without her.

So when he heard the knock, he almost didn't answer.

Until he heard her voice.

Sara.

"Chase, open the damn door."

He exhaled sharply, scrubbing a hand over his face before pulling it open.

And there they were.

Jaxon and Sara.

His best friend and the woman who had wrecked him before she had become his world.

Chase's stomach twisted. He didn't need to ask why they were here.

Mallory.—That meddling little shit must have called Sara.

Jaxon didn't speak right away. He just stood there, his gaze heavy, knowing. Because Jaxon had been here before.

He had lived through this. He had lost Sara once. And he knew exactly what Chase was going through.

Sara was the first to step forward, wrapping her arms around him. "I'm sorry," she murmured. "I tried to talk her into staying."

Chase didn't move. Didn't react. Just stood there, his body stiff, his breath shallow.

"Did she even think about it?" He asked hoarsely, his voice barely there.

Sara pulled back, her eyes filled with something that looked like pity. "Chase—"

And that was all the answer he needed. He exhaled sharply, shaking his head, stepping away.

Jaxon finally spoke. "Come on, man. We're taking you out."

Chase let out a bitter laugh, rubbing the back of his neck. "Not in the mood."

"You don't have a choice," Sara said, giving him a pointed look.

Chase opened his mouth to argue, but Jaxon was already pushing past him, grabbing his keys off the counter. "Low-Tide. Now."

Chase clenched his jaw but followed them out the door. Because what the fuck else was he supposed to do?

Sit here and drown in the memories of her? Sit here and keep checking his phone like some desperate asshole?

Because she wasn't calling.

She wasn't texting.

She had left. And she wasn't coming back.

The Low-Tide Tavern was packed.

People laughed, talked, lived.

And Chase?

He just sat at the bar, nursing his drink, barely listening to the band playing in the background.

Jaxon and Sara were somewhere in the crowd, giving him space.

But space didn't help.

Nothing helped.

Because this place?

It was still hers.

The booth in the corner? The one where he, Savannah, Mallory, and Nate had shared that perfect meal?

It was still there. Empty. Mocking him.

Chase took a slow sip of whiskey, his fingers tightening around the glass.

Jenna had stopped by earlier. She leaned in, smiled, traced a manicured nail down his arm.

"Miss me, Montgomery?" she had teased.

But Chase?

He had barely looked at her. Because he couldn't. Because the only woman he wanted wasn't here.

Jenna eventually took the hint and walked away, and Chase just sat there, drinking, staring at the table where she had once sat.

Laughing. Happy.

His chest ached.

He could have had that forever.

He should have had that forever.

But now?

Now he was just waiting.

For the day when he could walk into this bar, sit at this stool, and not think about her.

Because God help him—

Right now, he couldn't imagine a day when he wouldn't.

40

Tides Turning

CHASE BARELY REMEMBERED THE drive back from Low-Tide.

The road was a blur, streetlights flashing by in streaks of yellow and white, the hum of the engine nothing but a distant noise against the chaos in his head.

He had been lost in his own fucking mind.

Still seeing Savannah in every shadow.

Still hearing her laughter in the spaces between conversations that no longer interested him.

The world had kept spinning. People kept drinking, laughing, living.

But for him?

Time had fucking stopped.

Jaxon pulled the truck into Chase's driveway, the tires crunching against the gravel, the engine rumbling low before he cut it off. Neither of them moved at first. The silence was thick, heavy, pressing against Chase's chest like a goddamn vice. He was still staring out at the water, watching the tide roll against the dock, feeling that familiar ache in his chest settle even deeper.

He couldn't escape it.

Not here.

Not anywhere.

Savannah was everywhere and nowhere, haunting him in a way that left him raw, hollow, shattered from the inside out.

Sara, who had been uncharacteristically quiet most of the night, finally sighed and turned in her seat. "Alright, enough of this brooding bullshit. Let's go."

Chase shot her a look, his jaw tightening, but Jaxon was already pushing his door open, stepping out like he knew there was no arguing.

Chase had never fought a losing battle with Sara Stone.

He sure as hell wasn't about to start now.

So, he climbed out, following them both down toward the dock, the moon hanging heavy in the sky, reflecting off the water like liquid silver.

The air was thick with salt and regret, and Chase hated how much it reminded him of her.

Sara plopped down on one of the old wooden chairs, tucking her legs underneath her, the glow of the dock light casting soft shadows across her face. Jaxon leaned against the railing, arms crossed, his gaze sharp, unreadable, watching Chase with that same knowing look he had been giving him all fucking night.

Chase ran a hand down his face, dragging it over the stubble on his jaw.

"If you're here to give me some 'everything happens for a reason' bullshit, I'm gonna need you to save it," he muttered.

Jaxon smirked. "Oh, trust me. That is not why I'm here."

Chase exhaled sharply, dropping down onto the edge of the dock, letting his legs dangle over the water. The wood beneath him was worn, sun-bleached from years of salt air and storms.

Just like him.

Worn down. Weathered. Fucking tired.

Sara tilted her head, her voice softer now. "Mallory told me everything, Chase."

His stomach twisted.

He already knew that. Knew Mallory had been the one to drag Jaxon and Sara into this mess.

But hearing it out loud still stung.

"She's struggling too, you know," Sara continued.

Chase's jaw clenched.

"She's still gone, though, isn't she?" His voice was hoarse, thick with something he hated admitting.

Sara sighed. "Yeah. But that doesn't mean she wanted to leave."

Chase let out a bitter laugh, shaking his head.

"That doesn't change a damn thing, Sara."

Jaxon, who had been quiet up until now, let out a slow breath. "Yeah, it does."

Chase scoffed, but Jaxon didn't let him spiral. Instead, he walked over, dropped down next to him, his voice steady, unwavering.

"You think I don't know what this feels like?" Jaxon asked, his tone softer now. "That I don't know what it's like to wake up every fucking morning and feel like you're missing the best part of yourself?"

Chase didn't answer.

Because he knew.

Everyone knew what Jaxon and Sara had been through.

Sara had left once. Had walked away from him. And Jaxon had been just as wrecked as Chase was now.

The only difference?

Sara had come back.

"I was you once," Jaxon continued. "I sat right here, in this same damn spot, feeling like I'd never fucking breathe again without her."

Sara's expression softened as she leaned forward. "And you were the one who pulled him out of it, Chase."

Chase swallowed hard. He remembered that time too well. Remembered dragging Jaxon's ass out of bars. Remembered watching him fall apart.

He had been the one to remind Jaxon that Sara was still out there.

That it wasn't over.

And now?

Now, Jaxon was trying to do the same for him.

Chase let out a slow exhale, staring at the water. "Doesn't feel like she's coming back," he admitted, his voice barely above a whisper.

Jaxon was quiet for a long moment. "Neither did Sara."

Chase turned his head, his brows furrowing. "And yet, here she is."

Sara grinned, resting her chin on her knee. "What can I say? Jaxon is persistent."

Jaxon smirked. "You're damn right."

Chase huffed out a breath, shaking his head. "That was different."

Jaxon lifted a brow. "Was it?"

Chase didn't answer.

Because the truth?

It wasn't different at all. It was the same. And the fact that Jaxon knew exactly how this felt made Chase want to crawl out of his own fucking skin.

Because what if this really wasn't over? What if Savannah was just as wrecked as he was? What if she was sitting somewhere in Asheville, staring at her phone, aching to call him?

Chase sighed, dragging a hand down his face.

Sara sat forward, her expression softer now. "I know it hurts, Chase. And I know there's nothing anyone can say right now that's gonna make it hurt any less."

She reached over, squeezing his arm.

"But if I know Savannah—if I know you—this isn't how your story ends."

Chase swallowed against the tightness in his throat. He wanted to believe that.

God, he wanted to believe that so fucking bad.

But right now?

All he had was silence.

And that silence was fucking killing him.

Sara smirked, nudging his arm. "Besides, if your story really was over, you would've gone home with Jenna tonight."

Chase laughed.

An actual, real, fucking laugh.

Jaxon grinned. "There he is."

Sara smirked. "I was starting to think you died, but nope. Just depressed as hell. Love that for you."

Chase chuckled, shaking his head, feeling lighter than he had in days.

He looked between them, the two people who had been through this exact thing.

The two people who came out the other side.

And for the first time since Savannah left—

He let himself hope.

Even if just a little. Even if it hurt.

He could feel the tide turning.

Maybe her echoes didn't have to haunt him forever.

Maybe…

Just maybe—

He would get past this.

41

Distant Echoes

Days Ahead

Savannah didn't know how she made it back to Asheville. The highway stretched before her, mile after endless mile, but the drive was a blur. Nothing registered—the cars passing, the road signs, the soft hum of the tires against the pavement. It all felt distant, unreal, like she was floating somewhere outside of herself, trapped in a reality she didn't recognize.

Mallory had been silent for most of the trip. For that, Savannah was grateful. She couldn't talk about it. Not yet. Not when everything inside of her felt raw—like her chest had been split wide open, her heart left bleeding somewhere on Chase's dock.

But her mind wouldn't stop.

It kept replaying it.

The way his hands trembled when he held her.

The way his voice cracked when he said, I love you.

The way he whispered, If you leave, I might as well burn this whole place down.

And God, she felt like she was burning.

By the time they reached her apartment, the numbness had turned into something worse.

Regret.

It curled around her ribs, wrapped itself around her throat, squeezed until she could barely breathe. But she held it in. She kept it together—right up until she opened the door, stepped inside, and faced the unbearable, deafening quiet.

Her suitcase thudded to the floor.

Her breath left her in a sharp, broken exhale.

The walls that had once felt safe now felt like a prison. The space that had been hers for years now felt empty.

Because it was missing him.

Mallory hovered in the doorway, watching her carefully, arms crossed. "You okay?"

Savannah let out a bitter laugh, one that sounded so hollow, so unlike herself, that even she barely recognized it.

"No."

Mallory sighed, stepping forward. "Then why the hell did you leave?"

Savannah squeezed her eyes shut. Because I was scared.

"Of what? Being happy?" Mallory's voice was sharper now, tinged with frustration.

Savannah swallowed hard, trying to keep the tears at bay. "Of getting hurt," she admitted, voice barely above a whisper. "Of waking up one day and realizing it wasn't real."

Mallory let out a slow, deep breath. "Savannah." She stepped closer, placing her hands on her shoulders, forcing her to look at her. "You already hurt. And it was real. It is real."

Savannah shook her head, her voice breaking. "I don't know how to go back."

Mallory studied her for a long moment, then let her hands fall away.

"You don't have to know how." Her voice was softer now, less frustrated, more pleading. "You just have to want to."

Savannah did want to.

More than anything.

But how the hell was she supposed to undo what she had done?

Day Two

The morning came too soon. Savannah woke to a suffocating stillness, the weight of an empty bed pressing against her chest.

The sheets were cold. The pillow beside her was untouched. And worst of all?

It didn't smell like him.

She squeezed her eyes shut, fingers curling into the fabric, desperate for something—anything—to tether her back to the warmth she had left behind.

But there was nothing.

No trace of him. No rough hands pulling her close. No deep, raspy voice murmuring, "Morning, Monroe."

Nothing but silence.

She lay there for hours, staring at the ceiling, caught in the wreckage of what she had done, drowning in the echoes of what she had walked away from.

A soft knock at the door.

Then, the hesitant creak of it opening.

Mallory.

She stood there, holding a plate of food and a cup of coffee, her expression unreadable.

"You need to eat," she said softly.

Savannah didn't move.

Mallory sighed, setting the plate down before sitting on the edge of the bed.

"I know this is hard. But lying here all day isn't going to change anything."

Savannah finally turned her head, her voice hoarse.

"And what exactly am I supposed to do, Mal?"

Mallory studied her for a long moment before sighing.

"You could call him."

Savannah's stomach twisted violently.

She turned her face back toward the ceiling.

"I can't."

Mallory's brows furrowed. "Why the hell not?"

Because she was afraid.

Because if she called him and he didn't answer—It would be over.

Truly, irrevocably over.

And she wasn't ready for that—Not yet. Maybe not ever.

Mallory sighed and stood. "Fine. Sit here. Wallow. Torture yourself." She walked toward the door, pausing just before she left.

"But don't lie to yourself and act like this is what you want."

Then, she was gone.

Savannah exhaled shakily, staring at the ceiling until her vision blurred.

But sleep didn't help.

Because even in her dreams, Chase was there.

And when she woke up—her body reaching for something that wasn't there—

She was breaking all over again.

Day Three

By the time the sun set, Savannah had been staring at her phone for hours.

Still nothing.

No missed calls. No messages. No sign of him.

And why would there be?

She was the one who left.

Mallory sat beside her on the couch, watching carefully. "You're not okay."

Savannah let out a slow breath. "No."

Mallory pursed her lips. "Then maybe it's time you do something about it."

Savannah looked at her, something raw in her eyes.

"And if it's too late?"

Mallory shrugged. "Then at least you'll know. At least you won't spend the rest of your life wondering."

Savannah's stomach twisted.

Because she would wonder.

If she didn't fix this, she would spend every day for the rest of her life thinking about him.

Thinking about what they could have been.

Savannah sat in bed, staring at her phone, her fingers hovering over the call button.

Her pulse pounded so hard it drowned out every rational thought screaming at her to put the damn phone down.

She had no right to call him. She had no reason to. But she needed to hear his voice.

With a shaky breath, she tapped the number and quickly turned on private caller ID.

If he didn't answer, at least he wouldn't know it was her.

The line rang.

Once.

Twice.

Three times.

Her chest tightened, her fingers clenching the blanket in her lap.

And then—

His voicemail clicked on.

"You've reached Chase Montgomery, Montgomery & Associates. Leave your name and number, and I will call you back as soon as possible."

Savannah's breath caught, her entire body going rigid as his voice wrapped around her like a ghost.

Deep. Steady. Controlled.

Like he was perfectly fine. Like he wasn't wrecked. Like she hadn't left him standing on that dock with his heart in his hands.

But what truly shattered her—what made her drop the phone completely—was the sound.

The faintest rustling of wind.

The rhythmic lapping of water.

Like he had recorded the voicemail while sitting on his dock.

Their dock.

Her stomach twisted painfully as she sucked in a sharp breath, pressing a hand to her lips, swallowing back the sob clawing its way up her throat.

She had thought hearing his voice would make it better.

She had been so, so wrong.

Because now?

Now she missed him even more.

42

Mallory's Call

MALLORY HESITATED, HER THUMB hovering over Chase's name for far too long before finally pressing call.

She wasn't sure what she expected.

For him to answer? For him to ignore it? For her to chicken out at the last second and pretend like this wasn't the most important call she had made in a long, long time?

But when the line rang once, then twice, and she heard his voice on the other end—deep, rough, tired—it hit her like a freight train.

"Mallory?" He sounded—neutral.

Not relieved. Not angry.

Just existing.

And God, that was somehow worse than if he had been furious.

"Hey—Chase," she said softly, shifting on the couch, glancing toward the hallway where Savannah's door remained shut—silent, unmoving—a quiet reminder of how much she had disappeared into herself.

She didn't respond when Mallory knocked. Didn't respond when she sat beside her, trying to coax anything out of her.

She was just—gone.

Chase exhaled after a beat. "I'm guessing this isn't a social call."

Mallory let out a weak laugh. "That obvious?"

"Yeah." His voice wasn't cold, but it wasn't warm, either. Just there.

Like he was waiting. Like he was bracing for whatever the hell she was about to throw at him.

"Go ahead, Mal." His voice dropped lower, quieter. "Say what you need to say."

She hesitated.

Because now that she had him on the line, she wasn't sure where to start.

There was too much to say.

Too much to fix.

So she went with the only thing that mattered.

"She's miserable." The words tumbled out before she could stop them, before she could soften them, before she could find a way to make it hurt less. "She won't say it, but I see it. Every day. She doesn't eat, doesn't sleep—hell, she barely even talks to me anymore. She's not okay, Chase."

Silence.

A long, drawn-out pause where Mallory swore she could hear the sound of his breathing on the other end of the line.

And then—

"You want to know something, Mallory?" His voice was lower now, almost a whisper. "I've just started picking up the pieces."

Her stomach twisted.

"Chase—" She plead.

"She broke me." Chase admitted.

His words were quiet, but they held everything. And for the first time since Savannah had left, Mallory felt the full weight of what had happened.

Chase loved her. Loved her so deeply that when she walked away, she didn't just leave him behind—she left him in ruins.

"I know she's hurting," Chase admitted after a long pause. "I don't doubt that at all. But, Mallory, you have to see my side of this, too. I begged her to stay. I asked—And she still walked away."

Mallory inhaled sharply, pressing a hand to her forehead.

Because he was right. Savannah left.

She had a choice, and she made it. And now, she was drowning in the consequences.

"I get it," she whispered, voice tight. "I do. But, Chase, if she called you—if she said she wanted to come back—"

"I'd answer." His voice was steady.

No hesitation. No doubt.

Mallory's heart leapt. For the first time in weeks, she felt a tiny, fragile sliver of hope—

But before she could respond—before she could hold onto that lifeline—

A voice.

A woman's voice.

Soft. Muffled. But there.

Mallory's stomach dropped.

It was quick—just a few words, barely audible—but it was enough.

Enough to tell her Chase wasn't alone.

Enough to tell her Savannah had waited too long.

She heard Chase shift, his voice slightly muffled as he spoke to whoever was in the room with him.

Mallory clenched her jaw, trying to breathe through the tightness in her chest.

The phone rustled again, and then—

"You still there?"

She forced herself to answer. "Yeah. I just—"

She hesitated.

Did she really want to know? Did she want to ask who she was? Did she want confirmation that Chase was already moving on?

No.

Because she already knew. Already knew what the presence of that woman meant.

Mallory cleared her throat, desperate to end the call. "I should go."

Chase hesitated. "Mallory—"

"I'm glad you're doing okay," she said, voice tight, forced. A lie.

She was about to hang up when his voice stopped her. "Wait."

Mallory froze, pressing the phone back to her ear. "Yeah?"

Chase exhaled, his voice softer now. "Thank you."

Mallory frowned, confused. "For what?"

"For reaching out to Jaxon and Sara," he murmured. "For knowing what I needed, even when I didn't know."

Her heart twisted. Because as much as Savannah had needed her, as much as she had been by her best friend's side every step of the way—

Chase had needed someone, too. And somehow, she had been the one to make sure he wasn't alone.

She let out a quiet breath. "You'd do the same for me."

A pause.

Then, a soft chuckle. "Yeah. I would."

For the first time, the tension in Mallory's chest eased.

Maybe this was how it had to be—for now. Maybe Chase needed to move on.

Maybe Savannah needed to fight for him this time.

And maybe, just maybe—This wasn't the end.

But just as Mallory was about to say goodbye, Chase's voice cut through the silence once more.

"Mallory." He said called out, "One last thing."

She stilled. "Yeah?"

There was a beat of hesitation, like he was debating whether to say what was on his mind.

Then, in a voice so raw, so quiet it almost shattered her, he murmured— "Regardless of what does or doesn't happen—please make sure she's okay."

Mallory's heart leapt.

Because despite everything—

Despite how shattered Chase was, despite how much Savannah had hurt him—

He still loved her. Still cared. Still wanted to know she was safe.

And in that moment, Mallory saw it.

The kind of love that doesn't just go away.

She exhaled softly, blinking back the sting in her eyes. "I will," she promised.

And as she ended the call, she knew—

This wasn't over.

Not even close.

43

Breaking Point

THE SILENCE WAS SUFFOCATING.

Mallory stood frozen, her phone still warm in her palm, the weight of the call with Chase hanging in the air like the last crack of thunder after a storm.

She hadn't even tucked it away before Savannah stepped into the living room.

Mallory's stomach twisted.

Savannah's eyes—wide, glassy, desperate—locked onto hers, searching for something. Anything.

Mallory had no idea how much she had overheard.

She wished she could have one second—just one—to figure out how to do this without breaking her.

But Savannah wasn't going to let her.

The weight in her gaze demanded answers.

"How long have you been standing there?" Mallory's voice barely made it past the lump in her throat.

Savannah took a step forward. Arms crossed. Defensive. Bracing herself.

Like she already knew.

"Long enough," she whispered.

Mallory exhaled.

There was no delaying this. No sugarcoating it.

Savannah's voice was barely above a breath when she spoke again.

"You called him."

Not a question. Just a fact.

Mallory nodded. "Yeah."

Savannah's chest rose and fell, her fingers curling into fists against her sides. She had been waiting for this. For something. A sign.

She just never expected it to feel like this.

"And?" she croaked.

Mallory hesitated.

She wanted to lie. Wanted to find a way to soften it. To dull the blade before it struck.

But she couldn't.

Not when Savannah was already standing there, unraveling right in front of her.

"He said he's just started picking up the pieces."

The words landed between them like a dull, lifeless thud.

Savannah stilled.

A fracture. A break. A fucking wreckage. Mallory could see it happening in real time.

The way the color drained from Savannah's face. The way her shoulders curved inward. The way her breath hitched in her throat like she was seconds from collapsing.

And then—Mallory made it worse.

So much worse.

"The pieces you left behind."

Savannah sucked in a sharp breath.

She staggered back like Mallory had driven a knife straight into her chest, her hands trembling, her lips parting in a silent gasp. Her knees buckled, but she caught herself, fingers clutching the edge of the coffee table like it was the only thing keeping her upright.

Mallory clenched her jaw, hating herself for saying it.

For making Savannah hear it. For making her feel it.

But the truth was the truth. Savannah had wrecked him.

And now? Now, she was wrecking herself.

Her breathing was sharp, uneven, ragged—like she was seconds from breaking apart right in front of her.

The house was silent. Too silent.

The kind of quiet that presses down on your chest, that fills every inch of a room with the weight of what's left unsaid.

Savannah stood in the middle of the living room, arms wrapped around herself as if she could physically hold herself together. But she was unraveling, and she felt every thread pulling loose.

Mallory was still on the couch, her phone screen dark now, fingers gripping the fabric of the cushion beneath her.

The air between them was thick. Suffocating.

And then—

Savannah's phone buzzed.

The sound split the silence like a gunshot.

She flinched.

Mallory barely noticed it at first, too caught up in watching Savannah, bracing for the fallout.

But then—She saw it.

The way Savannah froze. The way her breath caught. The way her fingers trembled as she lifted her phone, staring at the screen as if moving would make it real.

Mallory frowned. "What is it?"

Savannah didn't respond. Didn't blink. Didn't breathe.

Her thumb hovered over the screen for a second—just one second—before she clicked the message open.

Chase: Take care of yourself, Monroe.

Savannah's stomach dropped.

Her fingers curled around the edges of her phone, gripping it like it was the only thing keeping her from completely falling apart.

It was Chase—-After all this time. After months of silence.

This was what he had to say?

Not a plea. Not an I miss you. Not a come back.

Just—take care. Like she was a stranger.

A distant memory. A past he had already put behind him.

The air left her lungs in a sharp, painful exhale.

She felt Mallory watching her, waiting for a reaction. For anything.

But Savannah couldn't move.

Because that?

That was final.

That was Chase walking away. That was him letting her go.

Savannah swallowed hard, forcing herself to breathe.

But the oxygen didn't help. Nothing helped.

She needed to move. To do something—anything—before the weight of it crushed her.

Slowly, she turned and walked toward the kitchen, her steps heavy, her hands numb.

Mallory didn't stop her. She didn't say anything.

Savannah gripped the edge of the counter, staring out the window, chest rising and falling unevenly.

The sky was dark now, city lights flickering to life in the distance.

But it didn't feel like home.

Not anymore.

Because home had never been Asheville.

It had been him.

She pressed a palm against the cool granite, grounding herself, fighting against the storm raging inside her.

And that's when she heard it—

His voice.

Her breath strangled in her throat.

At first, she thought she was imagining it. That grief had finally twisted into something cruel, warping the silence into the sound she missed the most. But then she turned.

And there—on the television screen—was him.

Chase.

Her lungs locked.

His name formed in her mind before she could stop it, before she could protect herself from what seeing him would do. He stood in front of a row of cameras, hands buried in his pockets, shoulders slightly tense beneath the weight of something unspoken. His head tilted slightly, his brow furrowed—not in anger, not in irritation, but in exhaustion.

A bone-deep kind of exhaustion. A kind she recognized.

"Shit," Mallory murmured, barely above a whisper.

But Savannah barely heard her. She barely heard anything over the dull, rushing sound in her ears.

Something about a state project. A contract. Logistics.

None of it mattered. She only cared about him. The way he looked. How tired he seemed. How the dark circles under his eyes told her that sleep had been just as cruel to him as it had been to her.

And then—

A reporter's voice cut through the air.

"Mr. Montgomery, some concerns have been raised regarding the previous company that relinquished the contract. Do you have any comments?"

Chase's response was smooth. Effortless. "You hear a lot of Whispered Echoes about backing out when things get tough, but with Montgomery? We make sure to see it through."

Savannah's stomach plummeted.

Her breath hitched.

Because she knew. She fucking knew.

That wasn't about the project.

That was about her.

That was him, standing in front of a camera, telling the whole fucking state of North Carolina, telling her what he couldn't bring himself to say before.

He wasn't waiting anymore.

Her fingers curled around her phone.

A tear slipped down her cheek.

She was too late.

Chase wasn't hers anymore.

44

Low-Tide Revival

CHASE SAT ON HIS dock, his elbows resting on his knees, the dim glow of his phone illuminating his face as he replayed the interview that had aired earlier that evening.

At the time, it had been just another statement—just another job, just another project, just another day. He'd stood there in front of the cameras, professional, collected, delivering his usual no-nonsense responses.

But now?

Now, watching himself, hearing the words fall from his own mouth, he felt the weight of them.

"You hear a lot of Whispered Echoes about backing out when things get tough, but with Montgomery? We make sure to see it through."

Jesus.

Chase scrubbed a hand down his face, realizing just how much power those words carried.

In that moment, standing under the bright lights, he hadn't realized exactly what he was saying.

But now?

Now, he knew.

He had just told the entire fucking state of North Carolina that he was moving forward.

That he was no longer holding onto the past. That he was no longer clinging to what could have been.

And yet—

He was still here.

Still sitting on this dock. Still feeling every ghost of her touch on his skin. Still haunted by her echoes.

His phone buzzed in his hand.

Jaxon: Just watched the interview. Dude, you look like hell.

Chase scoffed, shaking his head. "This motherfucker," he muttered, but there was no heat behind it.

Because Jaxon was right.

He sighed, thumb hovering over the keyboard before he finally typed a response.

Chase: I'm on it. Thanks, man.

That was all that needed to be said. Because there was nothing else to say.

Chase pushed up from the dock, stretching out muscles that had been coiled tight for months, making his way back inside the house, flipping on the bathroom light.

And what he saw in the mirror?

It wasn't him.

Not really. The man staring back at him looked hollowed out.

His beard had grown out too long, the dark scruff now borderline unruly. His hair was a mess, his skin looked tired, his eyes were weighed down by exhaustion. He looked like he had been rode hard and hung out to dry.

Jaxon was right.

Shaking his head, Chase turned on the clippers, trimming his beard back down to the length it had always been—sharp, clean, effortless. He brushed his teeth, ran his hands through his mess of hair, and stepped into the shower.

The water was hot, scalding even, but he needed it.

Needed to feel something other than the cold emptiness he'd been walking around with for two months.

When he stepped out, he wiped the fog from the mirror, staring at himself again.

Better.

Still broken. But better.

His phone buzzed on the counter.

Nate: You comin' to Low-Tide or what?

Chase exhaled slowly, staring at the screen for a long moment before finally typing back.

Chase: Yeah. I'll be there.

It was time.

The Return

Chase pulled on distressed-washed jeans, a black Henley that stretched across his broad frame just right, his worn ball cap, and his boots. Clean, freshly trimmed, and finally feeling like himself again, he grabbed his keys and stepped out the door.

By the time he pushed open the heavy doors of Low-Tide Tavern, he could already tell—

The tide was shifting.

The familiar scent of whiskey and fried food wrapped around him, the low hum of country music playing over the speakers blending with the loud, laughter-filled atmosphere.

And then?

He felt it.

The stares.

Not just from Nate, who was grinning like the bastard he was from across the bar. But from everyone else. Women. Friends. Locals who had watched him walk around like a damn ghost for the past two months.

They noticed.

They noticed the way he smiled. The way he laughed when Nate clapped him on the shoulder, already handing him a beer. The way he talked—really talked—without feeling like he was carrying the weight of the fucking world on his back.

And the women?

Damn if they didn't notice. One by one, they came up to him. Some brave enough to flirt outright. Some testing the waters, lingering close, hoping to be the one he set his sights on.

And for the first time in months?

He flirted back.

He talked, laughed, played the part. He even danced with a few of them—briefly, casually, harmlessly.

And then?

Then trouble walked in.

Jenna.

Fucking Jenna.

She didn't hesitate. Didn't even pretend like she hadn't seen him. No, she marched right up to him like she had been waiting for this moment.

Tight jeans. Red halter top. Heels that made her legs look longer than they already were.

"Well, well, well," she purred, running a manicured nail down his arm. "Looks like the real Chase Montgomery is finally back."

Chase chuckled, tipping his beer to his lips. "Didn't know I ever left."

Jenna smirked. "Oh, sweetheart, you left. But I'd say you've officially made your return."

Nate snorted from beside him, enjoying the show way too much.

Jenna slid closer. Too close.

She pressed a hand to his chest, tilting her head. "Dance with me."

Chase glanced toward Nate, who just lifted his beer in silent encouragement.

"Ahh—What the hell," Chase muttered, setting his drink down before leading Jenna to the dance floor.

And the second they started moving, Jenna took her shot.

"You know," she whispered against his ear, her fingers trailing up the back of his neck, "you could take me home tonight."

Chase chuckled, shaking his head. "Nice try, sweetheart."

Jenna pouted. "What? I'm just saying—"

"It's not happening," he cut in smoothly.

She sighed dramatically, leaning her head against his shoulder for a brief second. "Your loss."

But Chase?

He wasn't losing anything. Because for the first time in months—He felt free.

For the first time in months, he wasn't waiting for someone who wasn't coming back.

And as the night went on?

He had a good time. A true— good time.

He drank, danced, laughed, felt alive.

But when it came time to leave?

When Jenna tried one last time to get him to come home with her?

He turned her down.

Because no matter how much he was moving forward—

Some things?

Some things just weren't replaceable.

And when he walked out of Low-Tide Tavern that night, heading back toward home, back toward his empty bed—

He still felt her echoes.

45

Chasing Ghosts

One Year Later

SAVANNAH MONROE WASN'T THE same woman who had left Wrightsville Beach nearly a year ago.

She had tried to move on. Tried to convince herself that what she had with Chase was just a moment in time—a beautiful, fleeting thing that wasn't meant to last.

But the problem was, Chase Montgomery wasn't the kind of man you just forgot.

She had spent the last year pretending. Pretending she was okay. Pretending she was healing. Pretending that life had gone back to normal.

But it hadn't.

Nothing had felt normal since the day she left.

Her favorite coffee shop? It didn't taste the same. The city of Asheville? Too loud. Too suffocating. Her apartment? Too quiet. Too empty.

She had filled her days with work, trying to stay busy, trying to ignore the ache in her chest every time she saw a pickup truck that looked like his, every time she heard a song that reminded her of him, every time she saw the ocean in a movie and thought about what she had left behind.

And Chase?

She didn't know.

Not really.

She had done everything in her power to avoid finding out. She didn't check social media. She didn't ask Mallory for updates. She didn't call. Didn't text. Didn't give herself a single excuse to reach for him.

Because if she did?

She wasn't sure she'd survive it.

Tired of Pretending

Savannah Monroe was tired. Tired of pretending. Tired of smiling when she didn't mean it. Tired of dragging herself through the motions of a life that felt foreign without him.

She had tried to push through it.

She buried herself in work, forced herself into a routine, convinced herself that time would dull the ache in her chest.

But time wasn't healing anything. It was only making the silence louder, the loneliness heavier, the realization more brutal.

And Mallory?

She had seen enough. "You need to go on a date."

Savannah groaned, throwing her head back against the couch, already exhausted by the idea. "Mallory, no."

Mallory narrowed her eyes from across the kitchen, arms crossed over her chest, her patience wearing thin. "Yes."

"No," Savannah argued, dragging a pillow over her face.

"Yes."

"Mallory."

Mallory let out a long-suffering sigh, walking over to the couch and perching on the edge like she was gearing up for an intervention.

"Savy, I love you. But you have to start living again."

Savannah exhaled sharply, staring at the ceiling. "I am living," she muttered.

Mallory scoffed. "No, you're surviving. There's a difference."

Savannah swallowed hard, her throat tight. She hated that Mallory could read her so easily.

"I don't think I'm ready," she admitted, her voice smaller than she intended.

Mallory's expression softened. "I know."

Savannah blinked, caught off guard by her honesty.

"But, Savy, no one is telling you to replace him." Mallory's voice was gentle, but insistent. "No one can replace him. But you've been drowning for a year, and I just... I just want you to come up for air."

Savannah's chest constricted. She wanted to argue. Wanted to tell Mallory she was fine. But she wasn't.

And Mallory knew it.

So Savannah took a deep breath. And nodded. "One date," she whispered, barely convincing herself.

Mallory grinned, reaching over to squeeze her hand. "That's my girl."

A Mistake From the Start

Savannah knew it was a mistake the second she stepped into the restaurant.

Everything was wrong—The lighting was too bright. The music was too soft. The conversations around her felt hollow, scripted.

And her date? He wasn't Chase.

Ben Holman—owner of Holman Realty Group in Asheville. He'd been flirting with her for as long as she could remember. Eventually, she said yes.

He was polite. Charming, even. The kind of guy any woman would be lucky to sit across from—put-together, clean-cut, effortless.

But that was the problem.

Savannah had never wanted easy.

She wanted messy.

Chaotic.

Untamed.

She wanted Chase. And to his defense—Chase warned her about it.

She tried. God, she tried.

She smiled when she was supposed to. She laughed at all the right moments. She made small talk about work, about Asheville, about the latest movies and the changing seasons.

But her heart wasn't in it. Her heart was somewhere else. With someone else.

And when Ben leaned forward, offering an easy smile, and asked, "What do you do for fun?"

Savannah froze.

Because she didn't know how to answer.

Everything she had loved—everything that had ever made her feel alive—was tangled up in him.

Late-night drives? She and Chase used to pick random directions and just go, no destination, no plan—just the road and the promise of new places.

Old bookstores? Chase had taken her to that little shop near the marina once, had watched her get lost in the shelves, had memorized the way she traced the spines of books like they were sacred.

Dancing? The last time she danced, it had been barefoot on Chase's dock, wrapped in his arms, swaying to the sound of the waves.

She couldn't say any of that. So she forced a smile.

"You know," she said, forcing a casual shrug, "just—normal things."

Ben nodded, taking a sip of his drink. "Yeah? Like what?"

Savannah hesitated. And for the first time in a year, she realized—

She didn't have an answer.

A Truth Too Hard to Ignore

She barely made it through dinner.

Ben was kind.

Kind enough to notice when she wasn't really there. Kind enough to pick up the check without hesitation. Kind enough to offer a small, understanding smile when she apologized.

"Hey, it's okay," he said as they stepped outside into the crisp evening air. "You're clearly not ready."

Savannah exhaled sharply, guilt tightening in her stomach. "I'm sorry."

Ben smiled. "Don't be. Whoever he is... he set the bar high, huh?"

Her throat constricted. She nodded. "Yeah," she whispered. "He did."

Ben shoved his hands in his pockets, studying her for a moment before offering a small, knowing smirk. "Then don't settle for anything less."

Savannah blinked. She wasn't expecting that. But somehow, it was exactly what she needed to hear. She offered him a soft, grateful smile before getting into her car. And as she sat there, gripping the steering wheel, exhaling a shaky breath, she finally let herself accept the truth she had been running from for an entire year.

Maybe she wasn't supposed to move on. Maybe she wasn't supposed to force herself to be okay. Maybe she wasn't supposed to forget.

Maybe—She was supposed to find her way back.

And for the first time in twelve months, Savannah Monroe allowed herself to whisper the words she had been too afraid to say out loud.

She had left Wrightsville Beach—but she had never left him.

And she never would.

46

Old Friends

MALLORY SAT CROSS-LEGGED ON her couch, a half-full glass of cheap-but-does-the-job wine in one hand, her phone in the other. The apartment was quiet, save for the faint hum of the TV in the background—some crime show she wasn't really watching, the kind where the detective always figures it out in the last five minutes.

But she wasn't watching.

She was staring at Chase's name on her screen. Debating.

Because this wasn't just some casual check-in. This was poking a hornet's nest with a stick. But after Savannah's miserable attempt at a date, after the way she'd come home hollow and lost all over again, after the way she'd curled up on the couch, eating a single piece of pizza like it was punishment instead of dinner—Mallory couldn't take it anymore.

So she hit call.

The phone rang once. Then twice. And then—

"Mallory." That voice. Smooth. Steady. Relaxed.

And it caught her off guard. Because it had been a long time since she had heard Chase Montgomery sound like himself.

"Montgomery," she greeted, taking a slow sip of wine, letting herself listen for a second longer than necessary.

A beat of silence.

Then—

"To what do I owe the pleasure?"

Mallory smirked. "What, I can't just call an old friend?"

A low chuckle. "Mal, you and I both know you don't call just to check in."

She grinned, swirling her wine. "Fair." But she didn't get to the point right away. Instead, she let the moment settle, let herself take in the ease of this conversation. Because for the first time in a long time, Chase didn't sound like a ghost of himself.

And that? That was something.

"So," she started, stretching out her legs. "How's life?"

"Good." Chase said simply.

"Vague. Try again."

Another chuckle. "Life is... fine. Work is busy, the guys are good, the business is steady."

"Okay, and what about you?" she pressed. "The man, not the businessman. Are you happy?"

Chase exhaled, thoughtful. "I'm—better."

Mallory caught that hesitation. But she didn't push.

Not yet—

"And your love life?" she asked casually.

Chase scoffed. "Mal—"

"No, no," she interrupted, grinning. "I need to know. You dating anyone?"

"No." He said bluntly.

Mallory narrowed her eyes. "Let me rephrase—have you even tried?"

Chase sighed. "Damn, Mal."

"I mean, c'mon, Montgomery. It's been a year. Are you telling me you've just been sitting around sulking this whole time?"

"I don't sulk." He chirped back.

"Debatable," she teased.

Chase exhaled, shaking his head. "Look, it's not that I haven't been out. I've gone places, I've met people."

Mallory raised a brow. "And?"

"And... nothing." He said.

"Nothing?" She asked surprisingly.

"Mal—"

"Are you telling me," she cut in, sitting up straighter, "that you haven't had so much as a one-night stand in a year?"

Silence. Mallory blinked.

Then—

"Holy shit."

Chase chuckled. "You good?"

"No, I'm not good!" she practically shrieked. "You, Chase Montgomery, have gone an entire year without getting laid? Am I talking to Chase? Who the fuck are you?" She said laughing.

Chase smirked. "Mal, not that it's any of your business, but—I haven't."

Mallory sat back, stunned. Because Chase was never the kind of guy to ride the pine. He wasn't the type to sit around waiting for someone who wasn't coming back. He moved on.

He always moved on.

But this?

This wasn't just moving forward. This was proof that he never really let go.

And it damn near broke her.

She swallowed hard, deciding to lighten the conversation before it got too heavy. "Okay, let's shift gears before I start crying into my wine. How's life on the sound?"

Chase hesitated.

Just for a second.

"It's good. I've made some changes to the house."

Mallory raised a brow. "Like what?"

"Kitchen's different now. New floors, new cabinets. I redid the first-floor guest room, too."

Mallory inhaled sharply. She knew exactly what that meant—

Erasing memories.

She didn't say anything. But Chase must've read her silence.

"It looks different now," he murmured.

"Different," she echoed, voice soft.

"Yeah." A beat of hesitation.

Then—

"I'm thinking about selling it."

Mallory nearly dropped her wine glass. "Wait—what?" She questioned.

"It's just a house, Mal."

"No, it's not." Her voice firm.

Chase sighed. "I don't know. I just think—maybe it's time for something new."

Mallory bit her lip, unsure of what to say. Because this house? This wasn't just a place Chase lived. This was where he and Savannah happened. Where they danced barefoot on the dock. Where they made love the night before she left. And now he was thinking about walking away from all of it.

Chase took a deep breath. "Well... if it won't hurt her, tell Savannah that I said hey, and I hope she's doing good."

Mallory was silent for a long moment. Then, in a voice barely above a whisper, she said—

"Yeah. I'll do that." Mallory swallowed.

They both knew she wouldn't. Because he wasn't ready to reach out. And Savannah?

She wasn't ready to hear his name.

Another stretch of silence.

Then—

"You still traveling for work?"

Chase exhaled, shifting gears. "Yeah,. Actually—I'll be up that way in a month. I've got a project to scope out."

Mallory's heart jumped. "Wait, your coming to Asheville?"

"Yeah."

Mallory grinned. "Well, well, well. What a coincidence."

Chase huffed out a laugh. "Mal—"

"I'm just saying," she interrupted, grinning. "You might as well grab a drink with me while you're in town."

Chase smirked. "You never change."

"And you love me for it."

Chase chuckled. "That's debatable."

A pause.

Then, softer—"Mal—do me a favor?"

Mallory paused. "Depends on what it is."

Chase exhaled. "Same thing that I asked of you, a year ago—make sure she's okay."

Mallory's breath hitched. Because Chase wasn't asking for updates. He wasn't asking her to push Savannah in his direction.

He just wanted to know she was alright.

That was all.

Mallory smiled, her chest aching. "Yeah, Montgomery. I can do that."

A pause.

Then—

"Thanks, Mal."

She swallowed past the lump in her throat.

"Anytime."

And for the first time in a year? Chase Montgomery didn't feel like he was drowning.

And maybe, just maybe...

That meant Savannah Monroe was finally coming up for air, too.

47

Lingering Echoes

Savannah Monroe was already halfway through her glass of wine when Mallory walked through the door, shrugging off her jacket with an expression that screamed, "Buckle up—because, I have news!"

Savannah sat up straighter, her heart hammering before she could stop herself.

"What happened?" The words tumbled out before she could swallow them down. Too eager. Too desperate.

Mallory smirked, kicking off her shoes. "I talked to Chase."

Savannah froze.

The room went silent. Her wine glass hovering mid-air. Breath caught in her throat. "You what?" She stuttered out.

Mallory tossed her jacket over the back of a chair. "Called him."

Savannah blinked. "Out of nowhere?"

Mallory shrugged, like it was nothing. Like she hadn't just dropped a live fucking grenade in the middle of Savannah's world. "More like after weeks of debating. But yeah. I finally did it."

Savannah exhaled sharply, setting her wine down. "And?"

Mallory arched a brow. "That's it? No dramatic reaction? No 'Why the hell would you do that, Mallory?'"

Savannah let out a forced laugh, but it came out brittle. "I mean—you do dumb shit all the time. Why should this be different?" She took a quick sip of wine, hoping Mallory didn't notice how her fingers trembled.

Mallory smirked, sinking into the couch like this was any other night. "Okay then, I won't say anything about it." She picked up the remote, flipping through Netflix like she hadn't just set Savannah's entire nervous system on fire. "What are we watching?" She smirked.

Savannah's jaw dropped. "Excuse me?! Are you fucking serious right now?" She threw her arms in the air, nearly knocking over her wine. "You just casually announce that you talked to my ex—*the ex*—and now you want to talk about Netflix? No. No, no, no, Mallory, we are not doing this. You are going to tell me every single detail, right now!"

Mallory laughed, shaking her head. "That's what I thought."

She leaned forward, resting her elbows on her knees. "What do you want to know, Savannah?"

Savannah inhaled sharply, pretending she didn't already have an entire list prepared. "Everything. What did he say when he answered? Did he sound surprised? Annoyed? Happy?"

"Well, first off, he answered on the second ring."

Savannah's heart skipped. Second ring. He didn't let it go to voicemail.

Mallory gave her a knowing look. "Sounded like himself, which honestly threw me for a second."

Savannah narrowed her eyes. "Like himself? What does that even mean? Was he relieved? Did he sound like he missed—" She paused, "like he wanted to talk?"

Mallory's smirk deepened. "Not sad. Not overly eager. Just—like Chase."

Savannah swallowed hard but said nothing.

For the past year, she had been convincing herself that Chase was fine. That he had moved on. That he had let her go. That her absence hadn't wrecked him the way it had wrecked her. But hearing Mallory say that? That he was just now starting to feel like himself again?

It hurt.

Because she knew what that meant.

She had broken him. And he had just started putting the pieces back together.

Savannah swallowed past the lump in her throat. "What else did you guys talk about?"

Mallory hesitated. Like she was debating how much to tell her. But then she sighed, shaking her head. "Everything."

Savannah's jaw tightened. "Mallory—"

"He asked about you." Mallory admitted.

Savannah's breath hitched. Her world stilled. Those four words echoed in her head like a pulse. *He asked about you.* It had been a year. An entire fucking year. And he still asked about her?

Savannah's fingers tightened around the pillow, gripping it like it was the only thing keeping her grounded. "What did he say?"

Mallory hesitated again, then exhaled. "At first, he just asked how you were doing. If you were okay."

Savannah closed her eyes briefly, absorbing that.

But Mallory wasn't done. "And then he said—" Her voice softened. "'If it won't hurt her, tell her I said hey, and I hope she's doing good.'"

Savannah sucked in a sharp breath, her heart twisting in her chest. She hadn't realized how much she needed to hear that until now.

He wasn't bitter. He wasn't angry. He still cared. Savannah opened her mouth, but no words came out.

Mallory watched her carefully. "I swear, it was like I was playing 21 Questions."

Savannah let out a forced, half-smile. "What else did you ask him?"

Mallory, watching her carefully, continued. "Well, he's not dating anyone."

Savannah's eyes snapped up to hers, a flicker of something unreadable crossing her face. "What?"

Mallory smirked. "I asked him." Shrugging her shoulders.

Savannah's brows furrowed. "You asked him that?"

Mallory shrugged. "I may have phrased it as, 'Are you seeing anyone?' And, of course, in true Chase fashion, he gave me a vague-ass answer."

Savannah's pulse pounded. "Which was?"

Mallory grinned. "He said no."

Savannah's stomach flipped.

Mallory leaned in. "And then I said, 'Let me rephrase. I know you don't date, Montgomery.'"

Despite everything, Savannah let out a small breath of amusement.

Mallory continued, "He laughed. And then he said, 'Mal—not that it's your business, but...'" She hesitated.

"But what?" Savannah demanded.

Mallory exhaled. "He said that's not true. He just hasn't found his person. The person he wants to do life with."

Savannah inhaled sharply. Because she knew. She knew that he had found his person.

It was her.

He had told her. And she still walked away.

Mallory softened. "Sav, it's been a year. And he's still checking in on you."

Savannah looked away. "Is that all you guys talked about?"

Mallory hesitated again. Then—

"Oh, and one more thing."

Savannah lifted her head, pulse hammering. "What?"

Mallory inhaled deeply. "He's coming to Asheville next month."

Savannah's entire body locked up. Her stomach dropped. Her hands went cold.

"What?" she whispered, eyes wide in surprise mixed with panic.

"Work trip. He'll be in town. I may or may not have suggested we grab drinks."

Savannah's breath came fast. "Mallory—"

"Relax, I didn't set anything up. But, Sav..." Mallory's voice softened. "He's not over you. And if you're not over him either—" She tilted her head, watching her. "—maybe it's time to figure out what you want."

Savannah stared at her wine glass, pretending she wasn't already thinking about what it would be like to see him again.

Because maybe—

Maybe it was time.

48

Unspoken Loss

CHASE MONTGOMERY HAD LOST a lot in his life.

Lost games. Lost fights. Lost bets with his friends over the dumbest shit imaginable. Lost time chasing dreams that never quite took shape, hours slipping through his fingers like sand, leaving nothing behind but the weight of failure. Lost money on investments that seemed foolproof until they weren't. Lost sleep over decisions he couldn't take back. Lost parts of himself in the process, pieces chipped away by the relentless cycle of trying, failing, and forcing himself to keep going.

But none of it—none of it—came close to losing her.

Losing Savannah Monroe wasn't a single moment, wasn't a neatly contained tragedy with a beginning and an end. It wasn't just the night she stood on his porch, arms wrapped tightly around herself as if she was holding in all the things she couldn't say. It wasn't just the way her eyes shimmered in the porchlight, the way her voice wavered when she whispered words that shattered him. No, losing her was a slow, agonizing process, a cut that bled out over time, leaving him hollow long before she ever walked away. It was a wound that never quite healed, an ache that settled deep into his chest, constant and unrelenting.

Some days, he could almost fool himself into thinking he was okay. That he had moved on, that he had learned to live with the absence of her, with the spaces she used to fill. But then something small—a scent, a song, a laugh from across the room that sounded too much like hers—would unravel him all over again.

Now, he sat on the edge of the dock, elbows resting on his knees, fingers wrapped around a whiskey glass that he hadn't actually taken a sip from. The water stretched out before him, dark and endless, reflecting the fading light of the setting sun. It should have been calming. It used to be. The dock had always been his refuge—the one place where the world made sense, where the weight of everything could roll off his shoulders and disappear into the steady rhythm of the waves. But not anymore.

Now, it only reminded him of her.

Of the way she used to sit between his legs, back resting against his chest, her fingers tracing lazy patterns on his arms. Of the way she used to tilt her head back, letting the wind tangle in her hair, eyes closed, lips curling in quiet contentment. Of the way she used to laugh, that soft, unguarded sound that made him feel like maybe—just maybe—there was something good in this world meant just for him.

But she was gone.

And the dock was just wood and nails again.

The night was settling in now, the sky shifting from deep orange to navy, and the first hints of stars peeked through the darkness. The sound of crickets filled the silence, blending with the rhythmic lapping of water against the dock posts. He exhaled sharply, dragging a rough hand over the stubble on his jaw as if the motion could wipe away the thoughts that clung to him.

It had been a few days since Mallory called, and yet, her words still echoed in his mind. He hadn't expected it to matter. Hadn't expected her voice to stir up anything more than a mild irritation at hearing from someone who knew him too well. But it had been good to talk to her—better than he wanted to admit.

He had forgotten what it was like to have an easy conversation, to talk to someone who didn't need him to explain himself. Mallory had always been blunt, never one to dance around the truth, and maybe that was exactly what he needed. She didn't bullshit him. Didn't coddle him. And when she mentioned Savannah—when she said her name like it was just another name, like it wasn't a grenade tossed straight into his chest—he had asked about her before he could stop himself. The words slipped out, unintentional, instinctual.

And the second they left his mouth, he knew.

He still cared.

Still wanted to know if she was okay, if she was happy, if she had found whatever it was she had been looking for when she walked away. And for the first time in a long time, he let himself admit it—maybe, just maybe, he had been waiting for her to come back.

But she hadn't.

And she wouldn't.

Savannah Monroe had made her choice, and no matter how many times he replayed that night, no matter how many ways he tried to rewrite the past in his mind, the outcome never changed. She left. And he stayed. And that was that.

He was moving forward. That's what he told himself, anyway. But forward didn't mean forgetting. Not when every inch of this damn place was still tangled up with her memory. Not when his bed still smelled like her for weeks after she left. Not when he found strands of her hair in places they had no business being—woven into the fabric of his favorite hoodie, clinging to the bathroom tile, caught in the bristles of his damn toothbrush.

Not when he still caught himself scanning a crowded bar for her, knowing damn well she wouldn't be there.

Chase let out a slow breath, staring at the whiskey glass in his hand. The ice had melted, the liquor watered down and lifeless, but he wasn't drinking it anyway. He wasn't sure when the house had stopped feeling like home—maybe the second she walked out the door, maybe long before that. Without her, it was just walls and floors and furniture, just echoes of what used to be.

Which was why he was selling it.

The realtor was coming next week to take photos. Soon, someone else would live here, someone else would sit on this dock and make new memories, rewriting the ones he had been holding onto for too damn long. And maybe that was a good thing. Maybe it was time.

Pushing himself to his feet, he pocketed his phone and stepped inside. He moved through the house on autopilot, past the couch where she used to curl up with a book, past the kitchen where she used to steal sips of his coffee before making her own. He stopped in the bedroom doorway, staring at the empty bed, at the hollow space where she used to be.

Then, he turned.

Walked to the desk.

Grabbed a sheet of paper.

Picked up a pen.

The dock was quieter when he stepped back outside, the world slipping into the hush of night, the water smooth as glass beneath the moonlight. He sank into the chair, stretched his legs out in front of him, and stared out at the horizon.

And then—he started to write.

Not a text. Not an email. Not something easy, something he could delete before he ever had to send it.

No, this was real.

A letter.

Something she would never see. Something she would never read.

But he wrote it anyway.

Because even after all this time—after all the silence, after all the nights spent trying to forget—

She was still the only person he wanted to talk to.

Dear Savannah,

I don't know why I'm writing this. Maybe because it's easier than saying it out loud. Maybe because putting it down on paper makes it feel less like a confession and more like a release. Or maybe—

49

Written Regret

IT HAD BEEN NEARLY a month since Mallory told Savannah she had spoken to Chase. Since she had told her everything—the house, the fact that he wasn't dating, that he was thinking of selling, that he was coming to Asheville.

A month, and yet, the conversation still played in Savannah's head like a broken record.

She had done her best to push it aside, to move on like she told herself she was supposed to. But no matter how much she tried, his name still lingered in the air around her. His presence still wrapped itself around her like an old, familiar sweater she couldn't bring herself to take off.

Now, standing at her mailbox, a new weight settled in her chest.

She had just gotten back from lunch with Mallory, her stomach still full from too many fries and a milkshake she barely finished. It had been a good day. A light one. One where Chase wasn't at the forefront of her mind, at least for a little while.

But then—this.

Savannah sorted through the stack of mail absentmindedly as she walked toward her front door. A magazine, junk mail, a water bill—typical things she barely paid attention to. But then her fingers brushed over something different.

A handwritten envelope.

Her steps faltered.

The weight of the paper felt heavier than it should have. Her name was written across the front in a familiar, slanted scrawl. Her breath caught.

She turned it over, her fingers shaking, her pulse hammering in her ears as her gaze landed on the return address.

Chase Montgomery
124 Whispering Echoes Drive

Savannah sucked in a sharp breath, gripping the envelope tighter. The world around her blurred.

"Sav?" Mallory's voice barely registered as Savannah stepped inside, shutting the door behind her as if that alone could steady her.

She walked in a daze, straight to the couch, sinking down without a word. The envelope sat in her lap, heavy, haunting.

Mallory kicked off her shoes and glanced over, noticing the way Savannah was just sitting there, staring at it like it might disappear if she blinked.

"What is that?" Mallory asked cautiously, setting her purse down.

Savannah swallowed hard, not looking up. "It's from him."

Mallory went still. "Chase?"

Savannah gave the smallest nod. Her fingers traced the edge of the envelope, the rough ridges where it had been sealed.

Neither of them spoke.

The only sound in the room was the quiet hum of the air conditioning, the rhythmic ticking of the clock on the wall.

Mallory shifted closer. "What does it say?"

Savannah exhaled sharply, shaking her head. "I—I haven't opened it yet."

Mallory hesitated. "Do you want to?"

Savannah didn't know the answer to that.

She should have been prepared for this. Chase was coming to Asheville. She had known that. Had spent days debating whether she would see him, whether she would avoid him entirely.

But this?

This was unexpected.

This was terrifying.

Because Chase didn't write letters.

Not unless he had something to say.

Savannah closed her eyes for a moment, inhaling deeply before finally sliding her thumb under the flap, breaking the seal.

Her fingers trembled as she pulled out the folded page.

She hesitated once more, her breath catching, her heartbeat an unsteady rhythm in her chest.

Then, finally—

She read.

Dear Savannah,

I don't know why I'm writing this. Maybe because it's easier than saying it out loud. Maybe because putting it down on paper makes it feel less like a confession and more like a release. Or maybe—maybe because some words are meant to be written, not spoken. Because if I said them out loud, I don't think I'd ever stop.

I don't expect you to read this. Hell, I don't even know if I'll send it. But I need to get this out, even if it never reaches you.

It's been a year. A year of silence. A year of trying to convince myself that I'm fine. That you're fine. A year since you walked away, since I stood on that dock and let you go. A year since I swallowed every instinct screaming at me to fight, to beg, to do whatever it took to make you stay.

But I didn't.

I told myself I wouldn't be that guy—the one who clings to something that isn't his to hold. The one who makes it harder than it already was. And yet, here I am, writing a letter to a woman who isn't mine anymore.

I guess some things never change.

Mallory said you're doing okay. That you're finding your way. I don't know if that's true or if she was just trying to soften the edges of something that still cuts too deep. But I hope it is. God, I hope it is. I hope you've found whatever you were looking for when you left. I hope the restless ache in your chest isn't as heavy as it used to be. I hope that, wherever you are, you feel lighter. Freer.

And I hope—deep down—that you still think of me sometimes, too.

I hope you look back on those two weeks we had and smile. I hope you remember the way we laughed until we couldn't breathe, until our stomachs hurt and our faces ached, until the whole world outside of us didn't seem to exist. I hope you remember the stupid games we played in the truck, how you cheated at twenty-one questions and still lost. I hope you remember how you tried to beat me at pool and failed spectacularly, then made me promise never to bring it up again.

I hope you remember the way we sat on that dock, the way the water reflected the stars, the way the air smelled like salt and summer, the way you leaned into me like you never wanted to be anywhere else.

I hope you remember the night at Low-Tide, and smile about the embarrassment of Jenna. And I hope you remember how I told you that, no matter what, I'd always be in your corner.

And more than anything? I hope you're happy.

I wish I could tell you that I have been. That I woke up one morning and suddenly, *everything made sense again. That I stopped hearing your laugh in every damn song, stopped catching the faintest trace of you in my truck, stopped rolling over in bed, half-asleep, reaching for you like some fool who forgot that the love of his life walked out the door.*

But you and I both know I've never been good at lying.

I've gone out, if that's what you're wondering. I've been to Low-Tide, seen the same faces, danced with a few new ones. Women have tried to get my attention. Some of them probably should have.

But none of them have.

Because none of them are you.

And that's not me holding onto something that's already gone. That's just the truth.

The house isn't the same without you. It's just walls and floors and a roof now. Just a place where I sleep but never really rest. A place that used to feel like home, but now? Now it just feels like a reminder. A weight pressing in from all sides. So I'm selling it.

The realtor comes next week to take photos. Soon, someone else will live here. Someone else will stand on that dock and watch the sunrise. Someone else will fill this space with new laughter, with new memories, with something that isn't the ghost of us.

Maybe that's what needs to happen. Maybe I need to let this place go so I can finally let you go.

But before I do, I needed to say this.

I never called you—not because I didn't want to, but because I knew if I did, I wouldn't be able to stop. I wouldn't be able to hear your voice and pretend like we're just two people catching up. I wouldn't be able to ask how you're doing without wanting to get in my truck and drive straight to Asheville. I wouldn't be able to hear you say my name without wanting to pull you back into my arms and tell you that leaving was a mistake.

And I know that's not fair.

So I stayed quiet.

I told myself that if you ever wanted to come back, you would.

But you didn't.

And maybe that's the answer I've been looking for.

So this is me, finally saying the words I should have said that night, standing on that dock, watching you go.

I love you, Savannah. I never stopped.

But I think it's time I finally try.

It's time I stop just moving forward and actually move on.

No matter where life takes us, no matter who we become, no matter what paths we walk from here—there will always be the Echoes of Us.

Take care of yourself, Monroe.

-Chase Montgomery

Savannah read the last line over and over again, her breath coming in short, uneven gasps.

Take care of yourself, Monroe.

Her hands shook, gripping the paper so tightly it crinkled beneath her finger-tips, but she couldn't loosen her grip. Couldn't let go. Her vision blurred, tears welling and spilling down her cheeks in rapid succession, hot and unrelenting, like they had been waiting—aching—for permission to fall. Her heart, already splintered from a year of regret, cracked straight down the middle.

This wasn't just a letter.

This was goodbye.

The realization hit her like a punch to the gut, knocking the air from her lungs. She pressed her trembling fingers to her lips, but it did nothing to stop the sob clawing its way up her throat.

Somewhere in the background, she could hear Mallory calling her name, but it sounded far away, muted, like she was underwater. Like the weight of Chase's words had dragged her beneath the surface, leaving her gasping for air, fighting against a current too strong to escape.

He loved her. He never stopped.

And now?—

Now he was done.

A strangled sound tore from her lips, a sob so raw it felt like it had been buried inside her chest for months, waiting for this exact moment to break free.

Mallory was there in an instant, dropping onto the couch beside her, wrapping steady, grounding hands around Savannah's shaking shoulders.

"Savy," she whispered, her voice laced with concern. "Talk to me."

Savannah couldn't.

Couldn't find the words.

Couldn't breathe past the crushing weight in her chest, the unbearable truth suffocating her from the inside out.

Chase had waited. For an entire year, he had held on, hoping she would come back. Hoping she would give them another chance. And now, after twelve months of silence, after twelve months of forcing himself to move forward—

He was letting go.

She sucked in a shaky breath, her fingers curling tighter around the letter, as if she could somehow pull him back through the ink on the page. As if holding onto these words meant she could hold onto him.

But it didn't. She had already lost him.

"Savy," Mallory tried again, her voice gentle but firm. "What did he say?"

Savannah swallowed hard, her throat burning, her mind screaming at her to answer. But when she finally spoke, her voice was nothing more than a whisper, fragile and broken.

"He's selling the house."

Mallory stilled. "What?"

Savannah blinked rapidly as fresh tears blurred her vision, her lips trembling around the words she could barely force out. "He said—he's finally moving on." She swallowed against the ache lodged in her throat, shaking her head in disbelief. "The realtor is coming next week. Someone else is going to live there."

Mallory let out a slow, quiet exhale, her grip on Savannah's arm tightening like she was trying to anchor her. "Oh, Sav."

Savannah let out a breathless, broken laugh, swiping at her wet cheeks with the sleeve of her sweatshirt. "I should be happy for him, right?" she choked out. "That's what I'm supposed to feel?"

Mallory didn't answer. Because they both knew the truth. Savannah wasn't happy. She was gutted. She had spent an entire year convincing herself that Chase was fine. That he had moved on, that he was living his life without her the way she had convinced herself she needed to live without him. She had told herself that his silence meant he was okay.

That it meant he had let go. But that wasn't why he never called. Her breath hitched as the truth—the real truth—sank into her bones, carving through every defense she had built.

"He never called," she whispered, her fingers running over the slanted letters of his name on the page. "Not once. And I told myself that meant he was fine. That he was moving on."

Mallory swallowed hard. "He never called because he was waiting for you."

Savannah's breath caught. The words slammed into her, sharp and unrelenting, cutting deeper than she thought possible. Because that was the part that wrecked her the most.

Chase waited.

He had held on, thinking that if he reached out, she would run. That if he pushed, she would pull away. So he had done the one thing that went against every instinct in his body—He let her go.

And now, he was done waiting.

A sob ripped through her chest, her body curling forward as she tried—failed—to hold herself together.

Mallory's hands rubbed slow, soothing circles over her back, grounding her, keeping her from unraveling completely. She didn't say anything. Didn't try to fill the silence. She just let Savannah break. Let her feel every ounce of the heartbreak she had spent an entire year trying to bury.

It felt endless. Like she would never stop drowning in the weight of her own choices. But eventually, the sobs quieted. The air around her felt a little less suffocating. And after what felt like forever, Savannah finally lifted her head.

Her eyes, swollen and red-rimmed, met Mallory's.

And then—Her voice cracked.

"What kind of man waits, Mallory?"

Mallory blinked, lips parting, but Savannah wasn't done.

"What kind of man holds on this long?" Her voice wavered, thick with grief, with disbelief, with something she couldn't name. Another tear slipped down her cheek, her throat working against the emotion clogging it. "What kind of man has that much love inside him that he has to give up everything to finally let go?"

Silence stretched between them, thick and suffocating.

And then—

Savannah's face crumpled. "I fucked up, Mal."

Mallory exhaled sharply, shaking her head. "Yeah, babe. You did."

Savannah let out a breathless, humorless laugh, swiping at her wet cheeks again. "You're supposed to lie to me."

Mallory huffed. "You don't need me to lie. You need me to tell you the truth. And the truth is, you had something real. Something most people never get in their entire damn lifetime."

Savannah let her head fall back against the couch, staring up at the ceiling as another tear slipped down the side of her face.

"I was scared," she admitted, voice barely above a whisper.

Mallory sighed. "I know, sweetie."

Savannah closed her eyes, inhaling deeply, letting the weight of everything settle over her like a thick, inescapable fog. She had spent an entire year trying to outrun the truth. Trying to convince herself that leaving was the right choice. But Chase's letter had obliterated every single excuse she had clung to.

Because now?

Now, he was the one walking away.

And she had no one to blame but herself.

50

Love Language

SAVANNAH SPENT DAYS REREADING the letter.

Over and over, dissecting every word, as if somewhere between the ink and the paper, she could find an answer she didn't already know. As if, by some miracle, a hidden message would reveal itself, something—anything—that would change what she knew to be true.

But no matter how many times she read it, the conclusion was always the same.

She had never let him go.

She had ran.

That was the truth she had been hiding from for an entire year. The truth she had twisted and reshaped until it resembled something else, something easier to swallow. She had told herself that leaving was the right thing to do, that she had been saving herself from the inevitable heartbreak. That if she walked away first, if she severed the ties before they could tighten around her, she would be free.

But all she had done was bring the heartbreak forward. She had detonated the bomb before it even had the chance to go off.

And now? Now, she was the one left in the wreckage.

While Chase had moved forward.

She barely slept. She barely ate. Her apartment had become a maze she wandered endlessly, drifting from room to room like a ghost, haunted by memories she couldn't turn off. The way he used to look at her—like she was the only person in the world, like nothing else existed outside of her. The way his voice softened when he said her name, that slight rasp that always made her stomach tighten. The way he always tucked a strand of hair behind her ear, small and effortless but impossibly intimate, like touching her was second nature.

Like she belonged to him.

She had spent a year convincing herself she made the right choice. That she was healing. That time had dulled the edges of what they had.

But the truth?

She wasn't living. She wasn't healing. She was just—existing.

And then, just when she thought she had suffered enough, Mallory shattered the last fragile piece of her resolve.

"He has a meeting tomorrow," Mallory had said carefully, too carefully, like she knew exactly what she was doing. "But he's free after. He asked if I wanted to grab a drink and catch up."

Savannah's stomach twisted, nausea climbing up her throat so fast she had to grip the counter to steady herself. She had been debating ever since.

Should she go? Should she ask Mallory to trade places with her? Should she reach out? Should she—for once in her damn life—fight?

Or was it too late?

Was this letter just a farewell? One last piece of him before he finally, finally, closed the door for good?

Her mind was a battlefield of hope and fear, of what-ifs and should-haves, of maybes and never-agains.

Mallory hadn't invited her. Not because she didn't want her there. But because she knew. She knew Savannah would crumble.

She knew that seeing Chase—really seeing him, standing in front of her after all this time—would wreck her.

And now, as Savannah leaned against the fridge, arms crossed tightly over her chest, trying to keep herself together while the storm raged inside her, Mallory scrolled on her phone like she hadn't just dropped a bomb on her best friend's entire world.

Savannah exhaled sharply, trying not to spiral. Trying to breathe past the suffocating pressure in her chest—Say something. Her fingers curled around the fridge handle, nails biting into the cool metal.

"So," she forced out, her voice too even, too controlled, "where are you guys going?"

Mallory hummed, still scrolling, too casual. "Not sure yet. Maybe The Hollow. Maybe some place near his hotel."

The Hollow.

Savannah's stomach twisted violently.

The Hollow wasn't just any bar. It was the bar. The one in downtown Asheville that felt like a second home to some and a world away to others. It was weird, but in the best way—the kind of weird that made it feel alive. The warm glow of the lights softened the edges of the night, and the music—just right—filled the space without drowning out conversation.

It was the kind of place where time slowed down, where the clink of glasses and the low hum of chatter wove together like an unspoken rhythm. A place where artists, wanderers, and nine-to-fivers all coexisted in the same dimly lit booths, their lives momentarily overlapping. The décor was an eclectic mix of old and new, a little too mismatched to be intentional but somehow perfect. The drinks were strong, the stories stronger, and the regulars? Well, they were the kind of characters you couldn't make up.

The Hollow wasn't just in Asheville—it was Asheville. Strange, inviting, unforgettable.

And Chase was going there—With Mallory.

Savannah's grip tightened around the fridge handle, white-knuckled, her breath coming faster now.

She was about to say something—anything—to change the subject, to push this unbearable weight off her chest, when Mallory suddenly sucked in a sharp breath.

Savannah's heart stopped.

Mallory's eyes widened as she stared at her phone, something flickering across her face—something unreadable, something new.

Something that changed everything.

"Holy shit."

Savannah snapped to attention, her heart already hammering at the way Mallory's voice had gone tight, breathless.

Not good.

"What?"

Mallory didn't answer right away. Her brows furrowed, her expression unreadable as she stared at her phone like it had just betrayed her. Then, slowly, she turned the screen toward Savannah—"Look."

Savannah hesitated, pulse spiking, the air thick with something she didn't understand. But the second her eyes landed on the words, her lungs stopped working. Her heart slammed against her ribs.

Whispering Echoes on the Sound – A Legacy, now on the Market.

Her throat went dry as she snatched the phone from Mallory. Her fingers tightened around the phone as she scrolled, vision blurring at the sight of it.

The house.

His house.

The dock. The stairs. The kitchen.

Their kitchen.

Mallory exhaled beside her. "Wow. He really did some upgrades."

But Savannah wasn't listening. As her gaze scanned each image, the familiar and unfamiliar blended together in a cruel, perfect contradiction—like something sacred had been touched, reshaped. It was still Chase's house, but somehow, it wasn't. The kitchen had new cabinets, fresh paint. The living room looked brighter, the old furniture replaced, everything warm and polished, inviting but foreign. It was still him, but also not.

She kept scrolling, searching for something—anything—that still felt like him.

And then, she saw it.

Her breath caught.

"Oh my God." She exclaimed. Panic bloomed in her chest, spreading like wildfire.

Mallory jumped off the counter, alarmed. "What? What is it?"

Savannah froze, thumb hovering over the screen as her pulse roared in her ears.

"No."—"No, no, no." She repeated. Savannah could barely think, barely breathe, as she held up the phone with trembling fingers.

The guest bedroom on the first floor. Only—it wasn't a guest bedroom anymore.

The walls had been painted a soft, light gray with crisp white trim. The built-in shelves had been refinished and expanded—the same ones she had once imagined filling with stories.

But there were more now. Floor-to-ceiling shelves lined the walls, filled with books, some new, some worn from the touch of countless hands.

And the bay window?—A reading nook now.

Cushions, pillows, the perfect spot to get lost in a book.

It was beautiful.

It was exactly how she had pictured it.

But that wasn't what stole her breath.

No.

One detail shattered her. One detail sent every carefully constructed wall she had built around herself crumbling to the ground.

Centered on one of the shelves, nestled between the books, was an empty space.

And in that space, written in elegant, familiar script, was a single quote:

Books are my love language.

Savannah broke.

A strangled sob ripped from her chest as she slapped a hand over her mouth, body jolting forward from the sheer force of it.

Mallory stilled. She didn't know. She didn't understand.

Savannah's fingers curled around the phone, knuckles white, tears flooding her vision, drowning her in the weight of it.

She shook her head, voice shaking, breathless. "When we went on our getting lost trip—"

Mallory didn't move, but her eyes flickered with something fragile, something soft and knowing.

Savannah swallowed, her throat thick with emotion. "We found this old bookstore. It was beautiful. Chase just stood there, watching me, smiling like a fool as I went through hundreds of books."

Mallory inhaled sharply.

Savannah let out a shaky, breathless laugh, one that sounded nothing like joy. "I told him—" She wiped at her cheeks, but the tears wouldn't stop. "I told him his guest bedroom would make the perfect library. I told him to get built-in shelves. A nook under the bay window."

Her voice broke—"I told him that books were my love language."

Mallory gasped, "Oh my God." Her own eyes glossing over now.

Savannah pressed the phone to her chest, clutching it like it was the only thing keeping her from collapsing.

"Mallory," her voice fractured, barely above a whisper. "He did this for me."

Mallory let out a shaky breath, her voice thick, "Sav—he did this for you. After you left. After you shattered him."

Savannah covered her mouth with her hand, trying—failing—to keep the sobs at bay. But it was useless.

The weight of it crashed down on her.

The love he had poured into something she thought she had walked away from. The pieces of her that still lived in him, even after everything.

She had been running for so long.

And Chase?—

Chase had never stopped loving her.

Savannah sucked in a breath so sharp it physically hurt.

And then?

Then she sobbed. Because this?

This was love.

The kind of love that doesn't fade, doesn't waver, doesn't move on just because someone walks away. The kind of love that stays etched in the foundation of a home, waiting, hoping, even when it knows it shouldn't. The kind of love that builds bookshelves, paints walls, and leaves space—empty but expectant—knowing exactly who it was made for.

This was Chase.

Mallory sniffed, wiping a tear from her own cheek.

"That is the perfect man."

Savannah shook her head, her body trembling, her soul unraveling.

"And I let him go."

Mallory placed a firm hand on her shoulder, grounding her.

"Then don't."

Savannah's head snapped up. "What?"

"Don't let him go, Sav. You want to see him? Then see him. You want to talk to him? Then talk to him."

Savannah wiped at her face, exhaling shakily. "How? I can't just show up. What if he—"

Mallory cut her off, voice fierce, unwavering.

"We form a plan."

Savannah stared at her, uncertainty and hope waging war inside her.

"A plan?"

Mallory nodded.

"He's in Asheville. We know where he's staying. He told me he's free tomorrow night.

We make this happen. No more excuses. No more running."

Savannah hesitated for only a second longer before nodding.

"Okay."

She exhaled, resolve settling deep in her bones.

"Let's do it."

51

Planned Chaos

The Plan

SAVANNAH PACED THE LIVING room like a woman preparing for battle.

Mallory, meanwhile, was thriving—sitting cross-legged on the couch, laptop open, radiating the kind of unshakable confidence that only someone with absolutely nothing to lose could possess.

"Alright," Mallory announced, typing furiously. "We need a strategy. A solid, foolproof plan. We know Chase is in Asheville. We know he's free tomorrow night. And we know he has no idea you're about to waltz in and throw an emotional grenade at his life. So, we have to make this count."

Savannah stopped mid-pace, dragging a hand through her hair. "What if he doesn't want to see me? What if this just—hurts him all over again?"

Mallory didn't even look up. "Sav, I love you, but if you start spiraling, I will duct-tape your mouth shut and carry you to this bar myself."

Savannah blinked. "You don't have that kind of upper body strength."

Mallory arched an eyebrow. "Try me."

Savannah let out a strangled laugh, but Mallory pressed on, eyes gleaming with a mix of determination and unhinged enthusiasm.

"You want to see him. You need to see him. And we're making it happen."

Savannah exhaled, nodding. "Okay. What's the plan?"

Mallory spun the laptop around with a flourish, revealing a website with sleek black-and-white photos of Chase's hotel—a boutique spot in downtown Asheville that screamed classy but in a way that makes you wonder if the coffee costs $9.

"He's staying here. Fifteen-minute walk from The Hollow. And before you even think about pulling a mysterious hotel lobby run-in, I am begging you to have some dignity."

Savannah crossed her arms. "So what's your genius plan?"

Mallory's smirk was the stuff of legend.

"He's meeting me at The Hollow. He's never been there before, which means he'll be completely out of his element. That's where you come in."

Savannah narrowed her eyes. "Define 'out of his element.'"

Mallory's grin widened.

"Oh, you're gonna love this. This bar is... weird. And I mean weird. The regulars function like a chaotic little cult. The bartender, Gus, is convinced he can read your entire romantic history based on your drink order—he once told me I was 'destined for a love triangle, but only if I stopped ignoring my chiropractor's texts.'"

Savannah's lips twitched. "That's—unsettlingly specific."

"There's also Earl."

"—Who?" Savannah asked in confusion.

"Earl—A mysterious, elderly man who challenges every new male visitor to a round of darts. But here's the kicker—he only speaks in riddles."

Savannah groaned. "Oh my God."

Mallory held up a finger. "And the jukebox is cursed."

Savannah blinked. "Excuse me?"

"You don't pick the song. The jukebox chooses for you. And it has an unreal ability to expose your emotional state. One time I went in after a breakup and it immediately blasted 'It's Too Late' by Carole King. People applauded."

Savannah stared. "This sounds like an actual nightmare."

Mallory clapped her hands together. "Exactly. And when Chase inevitably looks like a lost puppy in the middle of all this chaos, you just happen to be there. Looking absolutely incredible. Offering to help him survive the madness."

Savannah let out a long, exhausted sigh, rubbing her temples.

"So, to summarize: you're throwing the man I love into a Twilight Zone-themed bar, hoping he panics, and my role is to be the sexy voice of reason?"

Mallory beamed. "Pretty much, yeah."

Savannah groaned, letting her head fall back. "And if he doesn't want to talk?"

Mallory shut the laptop, meeting Savannah's gaze dead-on, all humor gone.

"Then you walk away knowing you tried. But Sav... I don't think that's going to happen."

Savannah swallowed hard.

Because despite the absurdity of it all, despite the nerves eating away at her, despite the fear of what if—

Deep down, she already knew.

He still loved her.

And tomorrow night?

She was going to find out just how much.

Savannah squared her shoulders. "Alright."

Mallory grinned like a woman who had just engineered the world's most chaotic but effective romantic scheme.

"Now, go try on outfits. I refuse to let you have a Cinderella moment while wearing sad beige."

Savannah had spent the entire day in a state of slow, painful implosion.

It started that morning when she attempted to distract herself with coffee—a terrible mistake, in hindsight—and promptly forgot she had already filled her mug, sending a scalding tidal wave across the counter and onto her bare foot.

She screeched, nearly dropping the entire coffee pot in the process.

"Cool, love that for me," she muttered, hopping around the kitchen on one foot like an injured flamingo.

Then came her ill-fated attempt at being a functional adult.

She sat down at her desk, determined—determined, damn it—to focus. Emails. Spreadsheets. Anything but the existential panic currently screaming inside her brain.

Except when she went to search for a client's name in her inbox, her fingers betrayed her.

She stared at the search bar, horrified.

Chase Montgomery

"Oh, for the love of—Fuck—" She slammed the laptop shut like it had personally offended her.

By noon, she had officially abandoned all hopes of productivity and did the only thing she could think of—called Mallory, her personal agent of chaos, for emergency emotional support.

Mallory, bless her heart, was far too entertained by Savannah's breakdown.

"Okay, so what I'm hearing is that you're an absolute mess," Mallory said cheerfully over the phone, like she was discussing the weather and not Savannah's emotional collapse.

Savannah groaned, flopping onto her bed like a woman in distress. "I feel like I'm about to throw up and pass out at the same time. It's like my body is confused about whether I should be excited or terrified."

"Ah," Mallory mused. "Classic emotional whiplash. I've seen this before."

"Mallory, I cannot stress enough how NOT helpful you are right now."

Mallory chuckled. "Fine. I'll be serious. Take a deep breath. Eat something. Hydrate. And for the love of God, do not show up looking like a woman on the verge of a nervous breakdown. You need to radiate confidence."

Savannah huffed. "Confidence? I just tripped over my own pajama pants walking to the bathroom."

"Then maybe consider pants that don't try to assassinate you."

By 3 p.m., Savannah had stress-cleaned her entire apartment, gone on a walk to 'clear her head' (which accomplished nothing except making her look like a lunatic for muttering hypothetical conversations with Chase out loud), and tried on no fewer than eight different outfits.

None of them were right.

All of them screamed, I am having a full-blown emotional crisis.

So, at 6 p.m. sharp, Mallory arrived for damage control.

She plopped onto Savannah's bed like a judgmental fashion critic, laptop discarded, all business. "Alright. Show me what you've got."

Savannah grabbed the first outfit she had put together and did a slow, half-hearted spin. "This?"

Mallory grimaced. "Too corporate."

Savannah groaned, grabbing another option. "This?"

Mallory squinted. "Too 'I'm trying too hard.'"

Savannah threw up her hands. "I give up!" She said sarcastically.

Mallory let out a dramatic sigh and pushed herself up. "Move. Let the expert work."

After a flurry of activity—which included Mallory tossing half of Savannah's wardrobe onto the floor, muttering about how Savannah apparently had a hidden collection of tragic beige sweaters—the final result was in place.

Savannah stood in front of the mirror.

Fitted black top.

High-waisted jeans.

Casual. Effortlessly flattering. The kind of outfit that said, "Oh, I just threw this on," but actually took 45 minutes and a minor existential crisis to choose.

Mallory added a dainty necklace, a pair of ankle boots, and stepped back, smirking like a woman who had just solved a national emergency.

"There," she declared, satisfied. "Hot, but not too hot. Just hot enough to make him sweat."

Savannah swallowed, staring at herself, anxiety creeping in again. "What if he—"

"Nope." Mallory cut her off, holding up a hand like a traffic cop. "No spiraling. Get in the car before I drag you there myself."

7:15 p.m. | The Drive

Mallory drove like she was in a heist movie She wove through traffic with a level of aggression that was absolutely unnecessary, treating red lights as suggestions and lane markers as optional decor.

Savannah had been white-knuckling the door handle since they left her apartment, her body bracing for impact at every turn.

"Are you trying to kill us before I even get to see him?" she snapped as Mallory took a sharp left with zero warning, nearly launching Savannah into the passenger-side door.

"We're fine." Mallory said as she waved a dismissive hand, keeping one on the wheel like the reckless menace she was.

Savannah inhaled through her nose, trying not to scream. "I swear to God, if I die in this car before I even get to emotionally humiliate myself in front of Chase, I'm haunting you."

Mallory snorted. "Relax. I just need to get you there before you freak out and do something dramatic, like—oh, I don't know—text him instead."

Savannah froze, her grip tightening on her lap. "— wasn't going to text him."

Mallory's side-eye was immediate.

Savannah let out a heavy sigh, slumping in her seat. "Okay. I thought about texting him."

"Exactly." Mallory shot her a pointed look, eyes still laser-focused on the road like a woman on a high-stakes mission. "That's why I'm treating this like a hostage situation. You are not allowed to tip him off. No warning. No preemptive panic-texts. No last-minute exits. You are going in there, face-to-face, like a fully functional adult who just happens to be a little bit emotionally unstable."

Savannah stared out the window, the Asheville skyline looming closer, the familiar neon glow of The Hollow flickering in the distance.

Her stomach twisted.

"This is insane," she whispered, more to herself than anyone else.

Mallory reached over and patted her thigh reassuringly—a rare moment of gentle support amidst her usual chaos.

"Yeah, but it's our kind of insane."

Savannah let out a shaky exhale, the weight of the moment pressing hard against her ribs.

Because this was really happening.

For an entire year, she had avoided this exact moment, telling herself it was better this way—that distance was necessary, that time would dull the ache, that she could move forward without looking back.

But then Chase had written her that letter.

Then she had seen the library.

And suddenly, every excuse, every carefully constructed barrier she had put in place shattered.

She hadn't let go.

And neither had he.

Mallory swerved into a parking spot, cutting the engine without hesitation.

Savannah just... sat there.

Heart hammering.

Mouth dry.

Every possible worst-case scenario flashing through her head like a reel of disasters waiting to unfold.

What if he didn't want to see her?

What if he had moved on?

What if showing up like this hurt him more than it fixed anything?

"Sav—" Mallory's voice was softer this time, her usual mischief replaced with something more serious.

Savannah turned to look at her, expecting another sarcastic remark, another over-the-top pep talk.

Instead, Mallory studied her carefully, her expression unreadable.

And then—

"You're not just doing this for closure, are you?"

Savannah felt her throat tighten. She could lie. She could pretend that this was just about getting answers, about finally putting the past to rest.

But she knew better.

And so did Mallory.

"No."

The word felt heavier than it should have, like admitting it made all of this more real.

Mallory nodded slowly, like she had already known the answer but needed Savannah to say it out loud.

"Good." She glanced toward the glowing sign of The Hollow, her fingers drumming lightly against the steering wheel. "Because neither is he."

Savannah inhaled sharply, gripping the door handle so tight her knuckles turned white.

Inside, Chase was waiting.

He just didn't know it yet.

52

Miscalculated

MALLORY HAD PLANNED FOR chaos.

Not total disaster, not a train wreck, not an emotional meltdown of epic proportions—just enough chaos to shake Savannah loose from her spiral and get her back in the same room with Chase. It had taken weeks of listening to her best friend overanalyze, dissect, and ultimately self-sabotage every thought about Chase Montgomery. Weeks of witnessing Savannah build an entire mythology around the man, complete with tragic backstories and imagined regrets. Weeks of nodding along as Savannah convinced herself that the Chase she left behind was still nursing his wounds, stuck in the past, missing her the way she missed him.

So Mallory did what any rational, slightly meddlesome best friend would do—she manufactured the moment. She arranged the setting, nudged the right people, laid the groundwork for an inevitable, albeit mildly controlled, reunion. A foolproof plan.

Or at least, it had been.

Because there was one glaring flaw in all of it.

Chase Fucking Montgomery.

She should have accounted for this. She should have known. The man had always had a gravitational pull, a way of shifting the energy of a room to revolve around him, but somehow, even knowing that, she had underestimated just how effortlessly he could command a space.

And tonight, at The Hollow, Chase wasn't just in his element—he was thriving.

Mallory sat at the bar, fingers curled around the base of her drink, watching in a mix of horror and reluctant admiration as Chase did exactly what he had always done: walked into a room and owned it.

She had thought The Hollow might shake him, just a little. That the bar's unique brand of organized chaos—the neon lights buzzing just a touch too bright, the scent of old wood and spilled whiskey, the unpredictable crowd of regulars ranging from hipsters to bikers to maybe-sorcerers—would throw him off.

Instead, it was the opposite.

The Hollow didn't swallow Chase whole. It elevated him.

She watched as Gus, the all-knowing bartender, took one long, scrutinizing look at Chase when he ordered bourbon and attempted to dissect him, as he did with every new face that crossed the threshold.

"Alright, stranger," Gus said, rubbing his beard. "Let's try this again. You ordered bourbon. So that means—strong exterior. Carries old wounds. Little broody. Probably—"

Chase took a slow sip, tilting his head with lazy amusement. "Go on."

Gus narrowed his eyes. "Wait. No. You're—comfortable in it. You're not running from anything. You carry it, but you don't let it weigh you down."

Mallory almost choked on her drink. "Oh, shit." Gus was second-guessing himself. Gus never second-guessed himself.

Chase gave a slow, knowing grin, the kind that made it clear he was enjoying every second of the analysis. "Having a hard time with this one?"

Gus scowled. "Don't get cocky, son. I'm recalibrating."

But Chase just chuckled, shaking his head, and damn it, Mallory had to admit—he was stupidly attractive.

Savannah had spent months picturing a man wrecked by heartbreak, weighed down by regret, still mourning the way things had ended.

But this Chase?

This Chase was thriving.

His black button-up was fitted but effortless, sleeves rolled up just enough to reveal tattoos that were both intricate and devastatingly attractive. His jeans were worn in the way only well-loved denim could be, and his boots carried the scuffs of a man who actually used them for something other than aesthetics. The ball cap was pulled low enough to add an extra layer of mystery to his already ridiculous blue eyes, catching the dim bar lighting in ways that were downright unfair.

And worst of all?

He was fun.

Earl—the local cryptid, as the regulars affectionately referred to him—had already set his sights on Chase, issuing a challenge in the form of a cryptic riddle:

"The traveler seeks, but what he finds is written in the air. Take the aim, loose the flight, and tell me what is fair."

Mallory had barely finished rolling her eyes before Chase grinned, threw back the rest of his bourbon, and said, "Alright, Earl. Let's do this."

And just like that, Chase had won over The Hollow.

Earl was cackling between throws, Gus was refilling Chase's drink like he was some kind of honored guest, and even the usual barflies had stopped mid-conversation, drawn to the effortless charisma Chase exuded.

Mallory had to admit—she was impressed.

The man was seamless. He adapted, fit himself into the unpredictable energy of the bar like he had always belonged here. Where most outsiders would have stumbled, he moved with precision.

Earl fired off another riddle mid-game.

"What is strong but bends, light yet heavy, speaks yet makes no sound?"

Without hesitation, Chase threw his dart, nailed a bullseye, and deadpanned, "A book."

Earl howled with laughter. "A good answer! A clever man!"

Gus leaned over the counter, shaking his head. "This son of a bitch might actually belong here."

And Mallory?

Mallory was having too much fun.

Savannah had been so sure this place would throw Chase off his game, shake him, rattle him, maybe even humble him a little.

Instead, Chase became the game.

The Hollow wasn't a test for Chase. It was a stage. And he was absolutely owning it.

Mallory sat at the bar, drink in hand, amused and—against her better judgment—impressed.

And then—The Song Came On.

A familiar melody hummed through the bar, something low and smooth, the kind of song that made people want to move before they even realized it.

Mallory barely noticed at first. But then—

She saw it.

Chase froze.

Not in a bad way. Not like he was thrown off his game. But like something deep inside him recognized it. Like it unlocked a memory of some younger version of himself, probably standing in a crowded house party, beer in hand, dancing like he owned the place.

And then—he turned to her.

Slow. Purposeful. His bourbon still in hand, his smirk just a little softer now, just a little too knowing.

And then he held out his hand. "Dance with me."

Mallory blinked. Then let out a sharp laugh. "Excuse me?"

Chase cocked his head, waiting, damn near amused by her reaction. "You heard me."

She narrowed her eyes. "Do I look like the type of woman who gets up and slow dances in a bar?"

Chase shrugged. "You look like the type of woman who pretends that she's above it but actually loves it."

Mallory snorted. "Bold assumption."

He grinned. "Prove me wrong."

Damn it—She should say no. She should roll her eyes and tell him to take his charm elsewhere. But instead—she put her hand in his.

And just like that, Chase pulled her in effortlessly. And Mallory felt it immediately. His hand settled against her lower back, firm, warm, effortless, guiding her like he'd done this a hundred times before. It wasn't flashy. It wasn't one of those showy spins or exaggerated dips. It was just easy.

That was the fucking problem with Chase Montgomery—He made it look easy. Made it feel like something that you wanted to sink into.

Mallory exhaled slowly, forcing herself to focus on the moment and not the fact that he smelled ridiculously good.

She looked up at him. "Alright, points for confidence. But is this just part of the Chase Montgomery experience? Winning over bartenders, old men with riddles, and now charming unsuspecting women into dancing?"

Chase's thumb brushed the back of her hand absently, like he didn't even realize he was doing it. "First of all, I don't need to win over anyone. It just happens. Second of all, I don't just dance with anyone. You should feel special."

Mallory smirked. "Oh, should I?" She teasesd.

Chase spun her once, smooth as hell, then pulled her back against him. "Yeah. You should."

She barely caught herself from reacting—from letting out that breath she hadn't realized she was holding.

Damn him. Damn this.

She narrowed her eyes. "You're enjoying this way too much."

Chase grinned, low and lazy. "I really am."

Mallory shook her head, trying to regain some ground. "You know, I expected you to be a little more cocky about all of this."

Chase hummed. "That's the mistake people make. They assume I need to be cocky." His fingers flexed slightly against her back, a subtle movement, barely there, but she noticed it.

And now she was in trouble. Because, dammit, she got it now. She heard the stories. She understood why people talked about him the way they did. Because Chase wasn't about being the loudest guy in the room. He was about making you feel like you were the only one there.

And it fucking worked. Too fucking well.

The song began to fade, but Chase didn't move right away. He didn't let go. Not until Mallory finally exhaled, shaking her head with a smirk.

"Okay, Montgomery. I get it now." She said.

Chase laughed, slow and satisfied. "Took you long enough."

Mallory patted his chest, stepping back before she did something ridiculous, like admit this had been way too much fun. "Not bad, cowboy."

Chase took a slow sip of his bourbon, watching her with that same damnable ease.

She reached for her phone and asked if they could take a picture.

Chase laughed, but he didn't hesitate. He shifted closer, angling himself toward her as Mallory lifted her phone. The camera snapped, capturing him in all his heart-stopping, unfairly attractive glory.

The black button-up. Sleeves rolled, tattoos on full display. Worn jeans, perfectly broken in. Boots. Ball cap pulled low—just enough to cast shadows over those stupid, stupidly blue eyes.

Mallory barely resisted fanning herself. She pulled up Savannah's text thread and fired off a message.

Mallory: I'll let you know when to come in.

Mallory: And holy shit, he is looking so fucking fine.

She attached the picture and hit send.

A second later, three little dots appeared. Then disappeared. Then reappeared. Mallory grinned.

Savannah was losing her damn mind.

And honestly?

Fair.

53

Reckoning Echoes

SAVANNAH SAT IN HER car, gripping the steering wheel like it was the only thing keeping her from floating into the abyss. She had spent the last thirty minutes alternating between deep breathing exercises, cursing Mallory for convincing her to do this, and internally rehearsing exactly what she would say to Chase.

And then her phone vibrated. She didn't even have to check the name.

Mallory: I'll let you know when to come in.

Mallory: And holy shit, he is looking so fucking fine.

A second later, a picture popped up.

Savannah barely had time to process before her entire soul left her body.

Chase—Standing next to Mallory, looking unfairly, illegally good.

The black button-up stretched just right across his broad shoulders, the sleeves rolled up, showcasing those strong forearms and tattoos she had once traced with her fingers. Worn jeans that fit too well, just distressed enough to be effortlessly attractive. And the boots—because of course, Chase was still a boots guy.

But it was the hat that did her in.

A simple, old baseball cap, pulled low enough that his ocean-blue eyes glowed beneath the dim bar lighting.

Savannah stared at the picture, mouth slightly open, brain short-circuiting.

And then, without thinking, she did the dumbest thing possible.

She zoomed in. Why did she zoom in?!

Mallory's text bubble popped up again.

Mallory: Sav? You still breathing?

No. No, she was not.

She scrambled to type back, her fingers betraying her at every turn.

Savannah: This was a mistake.

Savannah: I cannot physically handle this.

Savannah: Mallory, I will pass away.

Mallory: lol.

Mallory: Listen, babe, if you don't get your ass in here, I might just keep him for myself.

Savannah gasped.

Savannah: You wouldn't dare.

Mallory: Try me.

Savannah groaned, letting her head fall back against the headrest.

This was so much worse than she had expected.

The plan was supposed to give her the upper hand. He was supposed to be out of his element, off balance. Instead, Chase was thriving. Gus and Earl loved him, Mallory was too comfortable, and now she was sitting here like a wreck because—

Because damn it, she wasn't over him.

Not even a little.

Her phone buzzed again.

Mallory: Savannah. Get in here. Now.

Savannah exhaled sharply.

This was it. Time to face him.

With one final, desperate pep talk "You will NOT die, you are a strong, confident woman, and if you panic, just order a shot and pray"—as she threw open the car door.

Her legs felt like jelly as she crossed the street, her pulse a chaotic drumbeat against her ribs.

Savannah stepped inside The Hollow, her pulse a frantic drumbeat in her ears.

The Hollow smelled like aged whiskey and warm candlelight, a heady mix of nostalgia and temptation that wrapped around her the moment she stepped inside. Neon lights flickered against the exposed brick, the hum of conversation rising and falling beneath the occasional burst of laughter.

And there, in the center of it all—was Chase.

Her breath stilled.

He hadn't seen her yet.

But she saw him. And she felt it.

That undeniable, gravitational pull. It wasn't fair how effortlessly he existed, how he commanded attention without even trying. People naturally gravitated toward him, drawn in by his easy confidence, his laugh—a sound she hadn't heard in over a year but still recognized instantly. He moved through the crowd like he belonged there, every nod of recognition, every quick grin, sending a fresh wave of longing through her.

Mallory caught sight of her from across the room, lifting a subtle brow as if to say well? Motioning for her to come over.

Savannah forced herself forward, her heart hammering with every step.

By the time she reached the bar, her mouth was dry, her throat tight.

"Drink?" Gus asked, leaning on the bar in front of her.

Savannah's mouth was too dry to answer, so she just nodded.

Gus, however, had already noticed something else.

His gaze flicked between Savannah and the man holding court across the room.

Savannah watching Chase.

Chase, oblivious.

A slow, knowing smirk curved Gus's lips.

"Well, damn," he muttered under his breath, shaking his head like he had just put together the final piece of a puzzle.

Savannah tore her gaze away from Chase long enough to glance at Gus. "What?"

Gus wiped his hands on a bar towel, looking entirely too amused.

"Nothing," he said. "Just—this is about to get real interesting."

Before she could ask what the hell that meant, Mallory spoke.

"You okay?"

Savannah turned to her, but Mallory wasn't looking at her.

She was looking at him.

And Savannah saw it.

The realization hit her square in the chest—Mallory liked Chase.

Not in a serious way, but—in a Mallory way. The way her eyes lingered on him, just a little longer than necessary. The way her lips curved just slightly as she watched him move through the crowd, laughing, joking, absolutely thriving in this moment.

Because Chase was fun.

That was what Savannah loved about him. And that was what she had been trying to pretend she didn't miss.

It wasn't just the way he looked at her, or the way he had once made her feel like she was the only girl in the world. It was the way he existed—fully, unapologetically, bringing energy to everything around him.

Mallory felt it too. And for the first time, Savannah saw him through someone else's eyes.

She had been so convinced that he had been suffering without her. That he had spent the past year as miserable as she had. But watching him now—laughing, confident, magnetic—she felt like she had stepped outside of her own perspective for the first time.

Had she actually believed he'd been standing still all this time?

Had she really thought he would have been stuck in place, waiting for her?

The realization hit her like a freight train. Her stomach twisted, a sharp, painful pull in her chest.

And then—

Then he saw her.

Chase turned, mid-laugh, looking for Mallory—and his gaze landed on Savannah instead.

And everything stopped.

54

Destined Echoes

CHASE'S LAUGHTER CUT OFF like a song abruptly stopped mid-note.

His easy, confident stance faltered—just slightly—but enough that Gus muttered, "Well, there it is."

For a second, Savannah swore the entire bar had gone silent.

Of course, it hadn't.

People were still talking, still drinking, still caught up in whatever chaos The Hollow had to offer. Glasses clinked. Someone near the jukebox let out a loud, rowdy laugh. A dart hit its mark against the board with a soft thunk. The world hadn't stopped.

But Chase had.

And for him, in that moment, everything else may as well have blurred into nothing.

His eyes locked onto hers.

Unblinking. Unmoving.

Like she was the last person he ever expected to see standing there.

Like she was the last person he wanted to see standing there.

Savannah's breath caught in her throat.

Because suddenly, she wasn't in The Hollow anymore.

She was back in time—standing on that dock, the night air thick with salt and regret, the water lapping softly against the wood beneath her feet. Watching him watch her. Memorizing every inch of his face because she knew, even if she didn't want to admit it, that she wasn't coming back.

That whatever they were—whatever they had been—was about to be severed.

And now?

Now, he was in front of her again, standing beneath the soft glow of neon lights, in a room full of strangers who adored him.

And he looked exactly the way he had when she had walked away.

Like she had stolen something from him.

Like she had taken more than just her absence with her when she left.

A flicker of emotion passed through his gaze—something too fast for her to catch, too layered to decipher. Frustration? Surprise? Something softer, something broken?

No. Not Chase.

He wouldn't let her see that.

Savannah's fingers curled around the edge of the bar, grounding herself, forcing her legs to stay still, to not run. Because, God help her, every instinct was screaming at her to turn around and disappear before he could say her name, before he could ask why.

But she didn't move.

Chase blinked, his Adam's apple bobbing as he swallowed, his hands flexing at his sides. A slow inhale. A slower exhale.

And then—

Then, in true Chase Montgomery fashion, the moment shifted.

Because instead of letting the weight of the past swallow him, instead of letting the tension consume them both, he did what he always did best.

He grinned.

Slow. Calculated.

Like he was amused. Like this was fun for him. Like he was already three steps ahead of her.

A smirk, just barely there, tugging at the corner of his mouth. A flick of his thumb against the brim of his cap.

And then, as if nothing in the world had changed—as if she hadn't just upended the fragile balance of this place, this night, his life—Chase turned back to his conversation.

He made her wait.

Savannah's stomach tightened.

Of course he did.

She could feel Gus watching the whole thing unfold, his hands idly wiping down the counter, his smirk as sharp as the tension in the air. He didn't say anything, but he didn't have to.

Because Chase hadn't come over. Hadn't made a scene. Hadn't demanded answers.

He just smiled.

And that—that damn smile—was somehow worse.

Because it meant the next move was hers.

Savannah didn't see Mallory motion to Chase. Telling him to come over.

She barely had time to process the grin—that damn grin—before Chase was moving.

Effortless. Smooth. Like this wasn't a reunion between two people whose pasts had been colliding in their dreams for the last year, but instead just another night, another moment, another game to play.

She couldn't breathe. She couldn't move.

Mallory went still beside her. Even Gus, who had probably seen every type of reunion imaginable, seemed to lean in, anticipating what came next.

The sounds of the bar faded—the murmur of conversation, the clink of ice against glass, the low hum of music vibrating through the walls—everything dulled beneath the weight of him.

Chase walked straight toward her, glass dangling loosely from his fingers, his boots moving over the worn wooden floor with a confidence that set every nerve in Savannah's body on high alert.

He wasn't rushing. No, that wasn't Chase Montgomery's style. He took his time, like he knew the moment was his to control, like he knew every step would only tighten the invisible thread that had always pulled them together, no matter how far she had run.

And then—He stopped.

Right in front of her.

Close enough that she could feel the faint warmth of his presence against her skin, close enough that the scent of him—leather, cedar, and something deeper, something infuriatingly familiar—wrapped around her, made her chest ache in ways she wasn't prepared for. Close enough that she had no choice but to look up at him.

His gaze never wavered. His shoulders relaxed, posture loose, unreadable. The brim of his baseball cap cast the slightest shadow over his face, but it did nothing to dim the sharp, electric blue of his eyes. He tilted his head just slightly, considering her, like he was seeing through every wall she had built, every excuse she had made for herself. Like he had been expecting her all along. Like this was all part of the plan.

His lips curved upward, slow and deliberate, voice low and easy—dangerously soft in a way that sent an unwelcome shiver down her spine. "You're late, Monroe."

Savannah's heart slammed against her ribs so hard it was a miracle she stayed upright.

Mallory actually choked on her drink, sputtering. "I—excuse me?!"

Chase didn't even look at her. His focus was locked entirely on Savannah, as if the rest of the room, the rest of the world, didn't exist.

And Savannah?

She didn't know whether to laugh, cry, or walk right back out the damn door.

Her grip on the bar tightened. This wasn't happening. This wasn't how this was supposed to go.

She had braced for shock. For tension. For an awkward, stilted, how-have-you-been conversation that neither of them would be prepared for. She had not, in any way, prepared for this. For Chase looking like he already knew how this night would go. For him not being thrown at all.

Savannah forced herself to swallow, to breathe, to fight against the pull of him. "I—what are you—"

Mallory suddenly grabbed Savannah's arm and shook it violently, like a woman on the verge of losing her mind. "No, no, no, you don't get to just brush past that. What the hell does you're late mean?"

Chase finally turned to acknowledge her, but his smirk didn't fade.

If anything, it deepened.

"It means exactly what it sounds like," he said simply.

Mallory narrowed her eyes, suspicion thick in her voice. "So, what—you just assumed she'd show up here eventually?"

Chase didn't hesitate. Didn't even blink. "I didn't assume anything."

Savannah felt it then—the weight of his words settling between them like a storm cloud about to break.

Her stomach twisted. Because he wasn't just talking about tonight. He was talking about all of it.

Like he had always known, somewhere deep down, that she would come back. Like this moment had always been waiting for them. The tension stretched thick between them, heavy and electric, the kind that sucked all the air from the room.

Savannah curled her fingers into her palm, nails pressing into her skin, grounding herself.

She should say something. She needed to say something.

Tell him he was wrong. Tell him she hadn't planned on seeing him again. That this wasn't inevitable. That she hadn't spent the past year replaying every memory, every late-night conversation, every touch, every damn look like a woman torturing herself with the past. That she hadn't ached for him in ways she didn't have words for.

But when she opened her mouth— Nothing came out.

Chase's gaze flickered—just the briefest hint of something unreadable passing through his expression before it disappeared behind that maddening, confident ease. And then, as if he had all the time in the world, as if he wasn't currently unraveling her piece by piece, he lifted his glass to his lips and took a slow sip, watching her over the rim.

Like he knew. Like he could see every thought racing through her mind.

And that damn grin?

It stayed.

Chase lifted his drink and smiled. "Mallory, don't take this the wrong way, but I knew you would tell her. I was counting on it."

Mallory blinked, brows knitting in confusion. "I—what?"

But Chase didn't elaborate. He just shrugged, impossibly calm, still looking like this entire night had unfolded exactly the way he expected.

Like he had been waiting for this moment.

"I hoped you would talk her into coming." He said, smugly.

Savannah's breath caught.

She had spent all day spiraling, agonizing over whether she should come. Whether it would be a mistake. Whether he would even want to see her. She had thought about every scenario, every possibility. Had imagined him looking at her with resentment, or worse—indifference. Had braced herself for impact, for the hurt that would come when she saw him moving on, moving forward, existing in a world where she was just a memory. And now—standing in front of him, hearing those words—He had hoped she would come. A warmth bloomed low in her stomach, unwanted but insistent, curling around her ribs and squeezing.

Mallory let out an exaggerated, almost offended gasp, smacking a hand against her chest. "Oh my God. Was I just played?"

Chase's grin turned wicked, effortless. "I'd never say that out loud."

Savannah wanted to be irritated.

She wanted to be annoyed that Chase knew her well enough to predict that she would eventually walk through that door. That he had been so sure of her, so certain of how this would unfold, that he had casually accounted for Mallory's meddling like it was just another step in the plan. But mostly? Mostly, she was staggeringly aware of how close he was.

The heat of him. The subtle flex of his forearm, where the edge of a tattoo peeked beneath his rolled-up sleeve. The way the dim lighting caught on the sharp cut of his jaw. The way he smelled—woodsy, clean, familiar in a way that sent her straight back to late-night drives and tangled sheets and whispered, half-laughed confessions.

She cleared her throat, forcing herself to focus. "So, let me get this straight." Her voice was steadier than she expected, but not by much. "You weren't surprised to see me?"

Chase tilted his head, watching her in that way that had always undone her, the way that made it feel like he saw everything. "Surprised? No." A pause. A flicker of something deeper in his gaze.

"Relieved? Yeah."

Savannah's heart stuttered.

Mallory, still dramatically recovering from her betrayal, turned to Gus in outrage. "Can you believe this? He used me."

Gus just chuckled, shaking his head as he wiped down the bar. "Darlin', you let yourself be used." His eyes twinkled with amusement as he tipped his chin toward Savannah. "We all knew this was happening before she did."

Savannah's mouth fell open. "You too, Gus?"

The old bartender smirked, slow and knowing. "You were bound to walk through that door one way or another."

Her stomach tightened. Because damn it, she hated that they were right. She hated that no matter how much she had told herself she wasn't ready for this, that she wasn't coming back, some part of her had already known the truth. That she would always come back to him. She groaned, turning back to Chase. "Unbelievable."

But Chase just looked pleased. Not smug. Not cocky. Just pleased. Just genuinely happy that she was here.

And that?

That was dangerous.

Because if he had been angry, if he had been cold, if he had given her something—anything—to hold onto, maybe she could have stood her ground. Maybe she could have convinced herself that leaving had been the right thing. But instead, he was this. Effortless. Smooth. The Chase Montgomery who had always been impossible to ignore.

She exhaled sharply. "Okay. Fine. You knew I'd come. What now?"

Chase's lips quirked, slow and deliberate, like she had just walked straight into his trap.

"Well, Monroe," he murmured, voice dipping into something rougher, something teasing, "you could buy me that drink."

Savannah fought the way her pulse roared in her ears.

Mallory cackled.

Gus poured another bourbon.

And Savannah?

She knew—she knew—she was in trouble.

Savannah inhaled slowly, willing her heart to settle. But it was impossible—not with him standing this close, not with the gravity of his presence pressing into every inch of her skin, not with the weight of his words still hanging in the air like a challenge she wasn't sure she could refuse.

She had spent the past year convincing herself she had made the right choice. That leaving had been necessary. That she and Chase had been doomed from the start, that some loves weren't built to last, that what they had had been nothing more than a fleeting, reckless, too-intense storm that had always been destined to burn out.

But now?

Now she was looking into the eyes of the man she had never stopped loving—eyes that had haunted her in dreams she refused to talk about, eyes that she had spent a year pretending didn't still hold a part of her.

And he was looking right back. No anger. No bitterness. Just– warmth.

And that?

That was so much worse than she had been prepared for.

Chase watched her carefully, the teasing edge that had laced his words all night fading, shifting into something deeper, something softer. Something dangerous.

"You really thought I wouldn't want to see you?" His voice was quieter now, the hum of the bar fading into nothing but static around them.

Savannah swallowed. "I didn't know what to think."

Chase tilted his head, eyes scanning hers, seeing too much—always seeing too much. "Yeah, you did."

She hated that he still saw through her so easily. She exhaled shakily, dropping her gaze to the drink Gus had placed in front of her, tracing the condensation on the glass with her fingertip, grounding herself in the coolness of it.

"I guess I thought... maybe it would be easier. If you had moved on. If you didn't care."

Silence stretched between them, thick and crackling.

And then—

"Sav," he said, gently, like he was speaking directly to the deepest, most hidden, most fragile part of her. Like he was touching her without ever lifting a hand. "I tried."

Her breath caught. She froze.

He tried.

Slowly, hesitantly, she lifted her gaze—and suddenly, the Chase standing in front of her wasn't the confident, easygoing man who had spent the night making The Hollow his kingdom.

No.

This was just Chase.

The man who had memorized her coffee order down to the extra pump of vanilla. The man who had stayed up with her on the dock until sunrise, talking about everything and nothing, about futures and fears and the kind of quiet hopes neither of them had ever spoken to anyone else. The man who had let her go. Even though she was pretty damn sure it had broken him to do it.

The weight of everything—the regret, the loss, the sheer aching missing of him—slammed into her all at once, stealing the air from her lungs.

Her fingers tightened around her glass, knuckles turning white. "Chase—"

But he just shook his head, a small, knowing smile tugging at his lips. "I'm not trying to make this hard on you, Savy. I just—I want you to know that you didn't imagine it."

Her throat tightened. "Imagine what?"

His gaze held hers, unwavering. "That I loved you."

Her breath stopped completely.

A sharp, dizzying kind of panic clawed at her chest, because he wasn't supposed to say that. He wasn't supposed to just put it out there like that—like it wasn't something fragile and breakable, like it wasn't something she had spent a year trying to bury beneath a thousand what-ifs and almosts and mistakes.

She hadn't realized she was gripping the bar like a lifeline until Mallory reached out under the counter, squeezing her knee—silent, supportive, grounding. The world around them was still moving. People were laughing, music was playing, drinks were being poured.

But they—Savannah and Chase—were in their own space. A world where nothing existed but this moment.

Savannah's voice was barely a whisper. "Loved?"

A heartbeat.

A flicker of something in Chase's gaze—something raw, something vulnerable, something that made her feel like the ground beneath her wasn't quite solid anymore. He studied her, slow and deliberate, as if searching for something—as if waiting to see if she could handle the truth before he gave it to her. And then—softly, honestly, devastatingly—

His lips quirked just slightly, but his eyes? They didn't waver.

"Still."

Savannah's chest tightened painfully, her pulse roaring in her ears. Because he wasn't playing games.

This wasn't flirtation. This wasn't Chase Montgomery trying to get a rise out of her. This was him. Standing in front of her. Telling her the truth.

No hesitation. No expectations. No regrets. Just honesty. Just Chase.

And for the first time in a year—

Savannah wasn't running.

She was standing still.

And maybe—just maybe—

she was finally ready to listen.

55

Echoes of Us

SAVANNAH HAD SPENT A year convincing herself that she had made the right choice. That leaving had been the only choice.

That what she and Chase had shared—intense, reckless, all-consuming—had been destined to burn out, leaving only embers behind. But now?

Now she was standing in front of the man she had never stopped loving, and every wall she had built to keep him out was crumbling at his feet.

And the worst part?

He wasn't even trying to tear them down. He wasn't pulling her in. He wasn't making any move to force her decision. He was just there. Like he always had been. Like he always would be.

And for the first time in a year, Savannah realized she didn't want to run.

She wanted to stay. She wanted to go home.

Her fingers curled into the fabric of her jeans, grounding herself in the reality of this moment, her pulse roaring in her ears as she met his gaze. Was this real? Could she have this again?

"Did you sell the house?" Her voice came out softer than she expected, barely audible over the thudding of her own heart.

Chase's lips quirked, slow and knowing, the kind of smile that had always made her stomach flip. "No."

She nodded, like she was working through something in her head, her heart knocking against her ribs, frantic and wild. "And you—" She exhaled, licking her lips, nerves twisting inside her. "You plan on keeping it?"

A shadow of a smile ghosted over his lips. "You tell me."

Her breath hitched. Because she had seen them. She's seen the life he built around her absence—the pieces of her that still lived in that house, in the walls, in the spaces where she once belonged.

"You built a library in the house?" she asked, her voice barely more than a whisper. "Why?"

Chase's expression softened, his voice steady, unwavering. "Because books are your love language." His eyes locked onto hers, no hesitation, no doubt. "And, well, you're mine."

Savannah's breath fluttered. The weight of those words, so simple yet so devastating, shattered through her like a storm breaking against the shore. He had remembered. Even after everything. Even after she had left, after she had run, he had built something for her—something he should have had no reason to believe she would ever see. It should have made her feel guilty. But it didn't. It just made her feel like she had one last chance to make this right.

She took a slow, measured breath, her heart pounding so hard she thought it might break her ribs. And then, finally—she made the choice.

Savannah set her glass down on the bar, pushed up from her stool, and took a single step forward—closer, close enough that Chase had to tilt his chin down to look at her, close enough that she could see the flicker of something raw and reverent in his eyes.

The smile faded from his lips, his throat working as he swallowed, his fingers twitching like he was resisting the urge to reach for her.

"Savy—" He said softly.

She lifted a hand, pressing it against his chest, feeling the steady thud-thud-thud of his heart beneath her palm. His breath stilled, caught somewhere between disbelief and hope.

"Take me home," she whispered.

Chase froze. Like he needed to process it, to make sure he hadn't imagined it. Like he needed to be sure this wasn't another dream he'd wake up from, aching and empty. And then—slowly, carefully—his hand covered hers, holding it there, holding her there.

"You sure?" he asked, his voice rougher now, quieter, like he was afraid to break whatever fragile moment they had just stepped into.

Savannah nodded, eyes shining. "I'm sure."

Chase exhaled. And she felt it.

The tension. The relief. The weight of every moment they had spent apart shattered under the choice she had just made.

A slow, beautiful smile spread across his lips, full of something deep, something unshakable. And Savannah—she couldn't wait any longer.

She surged forward before she could talk herself out of it, grabbing the front of his shirt, closing the space between them, and pressing her lips to his.

Chase inhaled sharply, like he hadn't expected it—like for all his confidence, for all the ways he had been three steps ahead of her tonight, he hadn't seen this coming. But then—then his hands were on her waist, pulling her closer, his grip firm, like he had been waiting for this moment since the second she walked away a year ago.

The world faded. The noise of the bar disappeared. The hum of conversation, the music, the laughter—none of it mattered. It was just them. Just Chase and Savannah and the ache of a year lost, colliding into a kiss that felt like a beginning and an ending all at once. He kissed her like he was memorizing her again. Like he had spent every night missing the way she fit against him, the way she used to pull him closer just like this, like she never wanted to let go.

Her hands slid up, fingers tangling into the soft fabric of his shirt, gripping like she was afraid this wasn't real.

But Chase—he wouldn't let her doubt it. He deepened the kiss, his hand sliding up her back, his other cupping the side of her face, tilting her just the way he knew she liked.

Savannah let out the smallest gasp, and he felt it, because Chase groaned, tightening his grip, erasing the space between them completely.

The moment stretched—heady. Electric. Charged with everything they hadn't said, everything they had been too afraid to admit. And then, finally—she pulled back just enough to catch her breath, her forehead resting against his, her fingers still curled in his shirt.

Chase was breathing just as hard as she was, his eyes dark and searching, like he was waiting—hoping—this wasn't just a moment.

Savannah let out a breathless, shaky laugh. "Okay."

Chase blinked. "Okay?"

Savannah nodded, her smile breaking wide—full of certainty, full of something new, full of something finally right. "Take me home, Montgomery."

Chase let out a slow, almost disbelieving exhale. His thumb brushed against her jaw, the touch featherlight, reverent.

And then, softly, his voice a whisper meant just for her, "Home isn't a place, Savannah. It's in the way you laugh, the way you dream, the way you love. It's every moment we've ever had and every one still waiting for us."

His lips ghosted over her forehead, the softest press of warmth, a kiss full of something deeper than words could ever say—

"It's—The Echoes of Us."

Epilogue

5 Years Later

I TOLD YOU THIS story.

I told you that love is messy. That it's raw, painful—the kind of thing that buries itself deep inside you and refuses to let go. That it will break you, reshape you, and leave you standing in the wreckage of who you used to be, wondering how the hell you're supposed to put yourself back together again.

And I meant every damn word.

Because love is all of those things.

But what I didn't tell you—what I couldn't tell you back then—was that love is also the thing that heals you.

It lingers. It seeps into your breath, into your bones, into the quiet spaces between your ribs that no one else has ever touched.

It stays.

Even when you try to forget. Even when you tell yourself you've let it go. Even when you run. Because love, real love, is never something you just walk away from.

And five years ago, I finally stopped trying.

It's been five years since I made that drive to Asheville.

Five years since I walked into The Hollow and saw her standing there, looking at me like I was both the past she couldn't escape and the future she wasn't sure she was allowed to have.

Five years since my world tilted on its axis, and I knew—right then, right there—that this was it. That this was us.

Did I know she was coming? No.

But God, I hoped.

I hoped so hard it hurt. I hoped with every damn breath in my body. I told myself that if what we had was real—if she really felt what I felt—then she'd show up.

And if she did? I'd never let her go again.

Mallory still calls– Still shows up unannounced. She still drinks my whiskey like she owns the place, kicks her feet up on my coffee table, and inserts herself into my life with that same shameless confidence she's always had.

And yes–She's still a pain in my ass.

But honestly? I wouldn't have it any other way.

She claims she knew all along that Savannah and I would find our way back to each other. Says it with a knowing smirk and a shrug, like she orchestrated the whole thing. And maybe she did, in her own way.

Not that I'll ever admit that to her.

And the house?

I kept it. I almost didn't. I Almost let my pride make me walk away from it, from her, from everything we had touched, everything we had built.

But love—real love—doesn't give you that option. Because it stays. And so did she.

That library Savannah once dreamed about? It's real. It's here.

And every morning, I wake up and find her sitting in that damn window nook, tucked into the cushions, legs curled beneath her, a book in one hand and coffee in the other.

It never gets old.

The way she loses herself in the words, the way her eyes soften when she finds a sentence that stays with her.

She loves all the books. The shelves are full of them. Classics, new releases, hardcovers, paperbacks— To surprise her, I even asked the bookstore clerk for recommendations.

Which, let me tell you, turned into an experience I wasn't prepared for.

Apparently, there is a thing called "smut." I had no idea what the hell that was when I asked.

Turns out, it's word porn.

And judging by the way Savannah's eyes lit up when she saw the stack, I have zero regrets. "I don't mind that kind of love language at all," she'd whispered, her fingers tracing the spines.

I'd never seen her look at anything the way she looked at those books. Except maybe me.

The house is still the same, for the most part. I've made a few updates.

The bedrooms have been redone. The dock—the one where I spent too many nights wondering if I'd ever see her again—is still my favorite place to sit when I need to breathe.

The difference is—I'm not sitting out there waiting anymore. I'm not chasing ghosts. I'm living. Because she's already here.

For all the good, and for all the bad, love changes us. It molds us into something new. It forces us to face the parts of ourselves we'd rather ignore. And if we let it—if we fight for it—it gives us something we never thought we'd have again.

Since that day all those years ago, I've become a better version of myself than I ever thought possible.

I don't take things for granted anymore. I don't let fear make my choices. And I damn sure won't let the best thing that ever happened to me walk away twice.

I still sit here on this dock most nights, listening to the tide roll in.

The difference is, now? I'm not listening for echoes.

I'm listening for her. For the way she laughs when our son refuses to go to bed and wants to sit on "Daddy's dock." I'm listening for the sound of her voice calling my name from the house, telling me that dinner's ready, or that I forgot to fold the laundry, or that I need to come inside because Carter won't go down without his daddy.

Yeah—our three-year-old can't fall asleep unless I'm the one to tuck him in.

I never thought I'd love anything more than her.

But then she gave me him. And God, if that didn't undo me completely.

Savannah still laughs about the way I cried the first time I held him. The way my hands shook when I traced his tiny fingers, the way I whispered, "I've got you, little man. You're safe."

The way I looked at her, completely wrecked, knowing I would never be the same.

I'm still not the same.

I'm better.

Because of her.

Because of him.

Because of us.

So I'll leave you with this—

Love is hard.

Love is impossible.

Love will wreck you.

It will break you.

It will make you question everything you thought you knew.

But if you're lucky—

If you fight for it, if you choose it, if you don't let go—

Love will put you back together.

Love is forever.

Love is this.

And this—

This was the ***Echoes of Us.***

      —Chase & Savannah Montgomery

Printed in Dunstable, United Kingdom

65134881R00170